PENGUIN ⓅCLASSICS

CANDIDE

FRANÇOIS-MARIE AROUET (1694–1778), who later took the name of VOLTAIRE, was the son of a notary and educated at a Jesuit School in Paris. His father wanted him to study the law, but the young man was determined on a literary career. He gained an introduction to the intellectual life of Paris and soon won a reputation as a writer of satires and odes – a not altogether enviable reputation, for the suspicion of having written a satire on the Regent procured him a term of imprisonment in the Bastille. On his release, his first tragedy, *Œdipe*, was performed (1718) in Paris with great success and soon after he published the poem he had written in prison, a national epic, *La Henriade* (1723), which placed him with Homer and Virgil in the eyes of his contemporaries. After a second term of imprisonment in the Bastille, Voltaire spent two and a half years (1726–8) in England, and returned to France full of enthusiasm for the intellectual activity and the more tolerant form of government he found there. His enthusiasm and his indictment of the French system of government are expressed in his *Letters Concerning the English Nation* (1733), published in France as the *Lettres philosophiques*, but whose sale was absolutely forbidden in France.

The next fifteen years were spent at the country seat of his friend, Madame du Châtelet, where he wrote his most popular tragedies and his *Zadig*, a witty Eastern tale, and started work on his *Century of Louis XIV*. After Madame du Châtelet's death in 1749, Voltaire was induced to pay a prolonged visit to the Court of Frederick the Great, with whom he had been in correspondence for several years. While there he completed his important historical work *Essay on Customs* (*Essai sur les moeurs et l'esprit des nations*) and began his *Philosophical Dictionary*. Voltaire and Frederick could not agree for long and in 1753 Voltaire decided to leave Prussia. But he was not safe in France. After two years of wandering he settled near Geneva and at last made a home at Ferney. It was during the last, and most brilliant, twenty years of his life that he wrote *Candide*, his dialogues and more tales, and published his widely read *Philosophical Dictionary* (1764) in 'pocket form', while conducting his ceaseless and energetic attack against what he called the 'infamous thing' – all manifestations of tyranny and persecution by a privileged orthodoxy in Church and State. He died at the age of eighty-four, after a triumphant visit to Paris, from which he had been exiled for so long.

THEO CUFFE was educated in Dublin and at the Sorbonne. He has translated Saint-Exupéry's *The Little Prince and Letter to a Hostage* and Voltaire's *Micromégas and Other Short Fictions* for Penguin.

MICHAEL WOOD was born in Lincoln in 1936 and attended grammar school there. He studied French and German at St John's College, Cambridge, and taught English and Comparative Literature at Columbia University, New York and at Exeter University. He is currently Straut Professor of English at Princeton. His books include *Stendhal, America in the Movies, The Magician's Doubts, Franz Kafka* and *The Road to Delphi*. He is a Fellow of the Royal Society of Literature and of the American Academy of Arts and Sciences.

VOLTAIRE

Candide

or *Optimism*

Translated and edited by THEO CUFFE
With an Introduction by MICHAEL WOOD

PENGUIN BOOKS

PENGUIN CLASSICS

Published by the Penguin Group
Penguin Books Ltd, 80 Strand, London WC2R ORL, England
Penguin Group (USA) Inc., 375 Hudson Street, New York, New York 10014, USA
Penguin Group (Canada), 90 Eglinton Avenue East, Suite 700, Toronto, Ontario, Canada M4P 2Y3
(a division of Pearson Penguin Canada Inc.)
Penguin Ireland, 25 St Stephen's Green, Dublin 2, Ireland
(a division of Penguin Books Ltd)
Penguin Books Australia Ltd, 250 Camberwell Road,
Camberwell, Victoria 3124, Australia (a division of Pearson Australia Group Pty Ltd)
Penguin Books India Pvt Ltd, 11 Community Centre,
Panchsheel Park, New Delhi – 110 017, India
Penguin Group (NZ), cnr Airborne and Rosedale Roads, Albany,
Auckland 1310, New Zealand (a division of Pearson New Zealand Ltd)
Penguin Books (South Africa) (Pty) Ltd, 24 Sturdee Avenue,
Rosebank, Johannesburg 2196, South Africa

Penguin Books Ltd, Registered Offices: 80 Strand, London WC2R ORL, England

www.penguin.com

This translation first published in Penguin Classics 2005

043

Translation and Notes copyright © Theo Cuffe, 2005
Introduction copyright © Michael Wood, 2005
All rights reserved

The moral right of the editor has been asserted

Every effort has been made to trace the
copyright holders. The publishers would be
interested to hear from any copyright holders
not here acknowledged.

Set in 10.25/12.25 pt PostScript Adobe Sabon
Typeset by Rowland Phototypesetting Ltd, Bury St Edmunds, Suffolk
Printed and bound in Great Britain by Clays Ltd, Elcograf S.p.A.

ISBN-13: 978-0-140-45510-6

www.greenpenguin.co.uk

Contents

Chronology

1694 Born 21 November at Châtenay, near Paris (Voltaire always claimed that he was born on 20 February), baptized François-Marie Arouet. His father was a wealthy notary; Voltaire would later describe himself as the illegitimate issue of a liaison between his mother, who died when he was seven years old, and an officer-gentleman-poet. His one brother was to become a priest and Jansenist, his sister would marry into the bourgeoisie and died young.

1697 Pierre Bayle publishes his *Dictionnaire historique et critique* (*Historical and Critical Dictionary*).

1704–11 Educated in Paris at the Collège Louis-le-Grand, the most famous of Jesuit colleges. Acquires a solid grounding in Latin literature, a religious education and a passion for the theatre. Many of his schoolfriends, who became friends for life, belonged to aristocratic families. Frequents the sceptical and libertine milieu of the Temple, ruled by an epicurean spirit and the fables of La Fontaine.

1710 Gottfried Wilhelm Leibniz's *Essais de Théodicée* (*Essays on Theodicy*) published.

1712–14 Law student; active social life in Paris and at various châteaux. Sent to Caen in 1713, and then to a position in the French embassy in Holland.

1715 Death of Louis XIV. Philippe duc d'Orléans becomes Regent.

1716 Returns to Paris and is exiled to Sully-sur-Loire for six months for writing a poetic satire against the Regent.

1717–18 Imprisoned in the Bastille for several months, on account of further scurrilities against the Regent.

1718 Banished for six months to Châtenay. Adopts the pseud-
onym of 'Voltaire'. His first tragedy, *Œdipe* (*Oedipus*), is
staged with great success.

1722 Travels in Holland.

1725 Three of Voltaire's plays are performed at the wedding
celebrations of Louis XV.

1726–8 Obliged to leave Paris and go into exile in England for
a spell of forced contemplation, following a quarrel with the
aristocratic chevalier de Rohan. Presented to George I at the
Court of St James. Meets Alexander Pope, William Congreve,
Henry Viscount Bolingbroke, and corresponds with Jonathan
Swift. Admires *Gulliver's Travels* (1726), and the works of
Isaac Newton. *La Henriade* (*The Henriad*), an epic poem on
religious intolerance, published in London in 1728, confirms
his reputation. Returns to Paris in October 1728.

1733–4 Publishes *Letters Concerning the English Nation*
(1733) in London, the French edition of which (*Lettres philosophiques*) appears in Paris in 1734. The French publisher is
arrested, the book is publicly burned on the orders of the
Paris *parlement*, and a warrant is issued for Voltaire's arrest;
he escapes to Lorraine, before settling at Cirey in Champagne, the home of his mistress Mme du Châtelet. Much of
the following decade is spent at Cirey: a period of extended
literary activity and philosophical speculation (starting
with the *Traité de métaphysique* (*Treatise on Metaphysics*),
written in 1734). Pope's *Essay on Man* published.

1736 Begins to correspond with Frederick, heir to the throne
of Prussia.

1738 Publishes his *Eléments de la philosophie de Newton*
(*Elements of the Philosophy of Newton*).

1740 Meets Frederick of Prussia, now Frederick II.

1741 War of Austrian Succession (1741–8). Sent on a secret
mission to rally Frederick II to the French cause.

1743–6 From 1743 Voltaire begins to enjoy temporary favour
at Louis XV's court at Versailles, with the support of Mme
de Pompadour. In 1744 Mme Denis, his widowed niece, becomes his mistress. Appointed Royal Historiographer (1745).
Elected to the Académie française (1746).

1747 Publishes *Zadig*, the first of the philosophical *contes*, or stories, to appear in print.

1748 Baron de Montesquieu publishes *De l'Esprit des lois* (*The Spirit of Laws*).

1749 Mme du Châtelet dies in childbirth.

1750–53 Accepts Frederick II's invitation to reside at the court at Potsdam.

1751–2 Publication of Volume I of the *Encyclopédie*; Voltaire contributes several articles to the early volumes. Publishes *Le Siècle de Louis XIV* (*The Age of Louis XIV*) and *Micromégas*.

1753–4 Leaves Potsdam after disputes with Frederick, and is held under temporary house-arrest at Frankfurt-am-Main. His return to Paris is blocked by Louis XV for some unspecified offence. There follows a period of wandering (Frankfurt, Schwetzingen, Colmar, Geneva).

1755 Settles at Les Délices, on the outskirts of Geneva. The Jesuit Order is expelled from Paraguay. Outbreak of Franco-British hostilities over Canada. Jean-Jacques Rousseau publishes his *Discours sur l'origine de l'inégalité* (*Discourse on the Origin of Inequality*). Lisbon earthquake (1 November); Voltaire writes his poem on the disaster (published 1756).

1756 Outbreak of the Seven Years' War, instigated by Frederick II. Voltaire publishes the first edition of his *Essai sur l'histoire générale et sur les mœurs et l'esprit de nations* (*Essay on General History and on the Manners and Spirit of the Nations*), an exercise in universal history, and continues to work on an expanded edition, which appeared in 1761; publishes the *Histoire des voyages de Scarmentado* (*History of the Travels of Scarmentado*).

1757 The *Encyclopédie* is suspended by the government, after its publication of controversial articles. Assassination attempt on the life of Louis XV by Robert François Damiens. Voltaire involved in secret negotiations between Frederick II and France in respect of a separate peace settlement.

1758 Writes *Candide* and acquires Château de Ferney and its estate, near Geneva, where he will remain for the rest of his life.

1759 (January or early February) publication of *Candide*. The Jesuit Order is expelled from Portugal.

1762-3 Rousseau's *Du Contrat social* (*The Social Contract*) and *Emile* published. Voltaire's campaign, eventually successful, to rehabilitate posthumously the reputation of Jean Calas, a Protestant cloth-maker of Toulouse groundlessly accused of murdering his son for wanting to convert to Catholicism. This initiates his protracted crusade against *l'Infâme* – the intolerance and persecution practised by the Catholic Church in alliance with the repressive French state – which will occupy him for the rest of his life; his *Traité sur la tolerance* (*Treatise on Toleration*) published in 1763.

1764 First edition of the *Dictionnaire philosophique portatif* (*Philosophical Dictionary*) published. Dissolution of the Jesuit Order in France.

1766 Campaign of protest over the execution of the Jean de la Barre on a charge of blasphemy; publishes a commentary on Beccaria's *Dei delitti e delle pene* (*On Crimes and Punishments*), which had appeared in 1763.

1767-8 Publishes *L'Ingénu* (*The Ingenu*, an attack on religious intolerance and persecution in France), *La Princese de Babylone* (*The Princess of Babylon*), and other philosophical *contes*, dialogues and miscellanies. Captain Cook's first voyage.

1769 Denis Diderot's *Le Rêve de d'Alembert* (*d'Alembert's Dream*) published.

1770 Baron d'Holbach's *Système de la nature* (*The System of Nature*) published.

1772 Diderot's *Supplément au voyage de Bougainville* (*Supplement to the Travels of Bougainville*) published.

1774 Death of Louis XV. Voltaire publishes *Le Taureau blanc* (*The White Bull*).

1778 Leaves Ferney to visit Paris for the production of his last tragedy, *Irène*, after an absence of nearly twenty-eight years. His return becomes a glorious apotheosis: he dies in Paris on 30 May. To avoid refusal of burial by the Parisian church authorities, his body is smuggled out of the city at night and buried in Champagne. (His remains were brought back to Paris and solemnly interred in the Panthéon in 1791.) Catherine the Great purchases Voltaire's library.

1789 Fall of the Bastille.

Introduction

*New readers are advised that this introduction
makes the detail of the plot explicit.*

The Best of All Possible Worlds

The word optimism, first used in print in 1737, represents
a philosophical position, a claim that in spite of errors and
appearances God's creation is as good as it could be, and
Voltaire's subtitle glances at just this doctrine. But the young
hero of this book is also an optimist in the modern sense.
Candide looks on the bright side when he can, and not one of
his many moments of discouragement can prevent his innate
cheerfulness from returning. Voltaire has not made it easy for
him. Candide inhabits a world which may seem freakishly full
of disasters, of war and earthquake, repeated rape and the
persistent exploitation of the frail and the innocent by the rabid
and strong. He suffers a good deal himself and carefully and
kindly notes the catastrophes of others. He despairs at the sight
of a slave in Surinam, who has lost an arm in a sugar-mill
accident, and a leg as punishment for an attempt to escape. The
slave is very forthright – 'It is the price we pay for the sugar
you eat in Europe' (chapter 19) – and provides one of the book's
coolest and wittiest condemnations of inhuman practices.
Dutch missionaries have taught the converted African slaves
that we are all, black and white, children of Adam, and therefore members of the same family. 'You must admit,' the slave
says, 'that no one could treat his relatives much more horribly
than this.' It is at this point – the only place in the book,
apart from the subtitle – that the word optimism is used. The
abomination of slavery, Candide cries, would make even his
teacher Pangloss renounce the doctrine of optimism. Candide's
servant Cacambo does not know the word. 'What is Opti-

mism?' he asks. Candide replies that 'it is the mania for insisting that all is well when all is by no means well'. Candide looks at the black man and weeps.

Voltaire, famously ridiculing the doctrine that all is for the best in the best of all possible worlds, is more subtly attacking (at least) three other, more insidious assumptions: that we can totally transcend our selfishness or provincialism; that a final accounting of the balance of good and evil in the world is achievable; that human philosophies bear some sort of direct relevance to human behaviour. Optimism is involved in all of these enterprises, and although our modern sense is anachronistic, and Candide's bitter definition is a mirror of his despair, these different meanings are not unrelated, as the mutilated slave might say; and it is their relation to each other and to the word's older, official meaning that matters to us. Indeed we scarcely see optimism in *Candide* except in the form of broad and damning travesties of it, and it takes an effort of the imagination to see that the doctrine isn't, or doesn't have to be, sheer parochial folly.

Theodore Besterman defines optimism as the theory 'that all that is and happens is for the best'.[1] 'For the best' already tilts the argument slightly. One meaning of 'All is well' is simply that all is as it has to be, that things could not be otherwise, and in this sense Voltaire had no significant quarrel with optimism. He merely regarded it as tautological and redundant. Thinking of English optimists like Henry St John Bolingbroke, the Earl of Shaftesbury, and Alexander Pope, he wrote in his *Philosophical Dictionary* (1764), 'their *All is well* means nothing more than that all is controlled by immutable laws. Who does not know that?'[2] The best of all possible worlds turns out to be the only possible world, there were never any other options. Free will is not subordinate to destiny, but certainly colludes with it in the long run.

But this is not optimism's most interesting claim. The idea that all is well implies a perspective – well for whom? – and may supply a useful corrective to limitations of vision. The world doesn't have to be a bad place because things are going badly for me. Voltaire himself was drawn to this view earlier in his career. 'What is bad in relation to you is good in the general arrangement,'[3] he wrote in his *Elements of the Philosophy of Newton* (1738). And of course the Christian notions of a benevolent God and a fortunate fall are optimistic in this sense: all is ultimately for the best even if there is nothing but a vale of toil and tears to be going on with. We may think of Alexander Pope's lines in *The Essay on Man* (1734):

> All Nature is but art, unknown to thee
> All chance, direction, which thou canst not see;
> All discord, harmony not understood;
> All partial evil, universal good[4]

When Candide quotes Pangloss as saying that the ills of the world are shadows in a beautiful painting, he is also quoting the German philosopher Gottfried Wilhelm Leibniz, a leading proponent of eighteenth-century optimism, who claimed that 'the shadows bring out the colours'.[5] This is not a negligible argument, even if we may feel closer to the position of Candide's dour companion Martin, who thinks such shadows are 'dreadful stains' (chapter 22). What turned Voltaire away from this more complex form of optimism was not a refusal of its logic or a conviction of its untruth but a perception of its potential heartlessness and a belief that the claim, even if true, couldn't be tested, and worse, couldn't be articulated without incurring some sort of complicity with the unacceptable, too eager an embrace of the idea that certain horrors are not only unavoidable but necessary. 'I respect my God,' Voltaire wrote in his *Poem on the Lisbon Disaster*, 'but I love the universe.' And elsewhere, thinking of Pope: 'A strange general good! composed of the stone, gout, all crimes, all suffering, death and damnation.'[6] Peter Gay, in *Voltaire's Politics*, goes so far as to say that 'Voltaire's objection to "whatever is, is right" was not to its complacent optimism but to its half-complacent, half-despairing pessimism . . . Voltaire's attack on "optimism" was an attack on pessimism in the name of a philosophy of activity'.[7] In other words, Voltaire saw pessimism as just too easy. The word pessimism, I should add, was not used until 1794, and appears to have been coined by Coleridge, although the frame of mind clearly existed long before, and Voltaire knew he didn't like it.

The book's first onslaught on optimism finds the doctrine in its crassest and most comfortable form: a combination of ignorance and complacency, which asserts that all is well everywhere because I'm doing pretty well in the tiny corner of the world I happen to know. Much of the fun here depends on Voltaire's parodies of sloppy argument, his deliberately loose connections between clauses, and an extravagantly restrictive sense of what a world is. The Baron von Thunder-ten-tronckh is 'one of the most powerful lords of Westphalia, for his castle had a gate and windows' (chapter 1). The relative sophistication of the baron's home – Westphalia is Voltaire's model of perfect backwardness – is the result rather than the cause of his greatness, but Voltaire's language mischievously pretends the reverse. And of course, as long as Westphalia is the world, this must be the best castle in the world. Candide too follows this lamentable style of inference when he thinks that Pangloss is the greatest philosopher in the province, 'and therefore in the whole world'. Voltaire has taken a grand phrase from Pope and toppled it into triviality. 'Whatever is, is right' becomes in *Candide* 'I like things the way they are because they suit me and because I don't know any better'.

This position is not only selfish but dependent on conditions beyond one's control, and it is rapidly rendered untenable by Candide's expulsion from the castle, by Pangloss's moral and physical ruin, and by the invasion of the castle by the Bulgars. Pangloss, undeterred, develops more complicated, if deeply muddled arguments as he and Candide start their travels: if Columbus had not brought syphilis from the New World we would not have chocolate in the Old; if private ills make up the general good, then the more private ills there are, the more all is well. In Pangloss's absurd assertions, we have our first inkling of what becomes fully clear only at the end of the book: Pangloss insists on his system not because he believes in it but because it is his system. It would not do for him to recant, he says, and in this statement Voltaire is offering us a sly definition of philosophy: never having to say you are wrong. 'I hold firmly to my original views,' Pangloss says in the last pages (chapter 28). 'After all I am a philosopher.' And Voltaire, in an uncharacteristically informative moment, tell us that Pangloss maintains his position 'while believing nothing of the kind' (chapter 30).

Candide is a philosopher too, in the sense that he loves to talk about philosophical ideas, but above all he is young, and his youth permits him attitudes which are not all that far removed from the initial provincialism of his native Westphalia. Candide is not complacent, and can't remain ignorant, but he does find it hard to believe the world is a bad place if his own affairs are going well. Voltaire remorselessly returns to this point, as strict with his likeable hero as he is with everyone else, but also interested in the *energy* of self-concern, as long as it is combined with curiosity and compassion. Candide's advantage over Martin, we learn, is that he has hope, 'for he still hoped to see Mademoiselle Cunégonde again, whereas Martin had nothing to hope for' (chapter 20). As well as hope, however, Candide has gold and diamonds, and he also has a good appetite. In the following stealthy sentence Mademoiselle Cunégonde is squeezed between money and food as only a part of what makes for the best of all possible worlds: 'when he thought of what remained in his pockets, and when he spoke of Cunégonde, especially at the end of a good meal, he still inclined towards the system of Pangloss'. And when Candide says 'once again I see that Pangloss was right: all is well' (chapter 27), he means nothing more than that he believes the desired end of his journey is near. Voltaire makes a slightly different point when he has Candide claim, while putting away a hearty meal, that he is too unhappy to eat, but the jokes all have the same theme: happiness and misery are contingent, local and material; philosophical optimism and conventional melancholy are postures. There is certainly a selfishness in Candide's repeated resorting to Pangloss's system; but there is also an ultimate moral health in his inability to be unhappy for long, even if his own intelligence says he should be.

The Worst of All Possible Worlds

To speak of the best of all possible worlds, as Pangloss and
Candide repeatedly do, is not only to espouse optimism as I
have described it, it is explicitly to compare worlds and impli-
citly to say what a world is. 'If this is the best of all possible
worlds,' Candide says after the Lisbon *auto-da-fé* in which he
has been flogged and Pangloss has been hanged, 'what must
the others be like?' (chapter 6). He is probably thinking of the
whole earth, but one can also think smaller, as we have seen.
If Westphalia is a world, then so are other regions and countries.
If Europe is a world, then so are the Americas, and Candide
himself says so. 'We are going to another world,' he remarks.
'No doubt it must be there that all is well' (chapter 10). He is
both right and wrong about this, as we shall see.

But persons are also worlds in *Candide*, each enclosed in a
circle of need and individual experience, and each convinced of
precisely the opposite of Pangloss's proposition, namely that
there is no world worse than his or hers. This is one of Voltaire's
favourite themes, and he elaborates it with the greatest relish.
Candide learns of Cunégonde's terrible fate from Pangloss: she
has been raped and disembowelled by Bulgar soldiers. The dis-
embowelling, it turns out, was something of an exaggeration,
since she did survive, and Voltaire later devotes a whole chapter
to her story, which she recounts to Candide. She became the
mistress of her rapist's superior officer, and was then sold to a
Jewish merchant, who shares her favours, or almost-favours,
with a Portuguese grand inquisitor. She and Candide and the
old woman who accompanies her have just finished supper
when the Jewish merchant arrives to exercise his proprietorial
rights. Furious at the sight of Candide, the merchant draws a
dagger, only to find that Candide is even swifter with his sword,
and 'his gentle disposition notwithstanding . . . lays the Israelite
out, stone dead at the feet of the lovely Cunégonde' (chapter 9).
Within minutes the Portuguese inquisitor arrives, and Candide,
thinking fast about the spot he finds himself in, decides he had
better kill him too. The situation gives rise to one of Voltaire's
most spectacular set-pieces, a stunning piece of absurdist

repartee. 'What on earth has got into you,' Cunégonde asks,
'you who were born so gentle, to do away with a Jew and a
prelate in the space of two minutes?' (chapter 9). It's hard to
think there could be a good reply to this question, but Candide
finds one. 'My dear young lady ... when you are in love, and
jealous, and have been flogged by the Inquisition, there's no
knowing what you may do.' The joke about Candide's gentle
nature is not a sarcasm, it is a suggestion that no one is gentle
all the time, and also glances more generally at the possibility
that anyone's nature can be radically altered by circumstance.
Voltaire returns to this thought, and to this tone, when Candide,
in another fit of self-defence, kills (or thinks he has killed)
Cunégonde's brother. This time it is Candide himself who
naively proclaims his surprise: 'I am the mildest man alive, yet
I have now killed three men, two of them priests' (chapter 15).
Is he still a mild man? How many killings will it take to change
this ascription?

Cunégonde's personal world seems pretty bad, but she has
some competition, and for some time now her companion the
old woman has been hinting that she too has a story to tell.
When Cunégonde insists she has been 'so horribly unhappy'
(chapter 10) in her world, the old woman says she herself has
suffered far worse misfortunes. Cunégonde almost has to laugh,
and lapses comically into that boasting about suffering which
so marks the book, and she multiplies everything by two, partly
for the sake of argument and partly no doubt because she feels
as if she has suffered everything twice.

Alas, my good woman ... unless you have been raped by two
Bulgars, been stabbed twice in the stomach, had two castles
demolished, had the throats of two mothers and two fathers slit
before your very eyes, and watched two lovers being flogged in
an *auto-da-fé*, I really cannot see that you have the advantage
over me. (Chapter 10)

The number of the Bulgars appears to be correct, the rest is
competitive accounting.

The old woman, of course, now tells her story and her

considerable travails put Cunégonde's into the shade. She is
Italian, the daughter of a pope and a princess and the mere
scenes of her sorrows cover much of the then known world:
Tunis, Tripoli, Alexandria, Smyrna, Constantinople; Moscow,
Riga, Rostock, Wismar, Leipzig, Kassel, Utrecht, Leiden, the
Hague, Rotterdam. The old woman also likes to boast, both
of her former beauty and fortune and of her later torments,
and she too indulges in absurd comparisons, insisting that
the plague is worse than the earthquake, as if there were anything to be said in favour of either. But she has her own form
of wisdom – 'I have lived, and I know the world,' she says
(chapter 12) – and makes a wager she knows she can't lose. She
suggests that Cunégonde ask each of their fellow travellers to
tell his story, 'and if you find a single one of them who has not
repeatedly cursed his existence, who has not repeatedly told
himself that he is the unhappiest man alive, then you may throw
me into the sea head first'. She is suggesting that everyone, in
a phrase Voltaire uses in his story *Zadig*, regards himself or
herself as 'the model of misfortune'. Later, Candide remembers
the old woman's proposition and organizes a competition. He
will take with him on his trip back to Europe the person who
is 'the most unfortunate and most thoroughly disgusted with
his condition in the whole province'. In the end he can't tell
which of the candidates is the most wretched, and chooses one
who is certainly miserable but probably more amusing than
most, the Manichean Martin. The very idea of supremacy in
sorrow or distress is self-defeating for all but the strictest misan-
thropes, and it is the old woman who has the most compelling
view of what we may call the theory of the worst of all possible
personal worlds. She says that there have been a hundred times
when she has wanted to kill herself, but she is still 'in love
with life'. She goes on to call this love a 'ridiculous weakness'
(chapter 12) but plainly it is a form of radical heroism, a love
that not only needs no reasons, but persists in spite of hosts of
counter-reasons. There is an echo here of Candide's inability to
sustain despair, however plausible the grounds. The old woman
has seen, she says, 'a prodigious number of individuals who
held their lives in contempt; but only a dozen who voluntarily

put an end to their misery: three negroes, four Englishmen, four Genevans and a German professor named Robeck'. The list is carefully designed. The negroes are presumably slaves, the English as melancholic as French myth would have them, the Genevans doubtless too dour and Calvinistic to live, and Robeck was a historical person who argued that loving life was ridiculous and sought to prove his point by deliberately drowning himself in 1739.

As for the New World, Candide is clearly wrong about this being the place where all is well, because cruelty, conflict and greed are not restricted to the Old World, and Cacambo points out to him that 'this hemisphere is no better than the other one' (chapter 17). But Candide is right in another sense, because in the Americas he does find Eldorado, a world where all really is well, a version of the utopia sketched out in Michel de Montaigne's essay on cannibals,[8] and echoed (and mocked) in Shakespeare's *Tempest*. Here in Eldorado there are no courts, prisons or lawyers, and no one is interested in gold and silver. The natives believe in God but they don't pray, in the sense of asking for help or grace or cure, because they already have all they need. Their form of prayer is simple worship and giving of thanks.

Yet the happiness and innocence of the citizens of Eldorado rests on total isolation, assured by an edict, to which they have all consented, that no one will ever leave this realm. And of course no stranger can enter it either, except by the kind of accident that brought Candide and Cacambo there. Voltaire seems to be saying that the best of all worlds can be found and enjoyed, but only at the cost of total separation from the turbulent and changing world humans have the habit of living and dying in, and in this context the remark made by Candide and Cacambo, both equally bemused and bewildered by Eldorado even before they have seen much of it, is exceptionally revealing. They say this is 'probably the land where all is well, for clearly such a place has to exist' (chapter 17). Has to exist? The place doesn't have to exist in material reality, and as far as we know it never has. But it does, it seems, have to exist as an expression of need and longing, because we cannot do without the dream of perfection it embodies. Voltaire includes it in his book for just this reason. 'All may be well,' he wrote in the *Poem on the Lisbon Disaster* (see Appendix 2), 'that hope can man sustain, / All now is well; 'tis an illusion vain'. Eldorado is the fictional illusion that represents the historical hope.

Well, not quite. Eldorado is perfect, but perfection itself is a problem in Voltaire's view, as his recurring allusions to the Garden of Eden also suggest. We can certainly wish that people might be less unhappy than so many of them are, less tormented by disease and poverty and the rabid violence of their neighbours, but should we hope for an ideal happiness for anyone? This goal may be not only unattainable but undesirable, because its achievement would leave no room for human restlessness and the intensity of our interest in the opinions of others. 'Nothing is so disagreeable,' Voltaire drily writes in an essay called 'Historical Praise of Reason', 'as to be hanged in obscurity'[9] – that is, without any public attention to one's martyrdom. And on the subject of happiness he offers one of the tersest and most complex statements in *Candide*. After a month in Eldorado, Candide decides the place is not for him because Cunégonde is not there, and also because he doesn't want to be like everyone else. If he takes a few sheeploads of gold and jewels with him back to Europe, he will be richer than all the kings there put together. Cacambo agrees: it's good to be on the move, we all like to go home and tell stories about our travels. Voltaire's comment is 'our two happy wanderers resolved to be happy no longer'. Why would anyone resolve to abandon happiness? Because it wasn't happiness? Or because it was? The paradox certainly contains an element of criticism, a measurement of folly: these two (genuinely) happy people don't know how to live with their happiness. But another and perhaps stronger reading will insist on the backhanded praise: the two are right to leave, happiness isn't everything, and a full life must include risk and adventure, and even a bit of pettiness.

And if Cacambo is ready to join his master in leaving Eldorado and happiness, he is also himself a model of goodness and loyalty, and a significant figure in the text for this reason.

Reading *Candide*, we become experts in suspicion, attuned to the obliquity of the book's language. An 'honest' person is someone who is about to do something crooked; 'good' or 'worthy' means naive or foolish. And so when Candide gives half his fortune to Cacambo and asks him to look for Cunégonde, with Voltaire telling us, for good measure, that 'he was a worthy fellow, this Cacambo' (chapter 19), we know what to expect. And when Candide says he trusts Cacambo as he trusts himself, that 'All is well, all goes well, all goes as well as it possibly can' (chapter 23), we merely wonder what form his terrible disappointment will take when it comes. Martin reinforces this idea by calling Candide 'a simpleton' for expecting 'a half-caste valet' to remain faithful when he has such an opportunity to defect. Ten pages later we are told there is still no sign of Cacambo. But then he turns up. He has been working for Candide all this time, he has found Cunégonde. 'The faithful Cacambo' turns out to be just what the epithet says he is: faithful. The interpretative rule in this deeply ironic text seems to be that the suspicious reading of words, persons and events is always correct – except when it is not. We certainly cannot count on human kindness, Voltaire is saying; but we cannot absolutely count on human betrayal either.

The Satirist's Garden

Italo Calvino remarks on the 'rhythm' and 'speed' of Voltaire's writing in *Candide*,[10] and Jean Sareil, in what is still the most subtle and far-reaching critical study of the book, asks a cluster of key questions.[11] If Voltaire is offering us such a disenchanted vision of the world, why is there so much gaiety in the writing? Why does the account of so many catastrophes have a happy ending? Why does this philosophical tale contain no real philosophical discussion? Why is Cunégonde the only person to age and become ugly?

Sareil himself offers an array of interesting responses. *Candide* is a satire, not a confession. Voltaire is not giving us his opinion about the universe; he is looking at persistent problems whose solutions, including the ones he has himself proposed,

do not satisfy him. He wishes to represent a world that is
not absurd and useless, but mysterious, forever inexplicable; a
world that is 'simultaneously livable and bad'.[12] And most
explicitly, Voltaire's 'lesson' is both that life is not worth much,
and that this 'not much' is of the highest value. These are
excellent answers. Voltaire's gaiety is a matter of style rather
than philosophy, the happy ending is at once ironic and an
invitation not to overdo our sense of misery. Voltaire's philosophy doesn't require philosophical discussion, indeed requires
its absence. There is plenty of confirmation of these claims in
Voltaire's other works. The hero of *Zadig* turns to philosophy
when he has a problem, but receives 'only knowledge', and no
relief. In his *Philosophical Dictionary*, Voltaire pretends to
wonder why we are arguing about the supreme or sovereign
good. 'You might as well ask what is the sovereign blue, or
the sovereign stew, or the sovereign way of walking, or the
sovereign way of reading ... There are no extreme pleasures
or extreme sufferings which will last a whole lifetime: the
sovereign good and the sovereign evil are chimeras.'[13] And
again (on the subject of destiny): 'Man can have only a certain
quantity of teeth, hair, and ideas. A time comes when he necessarily loses his teeth, his hair and his ideas'.[14] But there is more
to be said, and not only about the loss of Cunégonde's looks.
   It may help if we slow Voltaire down a little, look at the
details of his speed. Many critics have remarked on his strategic
use of the little word 'but'. In *Zadig* it represents an incomplete
discussion. An angel explains to the hero that things are what
they are, and if they were different, this would be a different
world. Zadig, wanting to argue and philosophize, says, 'But ...'
The angel is not listening, he is already on his way to another
sphere. In *Candide*, however, the use of 'but' usually indicates
not a wish to continue talking but the existence of a material
fact needing immediate attention, something that supersedes
talk. Does Candide believe, as certain Protestant zealots do,
that the Pope is the Anti-Christ? Candide replies that he has
not heard it said before, 'but whether he is or is not, I am in need
of food' (chapter 3). Meeting up with the syphilitic Pangloss,
Candide listens patiently to a long argument about the best

of worlds and sufficient reasons, then says, 'This is all very interesting . . . but now we must get you treated' (chapter 4). Caught up in the Lisbon earthquake, Pangloss seeks a scientific connection between this tremor and an earlier one in Peru. 'There must certainly be a seam of sulphur running underground from Lima to Lisbon' (chapter 5). Candide, trapped under fallen masonry and believing himself close to death, says, 'Nothing is more likely . . . but, for the love of God, some oil and wine!'. Pangloss says, 'What do you mean, "likely"?', and Candide passes out. On a milder note, but preserving the same corrective pattern, Voltaire has Candide say there is nothing certain in the world (the French literally says nothing solid in the world) but virtue and the happiness of seeing Mademoiselle Cunégonde again. Cacambo says, 'I agree . . . but we still have two sheep laden with more treasure than the King of Spain will ever own' (chapter 19). There are other uses of the word 'but' in *Candide*, moments of conventional argument or discussion, but the general tilt is obvious, and prepares us for the most famous 'but' of all. Pangloss, correctly but trivially, summarizes all their adventures as a chain of cause and effect. Candide answers, in the last words of the book, 'That is well said . . . but we must cultivate our garden' (chapter 30). The garden is what there is, beneath and beyond our words; and even philosophy is welcome in the garden, as long as it doesn't insist on having any consequences, or getting in the way of work, the active cultivation of that earth.

   To cultivate the garden, then, is not simply to mind one's own business, a wiser, more sophisticated version of the selfishness the book attacked at its outset. It is to decide not to seek answers to questions that can have none; to remember the concrete 'buts' that lie in wait for every grand abstraction. Still, it is hard not to feel there is a certain blandness in this philosophy that refuses philosophy, a betrayal of Voltaire's own best, angriest moments, and Roland Barthes, not intending a compliment, called Voltaire 'the last of the happy writers', or perhaps, given a certain fluidity in the meaning of the French word, 'the last of the lucky writers'. Voltaire was lucky, Barthes wrote, to have history on his side, a world of atrocities and

visible, idiotic villains, making way for the great wave of
improvement that ended in the French and American revolutions. And lucky to have been able to ignore another kind of
history, since he couldn't know anything about Hegel or Marx
or evolution. 'For Voltaire, there is no history in the modern
sense of the word, nothing but chronologies. Voltaire writes
historical works expressly to say that he didn't believe in history.'[15] History, for Barthes, is not simply what happens to
human beings in time but a particular, post-Enlightenment project of making sense of progress and its discontents. Voltaire's
third piece of luck or happiness, Barthes says, was the welcome
his contemporaries gave to his refusal of all systems. And not
only Voltaire's contemporaries, but those of Barthes too. Voltaire 'ceaselessly dissociated intelligence and intellectuality,
asserting that the world is an order if we do not try too much
to order it, that it is a system only if we renounce systematizing
it: this conduct of mind has had a great career subsequently:
today we call it anti-intellectualism'.[16]

'Today' for Barthes was 1964, and we may feel the idea of
history as change and evolution has taken a few hits since then.
But the charge of intellectual complacency retains its force, it
seems to me, only as long as we try to capture Voltaire's
thought, or more precisely, as long as we try to separate his
thought from the movement of his prose. Seeking to understand
Voltaire, we forget what it is like to read him. At the level of
the words, what Barthes calls luck turns into what Calvino calls
speed, and the gaiety of the writing, far from diminishing the
described horrors or providing an argument for ignoring them,
actually enhances them. They are beyond mere sentimental
condemnation, and beyond philosophy too, in another sense:
philosophy is not only helpless but tasteless, a form of unkind-
ness. Here, for example, is Candide, who is said to have
'trembled like a philosopher', escaping from Voltaire's version
of the Seven Years' War:

> Climbing over heaps of the dead and dying, he came first to a
> neighbouring village; it was in ashes ... Here old men riddled
> with wounds or lead shot looked on as their wives lay dying,

their throats cut, clutching their children to their blood-stained breasts; over there lay young girls in their last agonies, disembowelled after having satisfied the natural urges of various heroes; others still, half burned to death, cried out for someone to come and finish them off. Brains were scattered over the ground, amidst severed arms and legs. (Chapter 3)

A little later, in a village belonging to the other side in the war, Candide is said to be 'still stepping over twitching torsos'. 'Dead and dying', which sounds like a cliché, turns out to be an exact announcement of an enormity: this is what it means not to be dead yet, only shot, slashed, burned and dismembered. The anger is directed at those who lead people into war (we hear it especially in the sarcasm about heroes, which is merely another word for rapists), but we are also to remember that Candide, endlessly described throughout the book as a good person, is not stopping to help anyone, or even register his shock.

Late in the book, Candide, once again called 'the worthy Candide', meets up with Paquette, the chambermaid from the Westphalian castle, the one who gave Pangloss his syphilis. She is still pretty, and now a prostitute in Venice, having passed through the hands of a monk, a doctor and a judge, and is apparently some sort of expert on the professions:

Oh, Monsieur, if you could imagine what it is like to have to caress, with the same enthusiasm, an elderly merchant, a lawyer, a monk, a gondolier and an abbé; to be exposed to every insult and affront; to be reduced often to borrowing a petticoat so as to go and have it lifted by some disgusting man or other; to be robbed by one of what you have earned with another, or have it extorted from you by officers of the law; to have nothing to look forward to but a hideous old age, the poor house and the refuse-heap; then you would agree that I am one of the unhappiest creatures alive. (Chapter 24)

This is another worst-of-all-possible-worlds story, of course, but it is hard to argue with it, and Voltaire adds a cruel and subtle twist. Candide expresses his surprise that Paquette should seem so happy, and she points out that seeming happy is precisely part of her job, and not the least of its horrors: 'Ah! Monsieur . . . that is another of the miseries of our profession. Yesterday I was beaten and robbed by an officer; today I must seem in good humour to please a monk.'

In a short story called 'Adventure of Memory', Voltaire says the Muses don't compose satires because 'satires don't correct anyone, irritate the foolish, and make them even more mean'.[17] Does he believe this? He probably does, at least in part. He himself composes satires not because they work but because he is a writer, lucky or not. Pointless war, ubiquitous rape, endless prostitution, miserable dying, miserable living, the selfishness of even the best of men, good humour as the professional mask of pain – these are just a few features of the world Voltaire evokes for us, and I am not even mentioning natural disasters and ordinary human greed and crookedness. In such a universe cultivating one's garden is neither complacency nor wisdom, but a therapy of forgetting, a way of conjugating one's own good fortune and the distress of others. But if your garden happens to be the world of writing, then cultivating it is not even a work of forgetting. It is a work of unrelenting memory, a recurring assemblage of words that remind us what the world is like and invite us to think about which pieces of it we can change. Satires don't correct anyone, but some readers may find their mingled horror and laughter suggest work for them to do. That would be their garden.

There remains the question of Cunégonde's aging and becoming ugly. It is not strictly true that she is the only person this happens to – the old woman was once a beautiful princess – but she is the only person it happens to in the time of the immediate narrative, and the contrast with Paquette is important. Paquette needs to retain her looks so that the gap between the appearance of happiness and the hard grind of sexual labour can finally become clear, and in the economy of Voltaire's writing the situation alludes to the gap between many other bright appearances and dark realities. And Cunégonde needs to lose her looks so that . . . There are really too many possibilities.

Perhaps Cunégonde's aging happens simply so that Voltaire

can get a laugh out of this sour turn in what Candide, if no one else, keeps seeing as a fairy tale: the hero marries not the princess he dreamed of, but the old toad the princess has become. Voltaire does go to town on this subject. When Candide first hears that Cunégonde has become 'fearfully ugly' (chapter 27), he quickly strikes the correct posture: 'I am a man of honour, and my duty is to love her always.' At the end of the same paragraph, though, the change is still on his mind: 'What a shame she has become so ugly'. And, as Voltaire adds with mock gratuitousness, Candide sets out to catch up with her, 'however ugly she might be'. When he finally sees Cunégonde again, he is 'seized with horror', and recoils, before pulling himself together and stepping forward 'out of sheer good manners' (chapter 29). His surprise is not too surprising, since Voltaire has just described Cunégonde as 'all weather-beaten, her eyes bloodshot, her breasts sunken, her cheeks lined, her arms red and chapped'. She is clearly the victim of more than ordinary aging; the victim of her author, we might say. Not only has she not aged well, she has become an anti-beauty.

The fairy tale has turned sour, but the sourness has its reasons. The tale was deluded to begin with, a distracting dream or retarded fantasy. Cunégonde is the withered goal of Candide's longing, indeed she is what happens to all longing that pursues only an idea of a person or a passion. She has to change not in order to disappoint Candide or to allow him to do the right thing after all, but in order to remind us that the objects of our desire have histories of their own, and histories we may not like. She is the incarnation of the book's most cruel 'but'. Candide finds his great love again, but she is ugliness personified, and has become nasty into the bargain. The unfortunate Cunégonde loses her looks, it turns out, for precisely the same reasons as the unfortunate Paquette retains hers: appearances alter or don't alter, but they are never more than appearances, a place to start but not to end.

Michael Wood

NOTES

1. Theodore Besterman, *Voltaire* (London, 1969), p. 301.
2. Voltaire, *Philosophical Dictionary*, trans. Theodore Besterman (London, 1972), p. 72.
3. Voltaire, *Candide et autres contes* (Paris, 1979), p. 414.
4. Alexander Pope, *Poems*, ed. John Butt (New Haven, 1963), p. 515.
5. From Leibniz's *Theodicy*, quoted in notes to *Candide et autres contes*, p. 420.
6. *Philosophical Dictionary*, p. 72 (see Appendix 3: 'Bien (Tout Est): All Is Good').
7. Peter Gay, *Voltaire's Politics* (Princeton, 1959), p. 21.
8. Michel de Montaigne, 'Des Cannibales', *Essais*, book 1, chapter 30.
9. Voltaire, 'Eloge historique de la raison' (1775), in *Candide et autres contes*, p. 279.
10. Italo Calvino, 'Candide: An Essay in Velocity', in *The Literature Machine*, trans. Patrich Creagh (London, 1987).
11. Jean Sareil, *Essai sur 'Candide'* (Geneva, 1967).
12. Sareil, *Essai sur Candide*, p. 31.
13. *Philosophical Dictionary*, p. 67, entry 'Bien (Souverain Bien): Good (Sovereign Good)'.
14. *Philosophical Dictionary*, p. 173 (see Appendix 3: 'Destin: Fate').
15. Roland Barthes, *Barthes: Selected Writings*, ed. Susan Sontag, trans. Richard Howard (London, 1983), p. 154.
16. Barthes, *Selected Writings*, p. 156.
17. Voltaire, *Aventure de la mémoire* (1775), in *Candide et autres contes*, p. 275.

Further Reading

Editions of *Candide* and Other Texts by Voltaire

Romans et contes, ed. Frederic Deloffre and Jacques Van den Heuvel (Paris, 1979).

Candide, ed. André Magnan (rev. edn, Paris, 1984).

Contes en vers et en prose, vol. 1, ed. Sylvain Menant (Paris, 1992).

Candide, ed. René Pomeau (2nd edn, Paris, 1979).

Philosophical Dictionary, trans. Theodore Besterman (London, 1972).

Criticism on Voltaire and *Candide*

(*SVEC* refers to *Studies on Voltaire and the Eighteenth Century* (Voltaire Foundation, Oxford).)

Auerbach, Erich, *Mimesis. The Representation of Reality in Western Literature*, trans. Willard R. Trask, (Princeton NJ, 1968).

Barber, W. H., *Voltaire: 'Candide'* (London, 1960).

Barthes, Roland, 'The Last Happy Writer', Susan Sontag (ed.), *A Barthes Reader* (London, 1980).

Betts, C. J., 'On the Beginning and Ending of Candide', *Modern Language Review*, 80 (1985), pp. 283–92.

Bottiglia, W. F. (ed.), *Voltaire. A Collection of Critical Essays* (Englewood Cliffs, NJ, 1968).

—, *Voltaire's 'Candide': Analysis of a Classic* (2nd edn *SVEC* 7, 1964).

Calvino, Italo, 'Candide: An Essay in Velocity', *The Literature Machine* (London, 1985).

Davidson, Ian, *Voltaire in Exile: The Last Years 1753–78* (London, 2004).

Goldzink, Jean, *Roman et idéologie dans Candide* (Paris, 1982).

Havens, G. R., 'Some Notes on Candide', *Modern Language Notes*, May 1973, pp. 841–7.

Henry, Patrick, 'Sacred and Profane Gardens in *Candide*', *SVEC* 176 (1979), pp. 133–52.

Howells, R. J., 'The Burlesque as a Philosophical Principle in Voltaire's Contes', R. J. Howells and H. T. Mason (eds.), *Voltaire and His World: Studies presented to W. H. Barber* (Oxford, 1985).

Kavanagh, Thomas, *Enlightenment and the Shadows of Chance* (Baltimore, 1993).

Langdon, David, 'On the Meanings of the Conclusion of *Candide*', *SVEC* 238 (1985), pp. 397–432.

Magnan, André, *Voltaire, 'Candide ou l'optimisme'* (Paris, 1987).

Mason, Haydn T., *Voltaire* (London, 1975).

—, 'Voltaire's "Sermon" against Optimism: the Poème sur le désastre de Lisbonne', Giles Barber and Cecil Courtney (eds.), *Enlightenment Essays in Memory of Robert Shackleton* (Voltaire Foundation, Oxford 1988).

Mervaud, Christiane, *Voltaire en toutes lettres* (Paris, 1992).

—, 'Du Carnaval au carnavalesque: l'episode vénétien de Candide', Christiane Mervaud and Sylvain Menant (eds.), *Le Siècle de Voltaire: hommage à René Pomeau* (2 vols., Oxford, 1987).

Murray, Geoffrey, *Voltaire's Candide: The Protean Gardener, 1755–1762* (Geneva, 1970).

Pearson, Roger, *The Fables of Reason: A Study of Voltaire's 'Contes Philosophiques'* (Oxford, 1993)

—, *Voltaire Almighty: A Life in Pursuit of Freedom* (London, 2005)

Sareil, Jean, *Essai sur 'Candide'* (Geneva, 1967).

Starobinski, Jean, 'Voltaire's Double-barreled Musket', *Blessings in Disguise* (California, 1993).

—, 'On the Philosophical Style of Candide', *Comparative Literature*, 1976, vol. xxviii, pp. 193–202.

—, 'Candide et la question de l'autorité', Jean Macary (ed.), *Essays on the Age of Enlightenment in Honour of Ira O. Wade* (Geneva, 1977).

Valéry, Paul, 'Voltaire', in *Oeuvres*, 2 vols. (Paris, 1957–60), vol. I, pp. 518–30.

Wade, I. O., *Voltaire and Candide* (Princeton, NJ, 1959).

Waldinger, Renée (ed.), *Approaches to Teaching Voltaire's 'Candide'* (New York, 1987).

Weightman, John, 'The Quality of *Candide*', E. T. Dubois et al. (eds.), *Essays Presented to C. M. Girdlestone* (Newcastle, 1960).

Wolper, Roy, 'Candide, Gull in the Garden', *Eighteenth Century Studies* 3 (1969), pp. 265–77.

—, 'Voltaire's Contes: A Reconsideration', *Forum* 16 (1978), pp. 74–9.

Music and *Candide*

Bernstein, Leonard, *Candide, an Opera* (lyrics by Richard Wilbur and other lyricists) (1956).

Translator's Note

Stendhal, who loved comic opera, must have adored the little
novels of Voltaire, those peerless miracles of rapidity, energy
and terrible fantasy. In these nimble and cruel works, where
satire, opera, ballet and ideology are joined in an irresistible
rhythm, in these fables that were the scandalous delight
of the end of the reign of Louis XV, may we not see the
elegant ancestors of those operattas which so mercilessly
galvanized the last days of the reign of Napoleon III? But I
cannot re-read *La Princesse de Babylone*, *Zadig*, *Babouk* or
Candide without thinking I am hearing a music infinitely
more spiritual, more sceptical and more diabolical than that
of Offenbach or his like.

Paul Valéry, *Essai sur Stendhal*, 1927

There is no transposing Voltaire's notorious music into English.
John Butt, in his Preface to the earlier Penguin Classics translation of *Candide* (1947) wrote that 'a faithfully literal rendering
of the French would often offend an English ear by its very
baldness, and it has therefore been found necessary to expand
the French in such places . . . A translator must abandon something of Voltaire's rhythm in the effort to make him speak
modern English'. A difficult decision, since what is Voltairean
evaporates in paraphrase: his style inheres in its phrasing and
timing. The present translation attends closely to the words,
syntax, punctuation and other structural features of the original. It aspires to baldness, in the hope that some of the *allegro*
of the original will be transmitted, or overheard.

I have therefore tried to render Voltaire's sentences, rather
than break them up or run them together; and to retain rather
than elide the abrupt tempi of his prose, with its deliberate
repetitions and its suppression of connectives. I have also

followed where Voltaire dives in and out of the present tense to increase velocity, or to foreground the insubstantiality of his tale. Again, in the French text virtually all dialogue takes place inside the paragraph, which runs together different voices into a pattern of continuous dialogue; I have retained these paragraphs, although in the translation a new speaker is always preceded by a dash, so that it is clear who is talking. Voltaire's punctuation has likewise been followed, notably his expressive use of the semi-colon. More than many texts, *Candide* is a system of punctuation, and many of the story's effects are achieved by its compound sentences, at once brief and potentially interminable. As William Hazlitt said of *Candide*: 'every sentence tells, and the whole reads like one sentence' (*Lectures on the English Poets*, 1818, Lecture 6).

The vocabulary of *Candide* is formulaic, unresonating, casually exact. The translation has also tried to be faithful to this neutrality of surface. Voltaire's effects are achieved less at the level of lexical distinction than through syntax and its apparently innocent transitions. The tale's crisp rhythms combine abstinence and excess: parallelism, abbreviation and repetition on the one hand; accumulation (litanies, catalogues, genealogies, comic proliferation) on the other.

Finally, Voltaire's is a classical style, however mined and exploded from within; the translation has tried to respect the decorum of the original. *Candide* describes the facts of life in a new language of plain-speaking, but with a chaste scruple of phrasing. To offer a more demotically 'modern' version would be to collapse the distance between what is being said and the way in which it is being said.

A Note on the Text

Only one manuscript of *Candide* survives (discovered in 1959), copied in the hand of Voltaire's secretary, dictated in part by Voltaire, and with corrections in Voltaire's own hand. It probably dates from October 1758, and is known as the 'La Vallière' manuscript, named after the individual to whom Voltaire confided it. This manuscript presents intermediate states for chapters 19 and 22: thus the manuscript does not contain the meeting with the black slave in the former chapter, and it offers two versions of the latter chapter – or rather, subsequent to the first version of chapter 22, a second follows in which only the opening is rewritten, after which Voltaire returns to his first version. Other changes between the La Vallière manuscript and the first edition are not very numerous but occasionally significant. These have been noted in the explanatory notes.

The work was published pseudonymously (as written by a certain M. Le Docteur Ralph) on or shortly before 22 February 1759, and it appeared simultaneously in Geneva (published by Cramer), in Paris (supervised by La Vallière) and in Amsterdam, the three great publishing centres – so as to anticipate inevitable difficulties with the authorities, and to ensure the sale of as many copies as possible before the edition was inevitably pirated. Voltaire's authorship was soon exposed (he did not admit to being the author of *Candide* until 1768), whereupon the authorities attempted to suppress the work by seizing printed copies – in Paris on 25 February and in Geneva on 26 February. In the following months numerous other editions appeared: six in Paris, others in Liège, London and Lyons.

Over twenty editions were published in the course of 1759; three translations into English were published in London and Edinburgh, two of which appear to have been versions of manuscript copies sent by Voltaire, differing in minor respects from the original French edition.

For a new edition in 1761, Voltaire rewrote the Parisian episode in chapter 22, which had been criticized, adding the long passage discussing the theatre, and the account of Candide's adventures with Mme de Parolignac. After 1761 there were many further editions but no substantial corrections. Voltaire intended some further corrections, at the end of his life, of which his secretary Wagnière preserved a record. These have also been referred to in the notes.

The present translation follows the 1761 text, and indicates in the explanatory notes significant local divergences between this text and the 1759 edition.

A Note on Names

Voltaire plays on names, titles and honorifics throughout *Candide*. At the simplest level names are suggestive of nationality or race (thus **Issacar**), or they incorporate a Virgilian epithet: thus **Vanderdendur** – *de la dent dure*, 'of the hard tooth' – for the hard-bargaining Dutch merchant. But the names of the major characters are compounds as well as essences. Thus Pangloss, the apostle of optimism, gets his name from the Greek words *pan* ('all') and *glossa* ('tongue'): hence 'all tongue', or 'all talk', in counterpoint to Rabelais's protagonist Panurge (who is 'all energy', 'all work'). The name suggests 'one who glosses everything', and Voltaire in his notebooks accuses those 'who speak in order to say nothing' of *panglossie*.

If Pangloss closes everything inside a system, **Candide** (Latin *candidus*, 'white', 'pure', 'beautiful', and, by extension, 'honest', etc.) is he who is open to all experience. The term was used frequently in the contemporary French translation of Locke's *Essay on Human Understanding* to suggest the self as an innocent sheet of white paper on which experience will write its story. Voltaire often employs the word for its echoes of Horace, for whom *candidus* means unimpeachably 'sincere'; but elsewhere he also uses *candide* in an emergent modern sense, with a pejorative suggestion of gullibility.

The initial and final alliteration of Candide with **Cunégonde** is a notable aspect of the acoustic world of the tale. Cunégonde gets her name from St Kunigunde, wife of Henry II, Duke of Bavaria, who together with her husband took a vow of chastity. On his death she was restored a virgin to her parents. Unjustly accused of adultery, she had to prove her virginity through the

test of fire, for which she was canonized in 1200. The comic
incongruity of this choice of name, given the chequered fate
of Voltaire's heroine, is compounded by the sexual reference
embedded in the orthography of '*cu[l]*négonde' (Latin *cunnus*,
'cunt'; French *cul*, 'arse/ass'). The onomastic comedy is protracted, Cunégonde being referred to throughout the text as
'Mademoiselle Cunégonde'; George Saintsbury remarked that
'nobody will ever know anything about style who does not
feel what the continual repetition in Candide's mouth of that
Mademoiselle does' (*A History of the French Novel*, 1917,
vol. I, p. 382).

With **Cacambo**, Voltaire seems to conjure another name from
an alliteration with both Candide and Cunégonde. Or rather,
the onomatopoeia of 'Cacambo' (*caca* being a child's term for
excrement) is in cacophonous counterpoint to the romantic
aspirations of the story's hero and heroine. The name plays its
own characteristically optimistic tune: 'Le Caca-en-beau' – 'to
look on the bright side of *caca*', so to speak; and it also possesses
appropriate colonial connotations, by analogy with *cacao*
('cocoa') and *cacahuète* ('peanut').

Redolent of amorous intrigue, **Paquette** was a conventional
fictional name for domestic servants, perhaps originating with
the chambermaid Paquette in La Fontaine's fable about the
Curate and Death (*Fables*, Book 7, no. 10). A *pâquerette*
('daisy') is a flower that is both fresh and common, and the
pairing with **Girofleo** ('gillyflower') suggests two ironically
biblical flowers of the field, who neither toil nor reap.

Finally, **Pococuranté**, from the Italian *poco* ('little') and
curante ('caring'): hence one who 'cares about little', or 'the
bored-to-tears'. Pococuranté is dry-eyed – like Martin he is one
of the story's less deceived – with a name which in French
carries just a contrary hint of his being the more deceived (*cocu*,
'cuckold').

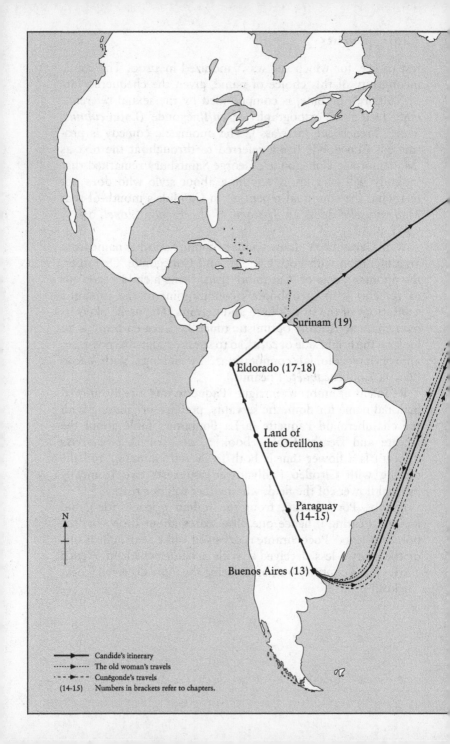

Surinam (19)

Eldorado (17-18)

Land of
the Oreillons

Paraguay
(14-15)

Buenos Aires (13)

N

——▶ Candide's itinerary
······▶ The old woman's travels
- - -▶ Cunégonde's travels
(14-15) Numbers in brackets refer to chapters.

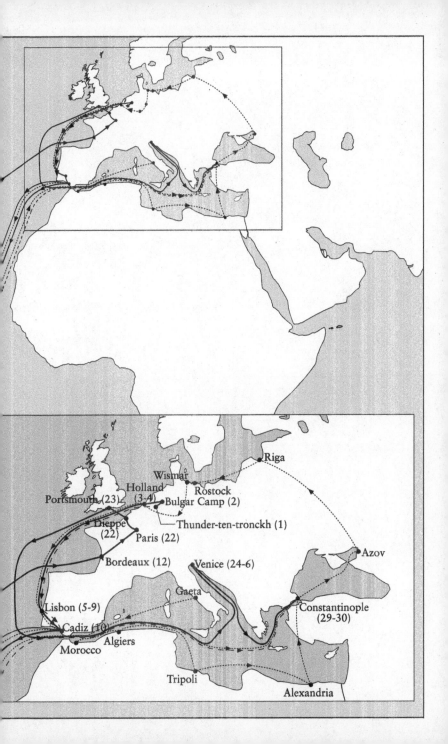

Riga

Wismar
Holland
(3-4)
Rostock
Portsmouth (23)
Bulgar Camp (2)
Thunder-ten-tronckh (1)
Dieppe
(22)
Paris (22)
Azov
Bordeaux (12)
Venice (24-6)
Gaeta
Constantinople
(29-30)
Lisbon (5-9)
Cadiz (10)
Algiers
Morocco
Tripoli
Alexandria

VOLTAIRE

Candide
or *Optimism*[1]

Translated from the German of Doctor Ralph[2]

WITH THE ADDITIONS[3] FOUND IN
THE DOCTOR'S POCKET WHEN HE DIED
AT MINDEN,[4] IN THE YEAR OF GRACE
1759

CHAPTER I

How Candide was brought up in a beautiful castle, and how he was driven from the same

Once upon a time in Westphalia, in the castle of Monsieur the Baron von Thunder-ten-tronckh, there lived a young boy on whom nature had bestowed the gentlest of dispositions. His countenance expressed his soul. He combined solid judgement with complete openness of mind; which is the reason, I believe, that he was called Candide. The older servants of the house suspected him to be the son of the Baron's sister by a kindly and honest gentleman of the neighbourhood, whom that young lady refused ever to marry because he could only ever give proof of seventy-one quarterings,[1] the rest of his genealogical tree having been lost through the ravages of time.

This Baron was one of the most powerful lords of Westphalia, for his castle had a gate and windows. His great hall was even hung with a tapestry. All the dogs in his barnyards made up a pack when the need arose; his stable boys served for huntsmen; the village parson officiated as his grand almoner. Everyone called him Your Grace, and everyone laughed at his jokes.

The Baroness, who weighed approximately three hundred and fifty pounds, and consequently basked in very great esteem, performed the honours of the house with a dignity that made her all the more imposing. Her daughter Cunégonde, seventeen years old and rosy-cheeked, was fresh, plump and appetizing. The Baron's son seemed in every respect worthy of his father.

Pangloss,[2] the tutor, was the oracle of the establishment, to whose lessons little Candide listened with all the good faith of his age and nature.

Pangloss taught metaphysico-theologico-cosmo-nigology.[3] He could prove to wonderful effect that there was no effect without cause,[4] and that, in this best of all possible worlds, His Lordship the Baron's castle was the finest of castles and Her Ladyship the best of all possible baronesses.

'It is demonstrable,' he would say, 'that things cannot be other than as they are: for, since everything is made to serve an end, everything is necessarily for the best of ends. Observe how noses were formed to support spectacles, therefore we have spectacles. Legs are clearly devised for the wearing of breeches, therefore we wear breeches. Stones were formed to be hewn and made into castles, hence his Lordship's beautiful castle, for the greatest baron in the province must perforce be the best housed; and since pigs were made to be eaten, we eat pork all year round; consequently, those who have argued that all is well have been talking nonsense: they should have said that all is for the best.'[5]

Candide listened attentively, and he trusted innocently; for he found Mademoiselle Cunégonde extremely beautiful, though he had never had the effrontery to tell her so. He concluded that, next to being born Baron von Thunder-ten-tronckh, the second degree of bliss was being Mademoiselle Cunégonde; the third was seeing her every day; and the fourth was listening to Maître Pangloss, the greatest philosopher in the province and, therefore, in the whole world.

One day, as Cunégonde was walking the grounds of the castle, in the little wood which everyone called *the park*, she caught sight through the undergrowth of Doctor Pangloss giving a lesson in experimental physics to her mother's chamber-maid, a very pretty and tractable little brunette. Mademoiselle Cunégonde had a natural aptitude for the sciences, and she noted breathlessly the repeated experiments to which she was witness; she saw clearly the doctor's sufficient reason,[6] both the effects and the causes, and she returned home very agitated, very thoughtful, and very much filled with desire to be a scientist, reflecting that she might yet prove to be the sufficient reason of young Candide, who might in turn prove to be hers.

She ran into Candide as she entered the castle, and blushed; Candide blushed in turn; she bade him good day in a faltering voice, and Candide answered without knowing what he was saying. The next day after dinner, as everyone was leaving the table, Cunégonde and Candide found themselves behind a screen; Cunégonde dropped her handkerchief, Candide picked it up; innocently she took his hand in hers, innocently the young man kissed the young lady's hand, doing so with a singular vivacity, sensibility and grace; their lips met, their eyes blazed, their knees trembled, their hands strayed. His Excellency the Baron von Thunder-ten-tronckh happened to be passing near the screen and, observing this cause and that effect, chased Candide out of the castle with great kicks to his backside; Cunégonde fainted; as soon as she came to her senses she had her face slapped by the Baroness, and all was consternation in the most beautiful and delightful of possible castles.

CHAPTER 2

What became of Candide among the Bulgars

Thus expelled from the earthly paradise, Candide wandered for a long time, not knowing where he was going, weeping, raising his eyes to heaven, then turning them frequently in the direction of the most beautiful of castles, containing the most beautiful of baron's daughters; he fell asleep finally in the middle of a field, with no supper, between two furrows; the snow fell in large flakes. Next morning, entirely numb, Candide dragged himself as far as the nearest town, which was called Valdberghoff-trarbk-dikdorff;[1] having no money, and faint with hunger and exhaustion, he paused forlornly at the door of a tavern. Two men dressed in blue[2] observed him: 'Well now, comrade,' said the first, 'there's a well-built young fellow, and he's of regulation height.' They approached Candide, and invited him very civilly to dine with them. 'Gentlemen,' said Candide with

engaging candour, 'you honour me greatly, but I lack the means
to pay my share.' – 'My good sir,' replied the second, 'a person
of your looks and quality never pays for anything: I'd say
you must be all of nearly six feet tall?' – 'That is my height,
gentlemen,' he replied, bowing. – 'Well then, good sir, sit yourself down and eat; not only do we invite you, but we shall make
sure that a gentleman like yourself does not go short of funds
either; after all, we men are born to look out for each other.' –
'You are right,' said Candide, 'that is what Pangloss always
told me, and now I see clearly that everything is indeed for the
best.' They press him to accept several écus;[3] which he takes,
and tries to make out a receipt; they refuse, and all three sit
down to dinner. 'Tell me,' says the first, 'do you not devotedly
love . . .' – 'Mademoiselle Cunégonde?' replies Candide. 'But
of course, devotedly.' – 'No, no,' says the second of these
gentlemen. 'What we mean is, do you not devotedly love the
King of the Bulgars?'[4] – 'Not in the least,' says Candide, 'since
I have never set eyes on him.' – 'What! But he is the most
delightful of kings, and we must drink his health this instant.'
– 'With great pleasure, gentlemen!' and he drinks the toast.
'That will do nicely,' says the first. 'You are hereby the support,
the defender, the mainstay, and, in a word, the hero of the
Bulgars; your fortune is made, and your glory is assured.'[5] They
immediately clap irons on his feet and march him off to the
regiment. He is made to do right turns, left turns, draw
the ramrod,[6] return the ramrod, take aim, fire and march at the
double, for which he receives thirty strokes of the birch; the
next day he performs his drill a little less badly, and receives
only twenty strokes; the day after that he is given only ten, and
is looked on by his comrades as a prodigy.

Candide, completely bewildered, had not yet figured out
quite what was meant by his being a hero. One fine spring day
he took it into his head to go for a long walk, simply by putting
one foot in front of the other, in the belief that it was a privilege
of the human as of the animal species to use its legs as it pleases.
He had not covered two leagues when he was caught up by
four other heroes, each over six foot tall, who tied him up and
marched him off to the cells. He was asked at his court-martial

which he preferred: to be flogged by the entire regiment thirty-six times, or receive twelve lead bullets in his skull simultaneously. In vain did he remonstrate with them about freedom of the will,[7] and protest that he preferred neither the one option nor the other; a choice had to be made; he determined, by virtue of that gift of God called *freedom*, to run the gauntlet thirty-six times.[8] He endured two runs. The regiment numbered two thousand men, which for Candide added up to four thousand strokes, which in turn laid bare the muscles and sinews from the nape of his neck to his buttocks. As they were lining up for the third run, Candide, who could take no more, politely asked if they would instead be so kind as to cave his head in; the plea was granted; he was blindfolded and made to kneel. At this moment the King of the Bulgars was passing by, and inquired as to the condemned man's crime; being a king of rare genius, he understood from everything he learned about Candide that here was a young metaphysician entirely unschooled in the ways of the world, and he granted him his pardon with a clemency whose praises will be sung in all the newspapers for all the ages.[9] An honest surgeon cured Candide in three weeks, with ointments prescribed by Dioscorides.[10] He had already grown back a little skin, and was able to walk, when the King of the Bulgars declared war on the King of the Abars.

CHAPTER 3

How Candide ran away from the Bulgars, and what became of him

Never was anything so gallant, so well accoutred, so dashing, so well drilled as those two armies. Trumpets, fifes, hautboys, drums and cannon produced a harmony such as was never heard in hell.[1] First the cannon toppled about six thousand men on either side; then the muskets removed from the best of possible worlds between nine and ten thousand scoundrels who were infesting its surface.[2] Next the bayonet proved sufficient reason for the death of a few thousand more.[3] The total may well have amounted to thirty thousand corpses. Candide trembled like a philosopher, and concealed himself as best he could for the duration of this heroic butchery.

Finally, while both kings were having victory *Te Deums*[4] sung in their respective camps, Candide resolved to go and think about effects and causes elsewhere. Climbing over heaps of the dead and dying, he came first to a neighbouring village; it was in ashes: it was an Abar village which the Bulgars had razed to the ground, in accordance with international law.[5] Here old men riddled with wounds or lead shot looked on as their wives lay dying, their throats cut, clutching their children to their blood-stained breasts; over there lay young girls in their last agonies, disembowelled after having satisfied the natural urges of various heroes; others still, half burned to death, cried out for someone to come and finish them off. Brains were scattered over the ground, amidst severed arms and legs.[6]

Candide fled as fast as he was able until he reached another village: this one belonged to the Bulgars, and the Abar heroes had dealt with it accordingly.[7] Candide, still stepping over twitching torsos or walking through ruins, finally left the theatre of war behind, carrying some meagre provisions in his knapsack and Mademoiselle Cunégonde's image in his heart. After a time he reached Holland, where his provisions ran out: but having heard that everyone in that country was rich, and that they were all Christians, he had no doubt that he would be treated there as well as he had been in the Baron's castle, before being chased out of it on account of Mademoiselle Cunégonde's beautiful eyes.

He begged alms of several solemn-looking individuals; they all replied that if he continued in this vein he would be locked up in a house of correction and be taught how to earn his living.[8]

He then approached a man who had just been holding forth to a large gathering for an entire hour, alone and unassisted, on the theme of charity. This orator[9] looked askance at him and said: 'What are you here for? Are you here for the good cause?' – 'There is no effect without cause,' replied Candide timidly, 'for everything is linked in a chain of necessity,[10] and arranged for the best. It was necessary that I be chased away from Mademoiselle Cunégonde, and have to run the gauntlet, and necessary that I beg for my bread until such time as I can earn it; none of this could have been otherwise.' – 'But my friend,' said the orator, 'do you believe that the Pope is Anti-Christ?'[11] – 'I've not heard it said before now,' replied Candide, 'but whether he is or is not, I am in need of food.' – 'You don't deserve to eat,' said the other. 'Be off, you wretch! Out of my sight, you miserable creature! And don't ever approach my person again.' The orator's wife, putting her head out of the window and catching sight of somebody who could doubt that the Pope was Anti-Christ, discharged over his head a chamber pot full of ... Heavens! To what extremes is religious zeal sometimes carried by the ladies!

A passer-by who had never been baptized, a good Ana-baptist[12] named Jacques, saw the cruel and ignominious logic thus being meted out to one of his brothers, a fellow being with two legs, no feathers and a soul;[13] so he took him back to his house, cleaned him up, gave him some bread and some beer, presented him with two florins, and would even have apprenticed him to work in his Persian fabrics workshops, such as are common in Holland. Candide, faint with gratitude, cried out: 'Maître Pangloss was quite right to tell me that all is for the best in this world; of which I am vastly more persuaded by your extreme generosity than by the harshness of that gentleman in the black cloak, and Madame, his lady wife.'

The next day, while out for a walk, he came across a beggar all covered in sores, his eyes glazed, the end of his nose eaten away, his mouth twisted on one side, his teeth black, who spoke in a strangled voice and was racked by a violent cough, spitting out a tooth with every spasm.

CHAPTER 4

*How Candide encountered his old philosophy
tutor, Doctor Pangloss, and what came of it*

Candide, moved even more by compassion than by disgust,
gave this frightful creature the two florins he had been given by
his honest Anabaptist, Jacques. The apparition stared at him
fixedly, began to weep, and threw its arms about his neck.
Startled, Candide recoiled. 'Alas!' said the one unfortunate to
the other, 'so you no longer recognize your beloved Pangloss?'
– 'What am I hearing! You? My beloved tutor? You, in this
horrible condition? What terrible thing has happened? Why are
you no longer in the most beautiful of castles? What has become
of Mademoiselle Cunégonde, the pearl of daughters, the
masterpiece of nature?' – 'I am worn out,' said Pangloss. At
once Candide led him to the Anabaptist's stable, where he made
him eat a little bread and, when he had recovered, said: 'Now!
What about Cunégonde?' – 'Dead,' was the reply. At this word
Candide fainted; his friend brought him to his senses with some
stale vinegar which happened to be in the stable.[1] Candide
opened his eyes. 'Cunégonde, dead! Ah, best of worlds, where
are you now? But what did she die of? Was it from seeing me
chased from their beautiful castle with great kicks from her
noble father's boot, by any chance?' – 'No,' said Pangloss. 'She
was disembowelled by Bulgar soldiers, after being raped until
she could be raped no more; they smashed in the noble Baron's
skull, as he tried to protect her; the Baroness was chopped to
pieces; my poor pupil received exactly the same treatment as
his sister; as for the castle, not one stone remains standing on
another,[2] not a barn, not a sheep, not a duck, not a tree; but
we had our revenge, for the Abars have done the very same to
the neighbouring estate of a Bulgar lord.'

On hearing this speech Candide fainted again; but having
recovered his senses and said all that was called for in such
circumstances, he inquired as to the cause, the effect and the
sufficient reason that had reduced Pangloss to so pitiable a

state. 'Alas,' said the other, 'love is its name: love, consoler of humankind, preserver of the universe, soul of all sentient beings, sweet love.' – 'Alas,' said Candide, 'I too have known this thing called love, this ruler of hearts, this soul of our soul; it has never earned me more than òne kiss and twenty kicks on the arse. But how can so beautiful a cause have produced so abominable an effect in your case?'

Pangloss replied thus: 'My dear Candide! You remember Paquette, the pretty lady's maid to our august Baroness; well, in her arms I tasted the delights of paradise, which in turn provoked the torments of hell by which you see me devoured; she was herself infected, and may now be dead. Paquette received this present from a very learned Franciscan,[3] who could trace it back to its source: for he had been given it by an old countess, who in turn had it from a cavalry captain, who was indebted for it to a marquise, who caught it from a page-boy, who contracted it from a Jesuit,[4] who, while a novice, had inherited it in a direct line from one of the shipmates of Christopher Columbus. As for me, I will pass it on to no one, for I am dying of it.'

'Oh Pangloss!' cried Candide, 'what a strange genealogy[5] is this! Surely the devil is its source?' – 'Not in the least,' replied that great man. 'It is an indispensable feature of the best of all possible worlds, a necessary ingredient:[6] for if Columbus, on an island off the Americas, had not contracted this disease – which poisons the source of all procreation, and often even prevents procreation, contrary though this be to nature's great plan – we would have neither chocolate nor cochineal;[7] it should be noted moreover that so far the disease, like religious controversy, has been peculiar to the inhabitants of our continent.[8] The Turks, the Indians, the Persians, the Chinese, the Siamese and the Japanese have yet to encounter it; but the sufficient reason already exists for them to know it in their turn, a few centuries hence. Meanwhile, it is making splendid progress amongst ourselves, and especially in those great armies of upstanding and well-bred mercenaries which decide the destiny of nations; you may be sure that when thirty thousand men engage in pitched battle against equal numbers, there are twenty thousand cases of pox on either side.'

'Well, that is certainly remarkable,' said Candide, 'but now we must have you treated.' – 'But how can we?' said Pangloss. 'I don't have a sou, my friend, and nowhere in this wide world can one get oneself bled or obtain so much as an enema without paying for it, or without someone else paying.'

This last remark decided Candide; he went and threw himself at the feet of his charitable Anabaptist, Jacques, and painted so affecting a picture of the state to which his friend was reduced, that the good man did not hesitate in taking Doctor Pangloss under his roof, and have him treated at his own expense. The cure was effected with only the loss of one eye and one ear. Pangloss could write legibly and his arithmetic was faultless, so the Anabaptist made him his bookkeeper. At the end of two months, being obliged to sail to Lisbon on business, he took his two philosophers with him on board. During the voyage Pangloss explained to him how all things are arranged for the best. Jacques was not of this view. 'Mankind must have corrupted nature just a little,' he would say, 'for men are not born wolves, yet they have become wolves.⁹ God gave them neither twenty-four-pounders nor bayonets,¹⁰ yet they have made themselves bayonets and twenty-four-pounders to destroy one another. Or I could instance bankruptcies, and the courts which seize the effects of the bankrupt only to cheat his creditors'¹¹ – 'All this is indispensable,' countered the one-eyed doctor, 'and private ills make up the general good,¹² so that the greater the sum of private ills the better everything is.' While he was reasoning thus, the sky darkened, the winds blew from the four corners of the earth, and their ship was assailed by the most terrible storm, all within sight of the port of Lisbon.

CHAPTER 5

*Storm, shipwreck, earthquake, and what
became of Dr Pangloss, Candide and Jacques
the Anabaptist*

Half of the passengers, weakened and expiring from the incon-
ceivable agonies that the rolling of a vessel induces in the nerves
and humours of a body being tossed in contrary directions,
were indifferent to the danger surrounding them. The other
half shrieked and said their prayers; the sails were torn, the
masts were broken, and the vessel was taking on water. Those
who could work did what they could, everyone shouted at once,
no one was in command. On the main deck the Anabaptist was
lending a hand with the rigging, when a crazed sailor struck
him a furious blow and laid him out flat on deck; but the force
of the blow jolted the sailor himself so violently that he went
overboard head first. He was caught in mid-air by a piece of
broken mast and left dangling. The good Jacques runs to his
assistance, hauls him back on board, and in doing so is himself
pitched into the sea in full view of the sailor, who leaves him
to drown without even a backward glance. Candide runs up,
and sees his benefactor resurface for a moment before being
engulfed for ever. He tries to jump in after him; Pangloss the
philosopher prevents him, arguing that Lisbon harbour was
built expressly so that this Anabaptist should one day drown
in it.[1] While he was offering *a priori* proofs[2] of this, the vessel
split and everyone perished, with the exception of Pangloss,
Candide and the same brute of a sailor who had drowned their
virtuous Anabaptist; the scoundrel managed to swim successfully to shore, while Pangloss and Candide were carried thither
on a plank.

When they had recovered a little, they set out in the direction
of Lisbon; they had a little money in their pockets, with which
they hoped to escape starvation having survived shipwreck.

Hardly do they set foot in the city, still weeping over the
death of their benefactor, than they feel the earth tremble

beneath them;[3] a boiling sea rises in the port and shatters the vessels lying at anchor. Great sheets of flame and ash cover the streets and public squares; houses collapse, roofs topple on to foundations, and foundations are levelled in turn; thirty thousand inhabitants without regard to age or sex are crushed beneath the ruins. 'There'll be things for the taking here,' said the sailor with an oath and a whistle. – 'What can possibly be the sufficient reason for a thing like this?' said Pangloss. – 'The end of the world is here!' shouted Candide. At which the sailor instantly dashes into the ruins, braving death in his search for silver; he finds some, seizes it, gets drunk, and, after sleeping it off, purchases the favours of the first willing girl he finds in the ruins of the fallen houses, in amidst the dead and the dying. But Pangloss caught him by the sleeve: 'My friend,' he said, 'this is no way to behave. You are flouting the laws of universal reason, and this is hardly the time or place.' – 'Hell and damnation!' replied the other, 'I am a sailor born in Batavia;[4] I've made four voyages to Japan, and four times I've trampled on the Cross;[5] you've picked the wrong man, with your drivel about universal reason!'

Candide had been injured by some falling masonry; he was lying in the street, covered with rubble. He called out to Pangloss: 'Help! Get me some oil and wine;[6] I am dying.' – 'But these earthquakes are nothing new,' replied Pangloss. 'The city of Lima in America experienced the same tremors last year; same causes, same effects: there must certainly be a seam of sulphur running underground from Lima to Lisbon.'[7] – 'Nothing is more likely,' said Candide, 'but, for the love of God, some oil and wine!' – 'What do you mean, "likely"?' retorted the philosopher, 'I regard the thing as proven.' At which point Candide fainted, and Pangloss brought him a little water from a nearby fountain.

The next day, having found some scraps of food while picking their way through the ruins, they recovered some of their strength. After which they worked alongside the others to bring relief to those inhabitants who had survived. Some of the citizens they had helped gave them as good a dinner as could be hoped for in such a catastrophe. The meal was a melancholy one, it is true, and the guests watered the bread with their tears; but Pangloss consoled them, assuring everyone that things could not be otherwise:[8] 'This is all for the best,' he said. 'For if there is a volcano beneath Lisbon, then it cannot be anywhere else;[9] for it is impossible for things to be elsewhere than where they are. For all is well.'

A little man in black, an agent of the Inquisition, who was sitting next to him, spoke up politely and said: 'It would seem that Monsieur does not believe in Original Sin; for if all is as well as you say, there has been neither Fall nor punishment.'[10]

'I most humbly beg pardon of your Excellency,' replied Pangloss still more politely, 'but the Fall of Man and Adam's curse are of necessity events within the best of all possible worlds.' – 'Then Monsieur does not believe in free will?' asked the agent. – 'Your Excellency will forgive me,' said Pangloss, 'but free will can coexist with absolute necessity; for it was necessary that we be free, since ultimately a predetermined will . . .'[11] Pangloss was in mid-sentence when the agent gave a nod to his armed flunkey, who was pouring him some wine from Porto, or rather Oporto.[12]

CHAPTER 6

How they had a magnificent auto-da-fé to prevent earthquakes, and how Candide was flogged

After the earthquake, which had destroyed three-quarters of Lisbon, the sages of that country could think of no more effective means of averting further destruction than to give the people a fine *auto-da-fé*;[1] it having been decided by the University of Coïmbra[2] that the spectacle of a few individuals being ceremonially roasted over a slow fire was the infallible secret recipe for preventing the earth from quaking.

Consequently they had rounded up a Biscayan[3] who stood convicted of marrying his fellow godparent, and two Portuguese who were seen throwing away the bacon garnish while

eating a chicken.[4] After dinner some men arrived with ropes
and tied up Doctor Pangloss and his disciple Candide – the one
for what he had said, and the other for having listened with an
air of approval: both were led away to separate apartments, of
a remarkable coolness never troubled by the sun: eight days
later each was dressed in a *san-benito*,[5] and crowned with a
paper mitre: Candide's mitre and *san-benito* were decorated
with inverted flames and with devils who had neither tails nor
claws; whereas Pangloss's devils had both tails and claws, and
his flames were upright.[6] Thus dressed, they walked in pro-
cession, and listened to a most affecting sermon, followed by a
delightful piece of plainchant monotony.[7] Candide was flogged
in cadence to the singing; the Biscayan and the two Portuguese
who did not relish bacon were burned to death; and Pangloss
was hanged, although hanging was not the custom at an *auto-
da-fé*.[8] That same day the earth quaked once more with a
terrifying din.[9]

Appalled, stupefied, distraught, covered in blood and shaking
uncontrollably, Candide said to himself: 'If this is the best of
all possible worlds, what must the others be like? I wouldn't
have minded the flogging; I was already flogged by the Bulgars.
But, oh my dear Pangloss! Greatest of philosophers! Did I have
to see you hanged, and for no reason I can understand? And
my dear Anabaptist, the best of men! Did you have to be
drowned in the port? And Mademoiselle Cunégonde, the pearl
of daughters, was it necessary for you to be disembowelled?'

He was turning away from the scene, scarcely able to stand,
having been successively preached at, flogged, absolved and
blessed, when an old woman approached him and said: 'Take
heart, my son, and follow me.'

CHAPTER 7

*How an old woman took care of Candide, and
how he was reunited with his beloved*

Candide did not take heart, but he did follow the old woman
into her hovel; she gave him a jar of ointment to rub on, and
set out food and drink for him; she then showed him a small,
fairly clean bed; next to the bed lay an outfit of clothes. 'Eat,
drink, and sleep,' she said, 'and may Our Lady of Atocha,
St Anthony of Padua and St James of Compostella watch over
you.[1] I will return tomorrow.' Candide, stupefied still by all he
had seen, all he had suffered, and most of all by the kindness
of the old woman, wanted to kiss her hand. 'It's not *my* hand
you should be kissing,' said the old woman. 'I will return
tomorrow. Rub yourself with ointment, eat, sleep.'

Despite his misfortunes, Candide ate and slept. The next day
the old woman brings him breakfast, examines his back, and
rubs it herself with a different ointment; later she brings him
dinner; and towards evening she returns with supper. The following day the same ritual was repeated. 'Who are you?' Candide kept asking her. 'Who has inspired such kindness in you?
How can I repay you?' The good woman never answered; she
returned the same evening, but this time without supper. 'Come
with me,' she said, 'and don't say a word.' She takes his arm,
and walks about a quarter of a mile with him into open country:
they arrive at an isolated house, surrounded by gardens and
ornamental canals. The old woman knocks at a little door. It
opens; she leads Candide by a secret staircase into a small gilt
room, sits him on a brocaded sofa, closes the door behind her,
and goes off. Candide thought he was dreaming; he thought of
his whole life thus far as a sinister dream, and of the present
moment as a very agreeable one.

The old woman reappeared shortly; she was supporting, not
without difficulty, a trembling woman, of noble stature, spark-
ling with jewels, hidden by a veil. 'Remove the veil,' said the
old woman to Candide. He stepped forward, and with a timid

hand lifted the veil. What a surprise! It was as if he was looking at Mademoiselle Cunégonde. But he was indeed looking at Mademoiselle Cunégonde, for it was she! His strength deserted him, he could not utter a word, he collapsed at her feet. Cunégonde collapsed on to the sofa. The old woman plied them with spirits; they came to their senses, they exchanged words: at first only broken phrases, questions and answers at cross purposes, sighs, tears, exclamations. The old woman suggested they make less noise, and left them alone. 'Is it really you!' said Candide. 'And alive! And in Portugal, of all places! So were you not raped after all? And were you not disembowelled, as Pangloss the philosopher assured me was the case?' – 'I most certainly was, in both cases,' said the lovely Cunégonde, 'but these things are not always fatal.' – 'But your father and mother, were they killed?' – 'It is all too true,' replied Cunégonde in tears. – 'And your brother?' – 'My brother was killed, too.' – 'And why are you in Portugal? And how did you know I was here? And by what strange means did you have me brought to this house?' – 'I will tell you everything,' the lady replied. 'But first you must tell me everything that has happened to you since the innocent kiss you gave me and those kicks you received for your pains.'

Candide obeyed her without question; and although he was bewildered, and his voice feeble and tremulous, and his spine still hurting a little, he described with the most artless simplicity what he had suffered since the moment of their separation. Cunégonde raised her eyes to heaven; she wept at the death of the good Anabaptist, and wept again over Pangloss; after which she spoke as follows to Candide, who did not miss a syllable, even as he devoured her with his eyes.

CHAPTER 8

Cunégonde's story

'I was in my bed, and sound asleep, when it pleased heaven to send the Bulgars to our beautiful castle of Thunder-ten-tronckh; they cut the throats of my father and brother, and chopped my mother to pieces. A huge Bulgar, over six feet tall, seeing that I had fainted at the sight of all this, set about raping me; this brought me to my senses, and I recovered my wits: I screamed, I struggled, I bit, I scratched; I tried to tear out the eyes of that huge Bulgar, not realizing that what was taking place in my father's castle was the custom on such occasions; the brute stabbed me in my left side, where I still carry the scar.' – 'Alas! I very much hope I shall see it,' said Candide, innocently. – 'You shall,' said Cunégonde, 'but let us continue.' – 'Pray continue,' said Candide.

She took up the thread of her story. 'A Bulgar captain came in, and saw me weltering in blood; the soldier carried on regardless, the captain fell into a rage at the lack of respect shown to him by this brute, and killed him while he was on top of me. Then he had my wounds dressed and and took me to his quarters as a prisoner of war. I used to wash the few shirts he owned, and cook for him; he found me very attractive, I must say; and I will not deny that he was well built himself, or that his skin was white and soft; otherwise not much wit, and even less philosophy: you could soon tell that he had not been educated by Doctor Pangloss. After three months, having lost all his money and his taste for me, he sold me to a Jew named Don Issacar, who had trading connections in Holland and Portugal, and was passionately fond of women. This Jew took a great liking to my person, but could not prevail over me. I resisted him more successfully than I had the Bulgar soldier. A person of honour may be raped once, but her virtue emerges all the stronger for it. In order to tame me, the Jew brought me to this country house, where you see me now. Hitherto I had believed there was nothing in the world as beautiful as the castle of Thunder-ten-tronckh; but my eyes have been opened.

'The Grand Inquisitor noticed me one day at Mass; he ogled me throughout the service, and then sent word that he had to speak to me on private business. I was taken to his palace; I informed him of my birth; he pointed out how far beneath my rank it was to be the chattel of an Israelite. A proposition was made on his behalf to Don Issacar, that he should hand me over to His Eminence the Inquisitor. Don Issacar, who is the court banker and a man of parts, preferred to do no such thing. The Inquisitor threatened him with an *auto-da-fé*. At last my Jew, intimidated, agreed to a compromise, whereby the house and my person would belong to both of them in common; the Jew would have Mondays, Wednesdays and the Sabbath, the Inquisitor would have the other days of the week. This arrangement has lasted for six months. It has not been without its quarrels, namely as to whether the night between Saturday and Sunday belongs to the old law or to the new.[1] For my part, I have so far resisted them both, which I am sure is the reason they both love me still.

'Finally, to avert the scourge of further earthquakes, and to intimidate Don Issacar, His Eminence the Inquisitor was pleased to hold an *auto-da-fé*. He did me the honour of inviting me. I had an excellent seat; refreshments were served to the ladies between the Mass and the executions. I was overcome with horror, I have to say, at seeing those two Jews being burned to death, and that honest Biscayan who had married his fellow-godparent; but imagine my astonishment, my dread and bewilderment when I saw a figure resembling Dr Pangloss dressed in a *san-benito* and a mitre! I rubbed my eyes, I watched, I saw him hang; then I collapsed. Scarcely had I come to my senses again, than I saw you standing there stripped naked: this was my worst moment of horror, of agony and despair. I can tell you now, by the way, that your skin is even fairer and rosier all over than my Bulgar captain's. The sight of it redoubled all the feelings that were overwhelming and devouring me. I cried out, and wanted to scream: "Stop! You barbarians!", but my voice failed me, and my cries would have been useless. "How can it be," I said to myself after you had been well and truly flogged, "that the loveable Candide and wise Pangloss are here in Lisbon, the one to receive a hundred strokes, and the other to be hanged by order of His Eminence the Inquisitor, whose beloved I am? Pangloss deceived me cruelly, after all, when he told me that all is for the best in this world.

'Distraught and desperate, beside myself with anger at one moment and the next moment ready to collapse, my mind was spinning with the massacres of my father and mother and brother; with the insolence of that vile Bulgar soldier and the knife wound he gave me; with my enslavement, my drudgery as a cook, my Bulgar captain, my disgusting Don Issacar and my abominable Inquisitor; with the hanging of Dr Pangloss, and that great plainchant *miserere*² they intoned while you were being flogged; and above all with the kiss I had given you behind the screen, the day I saw you for the last time. I praised God for bringing you back to me after so many tribulations. I ordered my old woman to take care of you, and to bring you here as soon she possibly could. She has faithfully carried out her commission, and I have the inexpressible joy of seeing you again, of listening to you, of talking to you. You must be ravenous, and I have a good appetite; let us begin with supper.'

So they both sit down to eat; after supper they resume their places on the beautiful and aforementioned sofa; where they are still to be found when Señor Don Issacar, one of the two masters of the house, arrives. It was the Sabbath day. He had come to enjoy his rights, and to protest his love.

CHAPTER 9

What became of Cunégonde, Candide, the Grand Inquisitor and a Jew

This Issacar was the most choleric Hebrew to come out of Israel since the Babylonian Captivity.¹ 'What!' he said, 'you Galilean whore! So the Grand Inquisitor is not enough for you? Do I have to share you with this ruffian too?' So saying, he draws a

long dagger that he always carried about with him, and, not
believing his adversary to be armed, hurls himself at Candide;
but our good Westphalian had been given a fine sword by the
old woman along with his suit of clothes. Out it comes, his
gentle disposition notwithstanding, and without more ado he
lays the Israelite out, stone dead at the feet of the lovely
Cunégonde.

'Holy Mother!' she cried. 'What will become of us? A man
killed in my house? If the watch arrives now, we are done for.'
– 'If Pangloss had not been hanged,' said Candide, 'he would
have given us some good advice in this extremity, for he was a
great philosopher. Since he is not here, let's consult the old
woman.' The latter was all prudence, and was beginning to
offer her opinion when another little door opened. It was
an hour after midnight: Sunday morning, therefore, and his
Eminence the Inquisitor's day. In he comes, to find the flogged
Candide, now with sword in hand, and a corpse stretched out
on the ground, and Cunégonde distracted, and the old woman
handing out advice.

Various thoughts went through Candide's head at this
moment: 'If this holy man calls for help, he will have me burned
at the stake without fail; he will probably do the same for
Cunégonde; he has already had me mercilessly whipped; he is
now my rival; I am already embarked on killing; there is no
choice.' This line of reasoning was clear-cut and rapid, and
without giving the Inquisitor time to recover from his surprise,
he runs him through and throws him down beside the Jew.
'There goes another one,' said Cunégonde. 'There will be no
pardon now; we are excommunicate, our final hour is at hand.
What on earth has got into you, who were born so gentle, to
do away with a Jew and a prelate in the space of two minutes?'
– 'My dear young lady,' replied Candide, 'when you are in love,
and jealous, and have been flogged by the Inquisition, there's
no knowing what you may do.'

The old woman now intervened and said: 'There are three
Andalusian horses in the stable, with as many saddles and
bridles: let our brave Candide harness them. Madame has some
*moidores*² and some diamonds. Let us get mounted immediately

– even though I have only one buttock for a seat – and ride for
Cadiz. The weather is perfect, and it is always pleasant to travel
in the cool of the night.'

At once Candide saddled the three horses. Cunégonde, the
old woman and he covered thirty miles without stopping. While
they were gaining distance, the Holy Hermandad[3] arrived at
the house. His Eminence the Inquisitor was buried in a beautiful
church, and Don Issacar was thrown on to the town refuse heap.

Candide, Cunégonde and the old woman were by now in the
little town of Avacena,[4] in the middle of the Sierra Morena
mountains, where they were having the following conversation
in an inn.

CHAPTER 10

In what distress Candide, Cunégonde and the old woman arrive in Cadiz, and of their embarkation

'But who could possibly have stolen my *pistoles* and diamonds?'
said Cunégonde in tears. 'What shall we live on? How will
we manage? Where shall I find the Inquisitors and the Jews to
give me more?' – 'Alas!' said the old woman, 'I strongly suspect
it was that reverend Franciscan who slept in the same inn as
us last night in Badajoz; God preserve me from making rash
judgements, but he passed through our room twice, and he set
off long before us.' – 'The good Pangloss often demonstrated
to me,' said Candide with a sigh, 'that the things of this world
are common to all men, and that everyone has an equal right
to them.[1] In which case, this Franciscan ought at least to have
left us enough to finish our journey. Do you really have nothing
left, my fair Cunégonde?' – 'Not a single *maravedi*,'[2] she said.
– 'What are we to do, then?' said Candide. – 'Let us sell one of
the horses,' said the old woman. 'I can ride on the croup behind
Mademoiselle, even though I have only one buttock for a seat,
and we shall reach Cadiz.'

In the same hostelry there was a Benedictine prior;[3] he

purchased one of the horses at a reduced price. Candide, Cunégonde and the old woman passed through Lucena, through
Chillas, through Lebrija, and finally reached Cadiz.[4] Here a
fleet was being fitted out and troops mustered, to bring to
their senses the reverend Jesuit fathers of Paraguay, who were
accused of having incited one of their local hordes to revolt
against the Kings of Spain and Portugal, raiding the town of
San Sacramento.[5] Candide, having served with the Bulgars,
performed the Bulgar drill before the general of this little force
with such grace, such celerity, such bearing, such pride and
dexterity that he was given a company of infantry to command.
He was now a captain; he went on board with Mademoiselle
Cunégonde, the old woman, two valets and the two remaining
Andalusian horses that had belonged to the Grand Inquisitor
of Portugal.

During the whole voyage they discussed endlessly the philosophy of poor Pangloss. 'We are going to another world,'[6] said
Candide. 'No doubt it must be there that all is well. For you
have to admit, there is reason to blench at some of what goes
on in our world, whether physically or morally.' – 'I love you
with all my heart,' Cunégonde said, 'but my mind is still reeling
from what I have seen, from what I have suffered.' – 'All will
be well,' Candide replied. 'The sea of this new world is already
superior to our European seas; it is calmer, its trade winds more
constant. No doubt about it, the New World is the best of all
possible worlds.' – 'God willing!' said Cunégonde. 'But I have
been so horribly unhappy in my world so far, that my heart is
almost sealed against hope.' – 'You two do nothing but complain,' said the old woman, 'but you have suffered nothing like
my misfortunes, I can assure you!' Cunégonde was on the verge
of laughter, finding it very droll of this good creature to claim
to be twice as unfortunate than herself. 'Alas, my good woman,'
she said to her, 'unless you have been raped by two Bulgars,
been stabbed twice in the stomach, had two castles demolished,
had the throats of two mothers and two fathers slit before
your very eyes, and watched two lovers being flogged in an
auto-da-fé, I really cannot see that you have the advantage over
me; to which I might add that I was born a baroness, with

seventy-two quarterings[7] to my coat of arms, and have been put to work in a scullery.' – 'My dear young lady,' replied the old woman, 'you know nothing of my birth; and were I to show you my bottom you would not talk as you do, and would suspend your judgement.' This speech aroused deep curiosity in the minds of Cunégonde and Candide; and the old woman continued as follows.

CHAPTER II

The old woman's story

'I did not always have red-rimmed and bloodshot eyes; my nose did not always touch my chin, nor was I always a servant. I am the daughter of Pope Urban X and the Princess of Palestrina.[1] Until the age of fourteen I was brought up in a palace, compared to which the castles of all your German barons would not have been fit to serve as stables; just one of my robes was worth more than all the assembled magnificence of Westphalia. I grew in beauty, grace and accomplishments, surrounded by privileges, amusements and hopes for the future. I had already begun to inspire love, and my breasts were forming. And what breasts! White and firm, sculpted like the Medici Venus. And what eyes! What eyelashes! What black brows! What fires flashed in my pupils, and outshone the glittering of the stars, as the local poets kept telling me! The women who dressed and undressed me fell back in ecstasies when they gazed upon me, from whichever angle, and all the men would have wished to be in their place.

'I was betrothed to the sovereign prince of Massa-Carrara.[2] What a prince! Of a beauty to match mine, compounding gentleness and charm, he sparkled with wit and he burned with love. I loved him as one does for the first time – to the point of idolatry, with passionate abandon. The wedding preparations were made, of an unheard-of pomp and extravagance; it was one endless round of feasts, tilting matches, comic operas; all of Italy composed sonnets in my praise, not one of which was any good. Just as my moment of happiness was at hand, an

aged marquise, who had been my prince's mistress, invited him
to take chocolate at her house. He died less than two hours later
in appalling convulsions. But this was a mere trifle, compared to
what followed. My mother, in despair – though far less afflicted
than I, of course – wanted to escape for a while from so oppres-
sive an atmosphere. She had a very fine estate near Gaeta.[3] We
embarked on a local galley, which was gilded like the high altar
of Saint Peter's in Rome. The next moment a pirate ship from
Salé[4] swept down and boarded us. Our men defended themselves as the Pope's soldiers usually do: they all fell to their
knees, threw down their weapons, and begged the pirates to
absolve them of their sins *in articulo mortis*.[5]

'They were promptly stripped naked as monkeys, as were my
mother, and our maids of honour, and I myself. The application
with which these gentlemen go around undressing everyone
they meet is truly remarkable. But what surprised me more,
they then took each of us and inserted their fingers into that
orifice which we ladies usually reserve for an enema syringe.
This procedure struck me as very strange, but that is how one
judges everything when one has never been out of one's own
country. I soon learned that its purpose was to discover if we
had hidden any diamonds there; it is a custom established
from time immemorial among the civilized seafaring nations. I
discovered that those religious gentlemen the Knights of Malta[6]
never fail to perform the same ritual when they capture Turks,
male or female; it is one article of international law that is never
neglected.

'I need not dwell on how painful it is for a young princess
and her mother to be taken to Morocco as slaves. You may
imagine what we suffered on board the pirate ship. My mother
was still very beautiful, and our ladies in waiting, even our
simple chambermaids, possessed more charms than are to be
found in the whole of Africa. As for me, I was ravishing, I was
beauty itself, grace incarnate – and a virgin to boot. Not for
long, of course; this flower which had been reserved for the
handsome Prince of Massa-Carrara, was plucked by the Corsair
captain, an abominable negro, who of course believed he was
doing me a great favour. Certainly, my mother the Princess of

Palestrina and I must have been made of stern stuff to endure what we endured before arriving in Morocco. But let that pass; such things are so commonplace as not to be worth describing.

'Morocco was knee-deep in blood when we arrived. The fifty sons of the Emperor Mulay Ismaël[7] each had their followers, which was in effect the excuse for fifty civil wars: blacks against blacks, blacks against browns, browns against browns, mulattos against mulattos. It was uninterrupted carnage from one end of the empire to the other.

'We had scarcely disembarked when some blacks, of a faction opposed to that of my pirate, presented themselves with a view to relieving him of his booty. Next to the diamonds and gold, we were the most precious part of his cargo. I was witness to a combat the like of which would never be seen in your European climes. Northerners do not have sufficiently hot blood. They do not have that raging lust for women so common in Africa. You Europeans seem to have milk in your veins; whereas it is vitriol, it is fire that courses through the inhabitants of Mount Atlas and the neighbouring countries. They fought with the fury of the lions, tigers and serpents of that region to decide who should have us. A Moor seized my mother by the right arm, while my captain's lieutenant held on to her left arm; another Moor grabbed her by one leg, while one of our pirates held her by the other. In an instant, almost all our ladies-in-waiting found themselves dragged likewise between four soldiers. My captain kept me hidden behind him. Scimitar in hand, he set to killing anyone who challenged his rage. At length, I saw all our Italian maids and my mother cut to pieces, torn apart, massacred by the monsters who contended over them. My fellow captives, and their captors – soldiers, sailors, blacks, browns, whites, mulattos and finally my captain – all were dead; and I remained alone, dying under a heap of dead bodies. Similar scenes were taking place, as everyone knows, over an area of more than three hundred leagues, without anyone ever omitting to say their five daily prayers as required by Mahomet.[8]

'I somehow managed to untangle myself from that great pile of blood-soaked corpses, and dragged myself to the shade of a tall orange tree at the edge of a nearby stream; there I collapsed from shock, from fatigue, from hunger, from horror and despair. Soon after, my exhausted senses surrendered to a sleep that was more like a trance than a rest. I was in this state of feebleness and insensibility, hovering between life and death, when I felt the pressure of something rubbing up and down on my body. I opened my eyes; I beheld a white man, rather attractive, who was moaning on top of me and muttering through clenched teeth: *O che sciagura d'essere senza coglioni!*[9]

CHAPTER 12

The misfortunes of the old woman, continued

'Astonished and delighted at hearing my native tongue spoken, and no less surprised by what this man was uttering, I replied that there were greater misfortunes than that of which he complained. I informed him in a few words of the horrors I had endured, and promptly fainted again. He carried me to a nearby house, had me put to bed, had food brought to me, looked after me, comforted me, flattered me, told me that never had he seen anything so beautiful as I, and that never had he so much regretted the loss of what no one could now restore to him. "I was born in Naples," he said, "where two or three thousand children are castrated each year; some die as a result, some develop voices more beautiful than any woman's, and some are sent off to govern provinces.[1] My operation was a great success, and I became soloist to the chapel of the Princess of Palestrina." – "The Princess my mother!" I exclaimed. – "The princess your mother!" he repeated, bursting into tears. "What! And are you that little princess whom I raised until she was six years old, and who already showed signs of becoming as beautiful as you are now?" – "The very same," said I. "And my mother lies not four hundred paces from here, torn to pieces, under a pile of corpses . . ."

'I told him everything that had happened to me; he told me his adventures in turn, and how he had been sent to the King of Morocco by one of the Christian powers, to conclude a treaty whereby the latter would be supplied with gunpowder, cannon and ships to assist him in destroying the trade of the other Christian powers.[2] "My mission is concluded," said this honest eunuch. "I am on my way to embark at Ceuta,[3] and I will take you back to Italy. *Ma che sciagura d'essere senza coglioni . . . !*"

'I thanked him with tears of gratitude – but instead of taking me to Italy he took me to Algiers, and sold me to the Dey of that province.[4] Scarcely had I been sold than the plague which has been doing the rounds of Africa, Asia and Europe broke out with a vengeance in Algiers. You may have seen earthquakes, Mademoiselle; but tell me, have you ever had the plague?' – 'Never,' replied the Baron's daughter.

'Otherwise,' continued the old woman, 'you would have to admit that it is far worse than any earthquake. It is very common in Africa;[5] and I was infected with it. Imagine my situation, the daughter of a pope, only fifteen years old, who in the space of three months had been exposed to poverty and slavery, had been raped almost daily, had seen her mother torn to pieces, had endured war and famine, and was now dying of the plague in Algiers. As it happens, I did not die. But my eunuch perished, and the Dey perished, along with almost the entire seraglio of Algiers.

'When the first ravages of this dreadful pestilence were over, the slaves of the Dey were sold off. A merchant bought me and took me to Tunis, where he sold me to another merchant, who sold me again in Tripoli; after Tripoli I was resold in Alexandria, after Alexandria resold in Smyrna, after Smyrna resold in Constantinople. I ended up as the property of an aga of Turkish janissaries,[6] who shortly afterwards was ordered to the defence of Azov against the Russians who were besieging it.[7]

'This aga, being very fond of women, brought his entire seraglio along with him, and housed us all in a small fort on the Maeotian Marshes,[8] guarded by two black eunuchs and twenty soldiers. A prodigious number of Russians were being killed, but they gave as good as they got. Azov was put to fire and sword, without regard for age or sex; all that remained was our little fort, from which the enemy determined to starve us out. The twenty janissaries had solemnly sworn never to surrender. But the extremes of hunger to which they were reduced forced them to eat our two eunuchs, rather than violate their oath. A few days later they resolved to eat the women-folk.

'We had a very pious and compassionate imam,[9] who de-livered an excellent sermon persuading them not to kill us outright. "Cut off one buttock," he said, "from each of these ladies, and you will be well provided for; if you have to come back for more in a few days' time, you can take as much again; heaven will smile on so charitable an action, and you will be rescued."[10]

'He was all eloquence; they were convinced; and we were subjected to this dreadful operation. The imam applied to our wounds the ointment they use on boys who have just been circumcised. We were all at death's door.

'Scarcely had the janissaries finished the meal with which we had supplied them, than the Russians arrived on flat-bottomed boats: not a single janissary escaped alive. The Russians paid not the slightest attention to the condition we were in. But wherever you go in this world there are French physicians; one of whom, who happened to be very skilful, took us into his care; he cured us, and as long as I live I shall never forget how, once my wounds had properly healed, he propositioned me. For the rest, he told us all to cheer up, and assured us that this sort of thing happened all the time in sieges, and that it was the rule of war.

'As soon as my companions could walk, they were made to travel to Moscow. As for me, in the division of spoils I fell to the lot of a boyar,[11] who made me his gardener and gave me twenty lashes a day. But two years later, after this gentleman was broken on the wheel along with thirty other boyars on account of some petty intrigue at Court, I took my chance and fled; I crossed the whole of Russia; for many years I served in taverns, first in Riga, then in Rostock, then Wismar, then Leip-zig, then Kassel, then Utrecht, then Leiden, then The Hague and Rotterdam. I have grown old in poverty and shame, having only one buttock, but always mindful that I was the daughter of a pope. A hundred times I have wanted to kill myself, but I was still in love with life. This absurd weakness is perhaps one of our deadliest attachments: can anything be more foolish than to keep carrying a fardel[12] and yet keep wanting to throw it to the ground? To hold one's existence in horror, and yet cling to it? In a word, to caress the serpent that devours us, until it has eaten away our heart?

'In those countries through which fate has led me, and in the taverns where I have served, I have seen a prodigious number of individuals who held their lives in contempt; but only a dozen who voluntarily put an end to their misery: three negroes, four Englishmen, four Genevans and a German professor named Robeck.[13] I ended up as servant to the Jew Don Issacar; he placed me in your service, dear young lady; I attached myself to your destiny, and have been more concerned with your adventures than with my own. Indeed I would never have spoken of my misfortunes, had you not provoked me somewhat, and were it not customary on board ship to tell stories to pass the time. In short, Mademoiselle, I have lived, and I know the world; why not amuse yourself and invite each passenger to tell his story; if you find a single one of them who has not repeatedly cursed his existence, who has not repeatedly told himself that he is the unhappiest man alive, then you may throw me into the sea head first.'

CHAPTER 13

How Candide was obliged to part from the lovely Cunégonde and from the old woman

Having heard the old woman's story, the lovely Cunégonde showed her all the courtesies owing to one of her rank and quality. She accepted the proposition, moreover, and engaged all the passengers, one after the other, to relate their adventures. In the end, Candide and Cunégonde had to concede that the old woman was right. 'It is a great pity,' said Candide, 'that

our wise Pangloss was hanged, contrary to the custom of an
auto-da-fé; he would have delivered a remarkable lecture on
the physical and moral evil that holds sway over land and sea,
and I might by now feel strong enough respectfully to venture
a few objections.'

As each story was told, the ship continued on its way. Presently they reached port at Buenos Aires. Cunégonde, Captain
Candide and the old woman went to call on the Governor, Don
Fernando d'Ibaraa y Figueora y Mascarenes y Lampourdos y
Souza. This grandee had the pride befitting a person who bore
so many names. He spoke to everyone with the most aristocratic
disdain, pointed his nose so loftily, projected his voice so rasp-
ingly, adopted so superior a tone and affected so haughty a gait
that all who met him were sorely tempted to thrash him. He
adored women to the point of mania. Cunégonde seemed to
him the most beautiful he had ever seen. The first thing he did
was to inquire whether she were not perhaps Captain Candide's
wife? The manner with which he asked this question disturbed
Candide, who dared not say yes, for she was not in fact his
wife, and who neither dared to call her his sister, for she was
not that either; and although this white lie was once very
fashionable among the Ancients, and could still have its uses
for the Moderns,[1] his heart was too pure to betray the truth.
'Mademoiselle Cunégonde,' he said, 'has promised to do me the
honour of marrying me, and we humbly beg Your Excellency to
conduct the ceremony.'

Don Fernando d'Ibaraa y Figueora y Mascarenes y Lampourdos y Souza twirled his moustache, smiled sardonically,
and ordered Captain Candide to go and review his company.
Candide obeyed, and the Governor stayed behind in the company of Cunégonde. He declared his passion to her, and assured
her that tomorrow he would marry her, with the Church's
blessing or anyone else's, however it pleased her charming
person. Cunégonde asked him for a quarter of an hour to collect
herself, to consult the old woman, and come to a decision.

The old woman said to Cunégonde: 'Mademoiselle, you have
seventy-two quarterings, and not a farthing to your name; it is
in your power alone to become the wife of the most powerful

nobleman in the Americas, who moreover has a very fine moustache; is this the moment for you to pride yourself on your
unswerving fidelity? You have been raped by Bulgars; a Jew
and an Inquisitor have both enjoyed your favours.[2] Misfortunes
confer their own privileges. I have to say that, were I in your
place, I should have no scruples about marrying His Excellency
the Governor – and making Captain Candide's fortune in the
process.' While the old woman was speaking, with all the prudence of age and experience, a small vessel was seen to enter
the harbour; on board were an alcalde and some alguazils,[3] and
here is what had happened.

The old woman had guessed shrewdly that it was the loose-
sleeved Franciscan who had stolen Cunégonde's money and
jewels in the town of Badajoz, when she and Candide were on
the run. This friar tried to sell some of the stones to a jeweller,
who recognized them as the property of the Grand Inquisitor.
Before he was hanged, the Franciscan confessed that he had
stolen them. He gave a description of the individuals involved
and the route they had taken. It was already known that
Cunégonde and Candide had fled. They were followed to Cadiz,
where no time was lost in sending a vessel after them. This
vessel was now in the port of Buenos Aires. Rumour spread
that an alcalde was coming ashore, and that he was pursuing
the murderers of the Grand Inquisitor. The canny old woman
immediately saw what had to be done. 'You cannot flee,' she
said to Cunégonde, 'and you have nothing to fear; it was not
you who killed His Eminence; and, besides, the Governor who
loves you will not allow you to come to harm. So stay put.'
Then she ran straight to Candide: 'Flee this instant,' she said,
'or within the hour you will be burned alive.' There was not a
moment to lose; but how could he part from Cunégonde, and
where was he to find refuge?

CHAPTER 14

How Candide and Cacambo were received by the Jesuits of Paraguay

Candide had brought with him from Cadiz a valet, of a type commonly found along the coasts of Spain and in the colonies. He was a quarter Spanish,[1] the son of a half-breed from the Tucuman,[2] who had been successively choir-boy, sexton, sailor, monk, commercial agent, soldier and lackey. His name was Cacambo, and he loved his master dearly, because his master was the best of men. He instantly saddled the two Andalusian horses. 'Hurry up, Master, let's do as the old woman says; let's get going, and with no looking back.' Candide burst into tears. 'Oh, my dear Cunégonde! Must I abandon you just when His Excellency the Governor was about to marry us! What will become of you, so far from home?' – 'She will become whatever she can,' said Cacambo. 'Women are never at a loss; God sees to that; let's go.' – 'Where are you taking me? Where are we going? What shall we do without Cunégonde?' repeated Candide. – 'By Saint James of Compostella!' said Cacambo. 'You were going to fight against the Jesuits; so let's go and fight for them instead: I know the roads well enough, I'll take you to their kingdom.[3] They'll be delighted to have a captain who knows the Bulgar drill; you'll make your fortune; when a man cannot get what he wants in one world, he finds it in another. And isn't one of life's great pleasures to see new places and do new things?'

'So you have already been to Paraguay?' said Candide. – 'But of course,' said Cacambo. 'I used to work in the kitchens at the college in Asunción,[4] and I know the ways of *Los Padres*[5] like I know the streets of Cadiz. It's a wonderful thing, their method of governing. To begin with, the kingdom is more than three hundred leagues[6] across, and they have divided it into thirty provinces. *Los Padres* own everything, and the people own the rest; it is a masterpiece of justice and reason.[7] For my money, nothing could be more god-like than *Los Padres*, who make war in this part of the world against the kings of Spain and Portugal, while being confessors to those same kings back in Europe; who kill Spaniards over here, and in Madrid send them to heaven: I find it all vastly amusing. But let's keep moving; you are about to become the happiest of men. How pleased *Los Padres* will be, when they discover there's a captain coming to join them who knows the Bulgar drill!'

When they reached the first border post, Cacambo told the lookout guard that a captain wished to speak with His Reverence the commanding officer. Word was sent to headquarters. A Paraguayan officer ran and knelt before the commanding officer with the news. Candide and Cacambo were first disarmed, then their two Andalusian horses were removed. The strangers were now brought forward between two files of soldiers; the commanding officer stood at the far end, wearing the three-cornered biretta, his cassock hitched up, a sword at his side, a spontoon[8] in his hand. He makes a sign; and twenty-four soldiers instantly surround the two newcomers. A sergeant explains to them that they must wait, that the commanding officer cannot speak to them, that the Reverend Father Provincial does not permit Spaniards to open their mouths unless he is present, or to remain in the country for more than three hours.[9] 'And where is the Reverend Father Provincial?' asked Cacambo. – 'He is taking parade after saying Mass,' replied the sergeant, 'and you will not have the privilege of kissing his spurs[10] for another three hours.' – 'Nonetheless,' replied Cacambo, 'the Captain, who like myself is dying of hunger, is not a Spaniard, but a German; so may we not have something to eat while waiting for His Reverence?'

The sergeant promptly went off to report this exchange to the commanding officer. 'The Lord be praised!' said the reverend gentleman. 'If he is German I can speak to him; have him brought to my arbour.'[11] Immediately Candide was led into a leafy summer house, decorated with a very pretty colonnade of green marble and gold, and with a trellis-work enclosing parakeets, colibris, humming-birds, guinea fowls and all manner of rare birds. An excellent lunch had been laid out in gold vessels;[12] and while the Paraguayans were eating maize out of

wooden bowls in the open fields, under a blazing sun, His
Reverence the commanding officer retired to the arbour.

He was a very fine-looking young man, round faced, quite
fair, with a florid complexion, arched eyebrows, piercing eyes,
red ears, crimson lips and a proud bearing – of a pride that was
neither quite Spanish nor quite Jesuit. Candide and Cacambo
had their weapons returned to them, along with their two
Andalusian horses; Cacambo gave the latter their oats near the
arbour, keeping his eye on them in case of surprise.

Candide first kissed the hem of the commanding officer's
cassock, then they sat down to lunch. 'So you are German?'
said the Jesuit to him in that language. – 'Yes, Reverend Father,'
said Candide. As they exchanged these words they both looked
at each other in extreme surprise, and with an emotion which
neither could conceal. 'And from what part of Germany?' asked
the Jesuit. – 'From the wretched province of Westphalia,' said
Candide. 'I was born in the castle of Thunder-ten-tronckh.' –
'Merciful heavens! Can it be possible?' cried out the commanding officer. – 'What miracle is this!' exclaimed Candide. – 'Can
it really be you?' said the commanding officer. – 'Can this really
be happening?' said Candide. They both drew backwards in
amazement, they embraced, they wept rivers of tears. 'What!
Can it really be you, Reverend Father? You, the brother of the
lovely Cunégonde? You, who were killed by the Bulgars! You,
the Baron's son! You, a Jesuit in Paraguay! This world is indeed
a strange place. Oh Pangloss! Pangloss! How happy you would
be at this moment, had you not been hanged!'

The commanding officer dismissed the negro slaves[13] and
Paraguayans who were serving drinks in goblets of rock crystal. He thanked God and Saint Ignatius a thousand times; he
clasped Candide in his arms; their faces were bathed in tears.
'You would be even more astonished, more moved, more beside yourself,' said Candide, 'if I told you that Mademoiselle
Cunégonde, your sister, whom you believed disembowelled,
is in perfect health.' – 'Where!' – 'Not far from here, with the
Governor of Buenos Aires; and I was coming here to wage
war against you.' Every word they uttered during this long
conversation piled marvel upon marvel. Their very souls

spoke through their tongues, listened eagerly at their ears, sparkled in their eyes. Being Germans, they sat at table for rather a long time, while waiting for the Reverend Father Provincial; and the commanding officer spoke to his dear Candide as follows.

CHAPTER 15

How Candide killed the brother of his dear Cunégonde

'Never while I live shall I forget that dreadful day when I saw my mother and father killed, and my sister raped.[1] When the Bulgars had gone, my adorable sister was nowhere to be found; my mother, my father and I were loaded on to a cart, along with two servant girls and three little boys whose throats had been cut, to be buried in a Jesuit chapel two leagues from our ancestral castle. A Jesuit sprinkled some holy water over us; it was fearfully salty; a few drops got into my eyes; the priest noticed a tiny movement of my eyelids; he placed his hand on my heart and felt it beating; I was saved, and at the end of three weeks I had completely recovered. You will recall, my dear Candide, how pretty I was; well I became even more so, to the point that the Reverend Father Croust,[2] who was Superior of the community, conceived the most tender affection for me; he initiated me as a novice; shortly afterwards I was sent to Rome. Our Superior General needed to recruit some young German Jesuits. The rulers of Paraguay try to admit as few Spanish Jesuits as they can; they prefer foreigners whom they think they can control more easily. I was judged suitable by the Reverend Father General to go and labour in this particular vineyard. So we set off, a Pole, a Tyrolean and myself. On arrival I was honoured with the posts of sub-deacon and lieutenant; I am now colonel and priest.[3] We shall be giving a hot reception to the King of Spain's forces, I can assure you; they will be thrashed and excommunicated. Providence has sent you here to assist us. But is it really true that my dear sister Cunégonde is not far

away, and staying with the Governor of Buenos Aires?' Candide
assured him on oath that nothing could be truer. Their tears
began to flow once more.

The Baron could not tire of embracing Candide; he called
him his brother, his deliverer. 'Ah! my dear Candide,' he said,
'perhaps we will enter Buenos Aires together as victors, and
rescue my sister Cunégonde.' – 'That is all I could wish for,'
replied Candide, 'for I was intending to marry her, and hope to
do so still.' – 'What an extraordinary piece of insolence!' retorted the Baron. 'So you would have the effrontery to marry
my sister, who has seventy-two quarterings on her coat of arms!
I consider it highly presumptuous of you to dare to speak to
me of so rash an intention!' Candide, whose blood turned cold
at this outburst, replied: 'Reverend Father, all the quarterings
in the world make no difference; I have rescued your sister from
the arms of a Jew and an Inquisitor; she has certain obligations
towards me, and she wishes to marry me. Maître Pangloss
always told me that all men are equal;[4] you may depend on it
that I shall marry her.' – 'We shall see about that, you dog!'
said the Jesuit Baron of Thunder-ten-tronckh, and with these
words struck him a great blow across the face with the flat of
his sword. Candide instantly drew his own sword and plunged
it up to the hilt in the Jesuit Baron's belly; as he withdrew it,
all steaming, he began to weep: 'Alas, dear God!' he said, 'I have
killed my former master, my friend, my future brother-in-law;
I am the mildest man alive, yet I have now killed three men,
two of them priests.'

Cacambo, who had been keeping watch at the door of the
arbour, came running. 'We have no choice but to sell our lives
as dearly as we can,' said his master. 'They are bound to come
into the arbour; let us die fighting.' Cacambo, who had seen far
worse in his time, kept his wits; he stripped the Baron of his
Jesuit cassock, put it on Candide, put the dead man's biretta
on his head, and forced him on to a horse. It was all done in
the blink of an eye. 'Let's get going, Master, at the double.
Everyone will take you for a Jesuit on his way to deliver orders;
we'll have crossed the frontier before they can come after us.'
He was already galloping as he said these words, and shouting

out in Spanish: 'Make way, make way for the Reverend Father
Colonel.'

CHAPTER 16

What became of our two travellers when they encountered two girls, two apes and the savages named the Oreillons

Candide and his valet were across the border post before anyone
in the camp had discovered the dead German Jesuit. The vigilant
Cacambo had taken care to fill his saddle-pack with bread,
chocolate, ham, fruit and a few bottles of wine. They forged
ahead on their Andalusian horses, deep into unknown country,
where they could find no sign of a track. At last a beautiful
grassland, traversed by streams, opened up before them. Our
two travellers allowed their horses to graze. Cacambo urged
his master to eat something, and he set him the example. 'How
can you expect me to eat ham,' said Candide, 'when I have
killed the son of his Excellency the Baron, and when I see myself
fated never to set eyes again on the beautiful Cunégonde? What
is the point of prolonging my miserable days, if I must drag
them out far away from her, in remorse and despair? And what
will the *Journal de Trévoux*[1] say?'

So saying, he ate nonetheless. The sun went down. The two
lost travellers heard faint cries, which sounded as if uttered by
women. They could not tell if these were cries of pain or of
pleasure; but they got to their feet rapidly, with that anxiety
and alarm which is so easily aroused in a strange country. The
shrieks were coming from two quite naked girls, who were
tripping lightly along the edge of the meadow, pursued by a
pair of apes snapping at their bottoms. Candide was moved to
sympathy; he had learned to shoot with the Bulgars, and could
bring down a hazelnut in a thicket without disturbing a leaf.
So he now raises his double-barrelled Spanish rifle, fires and
kills both apes. 'God be praised, my dear Cacambo! I have
delivered these two poor creatures from grave peril; if it was a

sin to kill an Inquisitor and a Jesuit, I have made ample amends by saving the lives of two girls. Perhaps they are young ladies of noble birth, and this episode may secure us some advantage in these parts.'

He was about to continue, but words failed him when he saw the two girls throw their arms lovingly around the two apes and collapse in tears over their corpses, filling the air with the most pitiful lamentations. 'I was not expecting quite so much tenderness of heart,' he said at last to Cacambo, who replied: 'You've excelled yourself this time, Master; you have just despatched the two lovers of these young ladies.' – 'Their lovers! Is it possible? You are making fun of me, Cacambo; how could anyone believe such a thing?' – 'My dear Master,' retorted Cacambo, 'you are always astonished by everything; why do you find it so strange that in some countries it is apes who enjoy the favours of young ladies? After all, they are one-quarter human, just as I am one-quarter Spanish.'[2] – 'Alas!' replied Candide, 'now I remember Maître Pangloss saying that in earlier times such things used to happen, and that these couplings had produced aigypans,[3] fauns and satyrs, and that several important personages of antiquity had set eyes upon them. But I took these stories to be fables.'[4] – 'Well, perhaps now you will take them to be true,' said Cacambo. 'It merely goes to show how people carry on when they haven't received a proper education. My only worry is that these same young ladies may land us in trouble.'

These solid reflections persuaded Candide that they must leave the prairie and plunge into the wood. There he made supper with Cacambo, and, both of them having cursed the Inquisitor of Portugal, the Governor of Buenos Aires and the Baron, they fell asleep on some moss. When they awoke they found they were unable to move their limbs; the explanation for which was that the Oreillon tribe,[5] who inhabit that country, and to whom the two women had denounced them, had tied them down during the night with ropes made of bark.[6] They were now surrounded by fifty or so stark-naked Oreillons, armed with arrows, clubs and flint axes: some were bringing a large cauldron to the boil; others were preparing spits, and all of them were chanting: 'It's a Jesuit! It's a Jesuit! We will be avenged! And we'll eat our fill! Let's eat Jesuit! Let's eat Jesuit!'[7]

'I told you so, my dear master,' exclaimed Cacambo sadly. 'I said that those two girls would play us a trick or two.' Candide, noticing the cauldron and the spits, cried out: 'We are going to be either roasted or boiled, for sure. Ah, what would Maître Pangloss say now, if he could see how men live in a state of nature?[8] All is for the best, no doubt, but I must say it is a cruel thing to have lost Mademoiselle Cunégonde and be roasted on a spit by Oreillons.' Cacambo was never one to lose his head. 'Don't despair,' he said to the dejected Candide. 'I am familiar with the gibberish these people speak. I will address them.' – 'Be sure to impress upon them,' said Candide, 'how frightful and inhuman it is to cook people alive, and how very unchristian.'

'Well, gentlemen,' said Cacambo, 'so you are thinking of eating Jesuit today? A splendid idea; nothing more proper than to treat your enemies in this fashion. In fact, natural law teaches us to kill our neighbour, which is how men behave the world over. If we Europeans choose not to exercise our right to eat our enemies, it is only because we have other means of eating well; but you lack such amenities, and it is certainly better to eat your enemies than to leave the fruits of one's victory to the ravens and crows.[9] On the other hand, gentlemen, you would not wish to eat your friends, would you? You think you are turning a Jesuit on the spit, but it is your ally, the enemy of your enemies,[10] whom you are about to roast. As for me, I was born in this very country; and the gentleman you see here is my master; and, far from being a Jesuit, he has just killed one, whose clothes he is wearing as the spoils of war: which is of course the origin of this whole misunderstanding. To check the truth of what I am saying, take his cassock and bring it to the nearest border post of the kingdom of *Los Padres*; inquire whether my master has not killed a Jesuit officer. It won't take long; if you find that I have lied, you can eat us anyway. However, if I have told you the truth, you are far too well acquainted with the principles, procedures and articles of international justice not to spare our lives.'

The Oreillons found this speech entirely reasonable; they dispatched two of their chiefs post-haste to find out the truth; the two delegates carried out their commission like men of sense, and returned shortly bearing the good news. The Oreillons untied their two prisoners, treated them with every civility, offered them girls, gave them refreshments, and escorted them back to the borders of their territory, gaily chanting: 'He's no Jesuit! He's no Jesuit!'

Candide could not stop wondering at the manner of their deliverance. 'What a people!' he kept saying. 'What men! What customs! If I had not had the good luck to run my sword right through Cunégonde's brother, I would have been eaten alive without fail. After all, it seems that the state of nature is a good thing, since these people, instead of eating me, showed me a thousand civilities just as soon as they knew I was not a Jesuit.'

CHAPTER 17

Arrival of Candide and his manservant in the land of Eldorado,[1] and what they saw there

When they had reached the frontiers of Oreillon territory, Cacambo said to Candide: 'You see, this hemisphere is no better than the other one: take my advice, let us go back to Europe by the shortest route possible.' – 'But how do we get back?' said Candide, 'and where would we go? If I return to my own country, I will find Bulgars and Abars cutting everyone's throats; if I return to Portugal I will be burned at the stake; and if we stay in these parts we may end up on a spit at any moment. And how could I bring myself to leave that part of the world containing Mademoiselle Cunégonde?'

'Let us make for Cayenne,'[2] said Cacambo. 'There we will find some Frenchmen, who are always to be found wherever you go; they will be able to help us. Perhaps God will take pity on us.'

Getting to Cayenne was by no means easy; they knew roughly which direction to take, but at every turn there were terrible obstacles in the shape of mountains, rivers, precipices, brigands and savages. Their horses died of fatigue; their provisions ran out; they survived for an entire month on wild fruits, and eventually found themselves by a small river fringed with coco-nut trees, which kept them alive and sustained their hopes.

Cacambo, whose advice was always as sound as the old woman's, said to Candide: 'We can't go on, we have walked enough; I see an empty canoe on the bank; let us fill it with coconuts, throw ourselves in, and let the current take us; a river always leads to human habitation of some kind. If we don't find anything pleasant, we are sure to find something new.' – 'Come on, then,' said Candide, 'and let us put our trust in Providence.'

They drifted for several leagues down-river, the banks of which were in some places level and covered with flowers, in others barren and steep. The river kept widening; at length it ran beneath a vault of terrifying rocks which seemed to touch the sky. The two travellers were bold enough to trust themselves to the current and be swept under this vault. The river, confined at this point, carried them along with dreadful noise and rap-idity. Only after twenty-four hours did they see daylight again; but their canoe smashed to pieces in the rapids; they dragged themselves from boulder to boulder for an entire league; finally they emerged into an immense open plain, bordered by inaccess-ible mountains. Here the land had been cultivated as much for beauty as from necessity, for everywhere the useful was joined to the agreeable.[3] The roads were crowded, or rather adorned with carriages lustrous in form and substance, bearing men and women of singular beauty, drawn with great rapidity by large red sheep[4] who surpassed the fleetest horses of Andalusia, Tetuan or Meknes.

'Now this, on the other hand,' said Candide, 'is a big improvement on Westphalia.' They put ashore at the first village they reached. Some local children, covered with tattered gar-ments of gold brocade, were playing quoits at the entrance to the settlement; our two visitors from another world stopped to observe them: their quoits were fairly large round objects, yellow, red and green, which gave off a singular light. The travellers felt an urge to pick up one or two of them; they proved to be gold, emeralds and rubies, the least of which would have been the greatest ornament in the Mogul Emperor's throne. 'Without any doubt,' said Cacambo, 'these children playing quoits are the sons of the King of this country.' At which moment the village schoolmaster appeared, to call them back to class. 'And that must be the tutor to the royal family,' said Candide.

The little urchins immediately abandoned their game, leaving the quoits and other playthings on the ground. Candide gathered these up, ran to the tutor, and respectfully handed them to him, giving him to understand by signs that Their Royal Highnesses had forgotten their gold and their precious stones. The village schoolmaster smiled and dropped them back on the ground, looked into Candide's face for a moment with great puzzlement and continued on his way.

Our travellers did not fail to pick up the gold, rubies and emeralds. 'What can this place be?' cried Candide. 'These royal children must be well brought up indeed, since they are taught to despise gold and gems.'[5] Cacambo was as taken aback as Candide. At length they drew near to the first house in the village; it resembled a palace in Europe. A crowd of people were pressing at the entrance, and there was an even larger crowd within. Strains of some delightful music could be heard, and a delicious aroma of cooking filled the nostrils. Cacambo went closer to the entrance, and realized that they were speaking Peruvian, which was his native tongue: for as everyone knows, Cacambo was born in the Tucuman, in a village where nothing else is spoken.[6] 'I will act as your interpreter,' he said to Candide. 'Let's go inside, for this is an inn.'

At once two boys and two girls, in uniforms of gold cloth, with ribbons in their hair, showed our visitors to a table of diners and offered them the menu of the day. Four different soups were being served, each garnished with a brace of parrots, followed by a boiled condor weighing two hundred pounds, two excellent roast monkey, a platter containing three hundred birds of paradise and another of six hundred humming-birds, together with some exquisite ragouts and delicious pastries; all of which was served on plates of what looked like rock crystal. The waiters and waitresses were serving a variety of beverages made from sugar cane.

Most of the diners were tradesmen and wagoners, all of them extremely polite, who questioned Cacambo with the utmost circumspection, and replied to his questions as fully as possible.

When the meal was finished, Cacambo assumed, as did Candide, that they would amply pay their share of the bill by tossing on to the table a couple of the large pieces of gold they had picked up; at which the landlord and landlady burst into peels of laughter, which continued for some time. At last their mirth subsided. 'Gentlemen,' said the host, 'I plainly perceive that you are foreigners. We are not accustomed to seeing your like; forgive us for laughing when you offered as payment the pebbles off our roadside. To be sure, you probably don't have any of our currency, but you do not need any money to dine here. All the inns established to further the trade of this nation are paid for by the government.[7] You have eaten indifferently here, for this is a poor village; but everywhere else you will be received as you deserve to be.' Cacambo translated the whole of this speech for Candide, who listened with the same wonder and bewilderment as his friend Cacambo showed in reporting it. 'What is this country,' said one to the other, 'which is unknown to the rest of the world, and where nature operates under laws so utterly different to ours? It is probably the land where all is well, for clearly such a place has to exist. And despite what Maître Pangloss may have said, I often noticed that everything went fairly badly in Westphalia.'

CHAPTER 18

What they saw in the land of Eldorado

Cacambo gave the landlord to understand that their curiosity was by no means satisfied. 'I am a very ignorant man,' said the landlord, 'and am happy to remain so; but there is an old fellow here, retired from the court, who is the most learned man in the realm – and its most talkative.' Whereupon he took Cacambo to meet the old man. Candide was now playing second fiddle, and accompanied his valet. They entered a very modest house, for the door was merely of silver and the panelling in the apartments merely of gold, though so tastefully fashioned that the most opulent of workmanship could not have surpassed it. To be sure, the antechamber was encrusted with mere rubies and emeralds; but the skill with which everything was arranged more than justified its bare simplicity.

The old man received the two strangers on a sofa upholstered with humming-bird feathers, and offered them refreshments in diamond goblets; after which he satisfied their curiosity as follows:

'I am one hundred and seventy-two years of age, and it was from my late father, equerry to the King, that I learned of the astonishing political upheavals which he himself witnessed in Peru. This kingdom in which we live is the ancient homeland of the Incas, who most imprudently left it to go and conquer an empire elsewhere, and were eventually wiped out by the Spaniards.[1]

'The princes of the royal house who stayed behind in their native land were wiser; they ordained, with the consent of the people,[2] that no inhabitant should ever again leave our little kingdom; and this is what has preserved our innocence and our happiness. The Spaniards had some confused knowledge as to the existence of this country, which they called El Dorado, and about a hundred years ago an Englishman named Sir Raleigh[3] even came quite close to here; but as we are surrounded by inaccessible mountains and precipices, we have so far been protected against the rapacity of the European states, with their irrational lust for the pebbles and mud of our land, for whose sake they would kill every last one of us.'

Their conversation lasted some time; it touched on the forms of Eldoradean government, on local customs, women, public spectacles, and the arts. At length Candide, whose taste still ran to metaphysics, asked through Cacambo whether the people of this country had any religion.

The old man flushed a little. 'But how could you suppose

otherwise!' he replied. 'Do you take us for ingrates?' Cacambo humbly asked what was the religion of Eldorado. The old man flushed again. 'Can there be more than one religion?' he replied. 'We have, I believe, the same religion as everyone else: we worship God from night till morning.'⁴ – 'Do you worship only one God?' asked Cacambo, who continued to act as the interpreter of Candide's doubts. – 'Evidently so,' said the old man, 'since there are not two Gods, or three, or four.⁵ I must say that the people from your world ask some very odd questions.' Candide was indefatigable in his questioning by proxy of this worthy old gentleman; he wanted to know how one prayed to God in Eldorado. 'We do not pray to him at all,' said the honourable sage. 'We have nothing to ask of him; he has given us everything we need; we thank him unceasingly.' Candide was curious to see some priests; he had Cacambo inquire where they could be found. The good old man smiled. 'My friends,' he said, 'we are all of us priests. The King and the heads of each family sing solemn hymns of thanksgiving every morning, to the accompaniment of five or six thousand musicians.' – 'What! You have no monks instructing and disputing, and governing and intriguing, and having everyone burned alive who is not of their opinion?' – 'We would have to be foolish indeed,' said the old man. 'Everyone here is of the same mind, and we cannot imagine what you mean by this talk of monks.' Each one of these answers sent Candide into raptures, and he said to himself: 'This is a far cry from Westphalia and my lord the Baron's castle: had our friend Pangloss seen Eldorado, he would not have kept saying that the castle of Thunder-ten-tronckh was the best place on earth; clearly, one has to travel in this world.'

After their long conversation, the good old man ordered a carriage and six sheep to be harnessed, and gave the two travellers a dozen of his servants to conduct them to the Court. 'Forgive me,' he said to them, 'for my age deprives me of the honour of accompanying you. You will not be displeased by the way our King receives you, and no doubt you will make allowances for any of our customs that do displease you.'

Candide and Cacambo climbed into the carriage; the six sheep raced along, and in less than four hours they arrived at the palace of the King, situated at the far end of the capital. The main portico was two hundred and thirty feet high and one hundred feet wide; it is impossible to describe the materials of which it was made, from which you may imagine their prodigious superiority over those pebbles and sand which we refer to as 'gold' or 'gems'.

Twenty beautiful women of the royal guard received Candide and Cacambo as they descended from the carriage; they conducted them to the baths, and dressed them in robes woven from down of humming-bird; after which the highest officers of the Court, both men and women, led them to the apartments of His Majesty, between two rows of musicians each a thousand strong, as custom dictated. When they drew near to the throne room, Cacambo asked one of the grand officers how he should go about greeting His Majesty: should he drop to his knees or prostrate himself on the ground; should he place his hands on his head or his behind; should he lick the dust off the parquet?[6] In a word, what was the correct form? 'The custom,' replied the grand officer, 'is to hug the King and kiss him on both cheeks.' Candide and Cacambo accordingly threw their arms around the neck of His Majesty, who received them with every grace, and invited them graciously to supper.

Meanwhile they were shown the city, its public buildings reaching to the clouds, its markets ornamented with a thousand columns, its fountains of spring water and its fountains of rose-water and sugar-cane liquors, all playing perpetually in the middle of large squares,[7] themselves paved with precious stones which gave off an odour of cloves and cinnamon. Candide asked to see the law courts and the court of appeal;[8] he was told that there were none, and that nobody ever went to court. He asked if there were any prisons, and was told that there were none. What surprised him even more, and pleased him most, was the palace of sciences, in which he saw a gallery nearly a mile long filled entirely with instruments for the study of mathematics and astronomy.

Having spent the whole afternoon seeing only a fraction of the city, they were taken back to the King. Candide sat down to dinner between His Majesty, his valet Cacambo, and several ladies. Never was entertainment more lavish, and never was there a more amusing supper-companion than His Majesty. Cacambo translated the King's witticisms for Candide, to whom they seemed witty even in translation. Of all the things that astonished Candide, this was by no means the least astonishing.

They spent a whole month in this place of hospitality. Candide kept saying to Cacambo: 'It is true, my friend, and I'll say it again: the castle where I was born cannot compare with where we are now; on the other hand Mademoiselle Cunégonde is not here, and doubtless you too have a mistress somewhere in Europe. If we remain here, we shall be just like everyone else; but if we return to the old world with only a dozen sheep loaded with Eldoradean pebbles, we shall be richer than all the kings put together, we shall no longer have Inquisitors to fear, and we shall easily rescue Cunégonde.'

This speech appealed to Cacambo: so pleasant it is to be on the move, to get ourselves noticed back home, and to boast of what we have seen on our travels, that our two happy wanderers resolved to be happy no longer and to seek His Majesty's permission to depart.

'This is a foolish scheme,' the King told them. 'I am well aware that my country is nothing to write home about; but when you are reasonably happy somewhere, you should stay put. I certainly have no right to prevent strangers from leaving; that species of tyranny has no place in our customs or our laws.[9] All men are free. Leave whenever you please, though you will have some difficulty in getting out. It is impossible to row back up the rapids which brought you here, so miraculously, and which run beneath the vaults of rock. The mountains which surround my kingdom on all sides are ten thousand feet high, and as perpendicular as walls; each of them is more than ten leagues across; the only descent is by sheer precipices. However, since you are absolutely set on leaving, I shall give orders to my engineers to make a machine that will transport you across in safety. When you have been conveyed to the other side of the mountains, no one may accompany you further; for my subjects have vowed never to set foot beyond our borders, and they are too wise to break their oath. You may ask of me otherwise whatever you please.' – 'All we ask of Your Majesty,' said Cacambo, 'is a few sheep loaded with provisions, with pebbles and with some of the mud of your country.' The King laughed. 'I cannot begin to understand the passion you Europeans have for our yellow mud; but take all you want, and much good may it do you.'

He immediately ordered his engineers to make a machine to hoist these two extraordinary persons up and out of his kingdom. Three thousand skilled engineers worked at the problem, for two weeks, at a cost of a mere twenty million pounds in sterling silver, which is the currency of that country.[10] Candide and Cacambo were placed in the machine, along with two large red sheep saddled and bridled for them to ride after they had cleared the mountains, plus twenty pack-sheep laden with provisions, thirty more carrying gifts of the richest native workmanship and fifty laden with gold and diamonds and other precious stones. The King embraced the two wanderers tenderly.

Their departure was a curious spectacle, as was the ingenious manner by which they were hoisted, men and sheep, to the top of the mountains. The engineers took leave of them, after seeing them safely across, and Candide had no further desire and no other object than to go and present his sheep to Mademoiselle Cunégonde. 'Now we have enough to pay off the Governor of Buenos Aires,' he said, 'if indeed a price can be placed on Mademoiselle Cunégonde. Let us make for Cayenne, take ship there, and then we'll see what kingdom we can buy ourselves.'

CHAPTER 19

What happened to them in Surinam,[1] *and how Candide made the acquaintance of Martin*

The first day's journey was pleasant enough. Our two travellers took heart from the thought of owning more treasure than could be mustered by Asia, Europe and Africa combined. Candide was in raptures, and carved Cunégonde's name on trees. On the second day, two of their sheep plunged into a swamp and were swallowed up, together with their entire load; a few days later two more sheep perished of exhaustion; seven or eight then died of hunger in a desert; and a few days later still more fell down a precipice. Finally, after a hundred days' march, they had only two sheep left. Candide said to Cacambo: 'My friend, you see how perishable are the riches of this world; nothing is certain but virtue, and the happiness of seeing Mademoiselle Cunégonde again.' – 'I agree,' said Cacambo, 'but we still have two sheep laden with more treasure than the King of Spain will ever possess, and I can see in the distance a town that I suspect to be Surinam, which belongs to the Dutch. We are at the end of our troubles, and the beginning of our happiness.'

As they drew near to the city, they came across a negro stretched out on the ground, with no more than half of his clothes left, which is to say a pair of blue canvas drawers; the poor man had no left leg and no right hand. 'Good God!' said Candide to him in Dutch.[2] 'What are you doing there, my friend, in such a deplorable state?' – 'I am waiting for my master, Monsieur Vanderdendur, the well-known merchant,' answered the negro. – 'And was it Monsieur Vanderdendur,' said Candide, 'who treated you like this?' – 'Yes, Monsieur,' said the negro, 'it is the custom. Twice a year we are given a pair of blue canvas drawers, and this is our only clothing. When we work in the sugar-mills and get a finger caught in the machinery, they cut off the hand; but if we try to run away, they cut off a leg: I have found myself in both situations. It is the price we pay for the sugar you eat in Europe.³ Yet when my mother sold me for ten Patagonian écus⁴ on the coast of Guinea, she told me: "My child, give thanks to our fetishes, and worship them always, for they will make your life happy; you have the honour to be a slave to our white masters, and therefore you are making the fortune of your father and mother." Alas! I don't know if I made their fortune, but they certainly didn't make mine. Dogs, monkeys and parrots are a thousand times less miserable than we are; the Dutch fetishes⁵ who converted me to their religion tell me every Sunday that we are all children of Adam, whites and blacks alike. I am no genealogist; but if these preachers are telling the truth, then we are all second cousins. In which case you must admit that no one could treat his relatives more horribly than this.'

'Oh Pangloss!' cried Candide. 'This is one abomination you could not have anticipated, and I fear it has finally done for me: I am giving up on your Optimism after all.' – 'What is Optimism?'⁶ asked Cacambo – 'Alas!' said Candide, 'it is the mania for insisting that all is well when all is by no means well.' And he wept as he looked down at his negro, and was still weeping as he entered Surinam.

They immediately inquired as to whether there was a vessel in port that one might send to Buenos Aires. The person they addressed happened to be a Spanish skipper, who offered to make them an honest deal. He arranged to meet them in a tavern. Candide and faithful Cacambo went to wait for him there, along with their two sheep.

Candide, who always poured out his heart, told the Spaniard of his adventures so far, and confessed that he intended to make off with Mademoiselle Cunégonde. 'In which case I will certainly not take you to Buenos Aires,' said the skipper. 'I would be hanged, and so would you. The beautiful Cunégonde is His Excellency's favourite mistress.' Candide was thunderstruck by this news; he wept for a long time; and at last he took Cacambo aside: 'Now, my dear friend,' he said to him, 'this is what you must do. We each have five or six millions' worth of diamonds in our pockets; you are cleverer than I; go and bring

Mademoiselle Cunégonde back from Buenos Aires. If the Governor makes difficulties, offer him a million; if he is still obstinate, offer him two. You have not killed any Inquisitors, so no one will be suspicious of you. I will have another ship fitted out; I will go and wait for you in Venice; it is a free state,[7] where we shall have nothing to fear from Bulgars, or Abars, or Jews, or Inquisitors.' Cacambo applauded this wise decision. He was in despair at parting from so good a master, who had become his close friend; but the pleasure of serving him prevailed over the sorrow of leaving him. Tearfully they embraced each other. Candide charged him on no account to forget the good old woman. Cacambo left the same day – he was a worthy fellow, this Cacambo.

Candide remained for a while in Surinam, waiting for another captain willing to take him and his two remaining sheep to Italy. He hired some servants, and purchased everything necessary for a long voyage; at length Monsieur Vanderdendur,[8] who owned a large vessel, came and presented himself. 'How much do you want,' Candide asked this character, 'to take me straight to Venice, along with servants, baggage, and those two sheep over there?' The skipper agreed on a price of ten thousand *piastres*.[9] Candide did not hesitate.

'Well, well!' said the careful Vanderdendur to himself. 'Here is a foreigner who parts with ten thousand *piastres* straight off! He must be fairly rich.' Returning a moment later, he informed Candide that he could not sail for less than twenty thousand. 'Very well, you shall have them', said Candide.

'Very well, indeed!' said the merchant softly to himself. 'This fellow parts with twenty thousand *piastres* as easily as ten.' Returning once more, he said that he could not take Candide to Venice for less than thirty thousand *piastres*. 'Then you shall have thirty thousand,' replied Candide.

'And so I shall!' said the Dutch merchant to himself again. 'Thirty thousand *piastres* are as nothing to this fellow; no doubt the two sheep are carrying immense wealth; but better not to press the point any further: let him pay up the thirty thousand first, and then we'll see.' Candide sold two little diamonds, the smaller of which fetched more than all the money the captain was asking. He paid him on the spot. The sheep were loaded on board. Candide followed in a small boat to join the vessel, which was riding at anchor. The skipper sees his opportunity, sets his sail and weighs anchor with a following wind; Candide, helpless and quite dumbfounded, immediately loses sight of him. 'Alas!' he cries out, 'now here is a trick worthy of the Old World!' He returns to shore, plunged in misery, having just lost what would have made the fortunes of twenty monarchs.

So he betakes himself to the Dutch residing magistrate, and, being a trifle agitated, knocks rather too brusquely on the door; he enters, explains what has happened, and shouts a little louder than is necessary. The magistrate begins by fining him ten thousand *piastres* for the noise he has made; he then hears him out with patience, promises to look into his case as soon as the merchant reappears, and charges him a further ten thousand *piastres* for the costs of the hearing.

This sequence of events completed Candide's despair; in truth he had endured misfortunes a thousand times more painful, but the cold-bloodedness of the magistrate, and of the captain who had robbed him, raised his spleen, and plunged him into the blackest melancholy. The wickedness of man now revealed itself to him in all its ugliness; his mind fed exclusively on gloomy thoughts. Finally, hearing of a French vessel ready to sail for Bordeaux, and having no more diamond-bearing sheep to transport, he paid for a cabin at the going rate, and let it be known in the town that he would pay the passage and board of any honest man who cared to make the journey with him, and two thousand *piastres* besides, on condition that this person be the most unfortunate and most thoroughly disgusted with his condition in the whole province.

A crowd of candidates came forward, such as an entire fleet could not have carried. Candide, determined to select the worthiest of these, picked out twenty individuals who seemed to him fairly companionable, each of whom naturally claimed to deserve preference. He assembled them at his inn and gave them supper on condition that each took an oath to give a faithful account of his life-story; promising in return to choose the one who seemed to him most to be pitied and to have most cause for being discontented with his lot, and to give each of the others a small consideration.

The sitting lasted until four o'clock in the morning. As he listened to their adventures, Candide called to mind what the old woman had said to him on the boat to Buenos Aires, and her wager that there was not a single person on board who had not suffered very great misfortunes. Each story he heard put him in mind of Pangloss. 'That Pangloss,' he said, 'would be hard pressed to prove his system now. I wish he were here. What is certain is that if all is well, then it is so in Eldorado and nowhere else on earth.' He finally decided in favour of a poor scholar who had worked ten years for the publishing houses of Amsterdam, taking the view that there was no occupation in the world which could more disgust a man.[10]

This scholar, who was moreover a very decent fellow, had been robbed by his wife, beaten by his son, and deserted by his daughter, who had eloped with a Portuguese. He had just been done out of a small sinecure on which he subsisted; and the preachers of Surinam were persecuting him because they had decided he was a Socinian.[11] It has to be said that the rival candidates were at least as wretched as he; but Candide was hoping that the company of a scholar would keep him amused during the voyage. The others all considered that Candide had done them a new injustice; but he pacified them by giving each a hundred *piastres*.

CHAPTER 20

What happened to Candide and Martin at sea

So the old scholar, who was called Martin, embarked for Bordeaux with Candide. Both had seen and suffered much; and even had their ship been scheduled to sail from Surinam to Japan via the Cape of Good Hope, they could still have occupied the whole voyage discussing moral and physical evil.

Candide had one great advantage over Martin, however, for he still hoped to see Mademoiselle Cunégonde again, whereas

Martin had nothing to hope for; moreover, Candide had some gold and diamonds; and although he had lost a hundred large red sheep laden with the greatest treasures on earth, and although the knavery of the Dutch captain gnawed at his heart, nevertheless, when he thought of what remained in his pockets, and when he spoke of Cunégonde, especially at the end of a good meal, he still inclined towards the system of Pangloss.

'But you, Monsieur Martin,' he said to the scholar, 'what do you make of all this? What is your idea of physical evil and moral evil?'[1] – 'Sir,' replied Martin, 'the priests accused me of being a Socinian; but the truth of the matter is that I am a Manichean.'[2] – 'Now you are making fun of me,' said Candide, 'there are surely no Manicheans left in the world.' – 'Well, here is one,' said Martin. 'I cannot help it, but I cannot see things in any other way.' – 'Then you must have the devil in you,' said Candide. – 'He takes so great a share in the affairs of this world,' said Martin, 'that he may well be a part of me, as of everything else; but I assure you, when I look around at this globe, or rather this globule,[3] I think that God has indeed abandoned it all to some malign being – all except your Eldorado, of course. I have scarcely seen a town that did not desire the ruin of the next town, nor a family that did not wish to exterminate some other family. Everywhere the weak loathe the strong, before whom they cringe, and the strong treat them like so many sheep to be sold for their meat and their wool. A million assassins in regimental formation[4] run from one end of Europe to the other, murdering and pillaging under orders, as a way of earning their bread, since there is no profession more honourable; and even in those cities which appear to enjoy peace, and where the arts flourish, men are more devoured by envy, cares and anxiety than all the tribulations visited upon a citadel under siege. Private griefs are crueller even than public miseries. In short, I have seen so much, and endured so much, that I am become a Manichean.'

'And yet there is some good in the world,' Candide would reply. – 'That may be so,' Martin would say, 'but I have not experienced it.'

In the midst of this discussion the sound of cannon was heard.

The noise grew louder with each passing moment. Everyone reached for their spyglasses. Two vessels were to be seen engaging in combat at a distance of about three miles: the wind brought them both so close to the French vessel that everyone had the pleasure of watching the engagement in complete comfort. Presently one of the vessels fired a broadside, so low down and so accurate as to sink the other outright. Candide and Martin could distinctly make out a hundred or so men on the deck of the sinking vessel, all raising their arms to heaven and uttering the most fearful shrieks; the next moment everything was swallowed.

'Well, there you have it,' said Martin. 'That is how men behave towards each other.' – 'Certainly,' said Candide, 'the devil had a hand in this business, at least.' As he was speaking, he noticed something bright red in the water, swimming close to their ship. The launch was lowered to see what it might be. It was one of Candide's sheep. He felt more joy at recovering this one sheep than the affliction he had suffered at losing a hundred, each laden with the fat diamonds of Eldorado.

The French captain soon ascertained that the captain of the ship doing the sinking was a Spaniard, and that the captain of the ship being sunk was a Dutch pirate: the very same who had robbed Candide. The immense riches seized by this scoundrel were engulfed along with him, and nothing saved but a single sheep. 'You see,' said Candide to Martin, 'crime is sometimes punished; that blackguard of a Dutch owner got the fate he deserved.' – 'Yes,' said Martin, 'but did the passengers on board have to perish too? God punished the thief, the devil drowned the rest.'

Meanwhile the French and Spanish ships continued on their way, and Candide continued his conversation with Martin. They disputed for fifteen days in a row, and at the end of fifteen days were as far from agreement as on day one. But they talked, after all, they exchanged ideas, they consoled one another. Candide stroked his sheep: 'Since I have found you again,' he said, 'I may well find Cunégonde.'

CHAPTER 21

Candide and Martin approach the coast of France, philosophizing all the way

At last the French coast came into view. 'Have you ever been to France, Monsieur Martin?' said Candide. – 'Yes,' said Martin, 'I have travelled through several of its provinces. In some of which half the population are lunatics, whereas in others they are too cunning by half; in some parts they are quite good-natured and rather simple-minded, while in others they sharpen their wits. But wherever you go, the principal occupation is making love, the second is spreading scandal, and the third is talking non-sense.'[1] – 'But have you been to Paris, Monsieur Martin?'[2] – 'Yes, I've been to Paris; it combines all of the above categories; it is a chaos, a throng in which everyone pursues pleasure and almost no one finds it, or at least so it seemed to me. I stayed there only briefly; on my arrival I was robbed of all I had by pickpockets at the Saint-Germain fair;[3] I was then taken for a thief myself, and spent eight days in prison; after which I took a job as a printer's proofreader to earn enough to return to Holland on foot. I came to know all sorts of rabble – the hacks and scribblers, the political intriguers, and the holy rabble who trade in religious convulsions.[4] I am told there are some civilized people in that city; I should like to think so.'

'For my part, I have no interest in seeing France,' said Candide. 'You will appreciate that when a man has spent a month in Eldorado, he no longer needs to see anything in this world except Mademoiselle Cunégonde; I am going to wait for her in Venice; we shall be travelling to Italy by way of France: why don't you accompany me?' – 'With pleasure,' said Martin. 'They say that Venice is strictly for the Venetian nobility, but that foreigners are nevertheless well received when they have plenty of money; I have none, and you have lots; I will follow where you lead.' – 'Incidentally,' said Candide, 'do you think the earth was originally a sea, as we are told in that fat volume belonging to the captain?'[5] – 'I believe nothing of the kind,' said Martin, 'no more than I believe all the other idiocies that are put about these days.' – 'But to what end was this world created, then?' said Candide. – 'To make us mad,' replied Martin. – 'And are you not amazed,' Candide went on, 'at the emotions displayed by those two Oreillon girls for their apes, which I told you about?' – 'Not in the least,' said Martin. 'I see nothing strange in their passion; I have seen so many extraordinary things that nothing seems extraordinary to me any more.' – 'Do you think,' said Candide, 'that men have always massacred one another, as they do today? That they have always been liars, cheats, traitors, ingrates and brigands, as well as weaklings, shirkers, cowards, backbiters, gluttons, drunkards, misers and social climbers, in addition to being bloodthirsty, slanderous, fanatical, debauched, hypocritical and downright stupid?' – 'But don't you accept,' replied Martin, 'that hawks have always killed pigeons when they come across them?' – 'Without a doubt,' said Candide. – 'Well, then,' said Martin, 'if hawks have always had the same nature, why do you expect men to change theirs?'[6] – 'Oh,' said Candide, 'but there is a crucial difference, because free will...' And philosophizing thus, they arrived in Bordeaux.

CHAPTER 22

What happened to Candide and Martin in France

Candide stopped off in Bordeaux only for as long as it took to sell a few Eldoradean pebbles, and equip himself with a fast post-chaise – with two seats, for he could no longer be without his philosopher Martin; he was only grieved to be parting from his sheep, which he left to the Academy of Science in Bordeaux; they offered as the subject of that year's essay prize the question: 'Why is the wool of this sheep red?' The prize was awarded to a scholar from the North, who proved by means of A plus B minus C divided by Z[1] that the sheep must of necessity be red, and must in due course die of sheep-pox.

Meanwhile, all the travellers Candide encountered in taverns along the way said to him: 'We're going to Paris.' Such general eagerness finally decided him to see this capital for himself; it would not involve too much of a detour off the road to Venice.

He entered by the Faubourg Saint-Marceau,[2] and felt like he was in the meanest village in Westphalia.

Scarcely had Candide reached his inn than he came down with a minor ailment brought on by his exertions. Since he had an enormous diamond on his finger, and since a prodigiously heavy strong-box had been noticed among his luggage, he soon had by his side two doctors whom he had not sent for, a number of intimate friends who never left the room, and two philanthropic ladies to warm his broth for him. Martin said: 'I remember being ill myself when I first came to Paris; I was very poor, so I had neither intimate friends nor philanthropic ladies nor doctors. And I got better.'

However, by dint of many enemas and much bloodletting, Candide's illness worsened. A parish curate called, and asked him meekly for a note of confession,[3] payable to the bearer in the next world; Candide would have none of this. The philanthropic ladies assured him that it was all the fashion; Candide replied that he was not fashionable. Martin was all for throwing the curate out of the window; the clergyman swore that Candide would be buried without rites; Martin swore that the clergyman would be buried above ground if he continued to bother them. The dispute grew heated; Martin took the clergyman by the shoulders and ejected him without ceremony; which caused a great scandal, and was reported to the authorities.

Candide recovered. And during his convalescence he had some genteel company to supper. There was gambling for high stakes. Candide was quite amazed that he never drew any aces; Martin was not amazed.

Among those who did the honours of the city for Candide was a little abbé from Perigord,[4] one of those assiduous types, alert, endlessly obliging, impudent, fawning, adaptable, who are always on the lookout for strangers passing through, for whom they rehearse all the scandals of the town, and procure its pleasures at a range of prices. This creature began by taking Candide and Martin to the theatre. A new tragedy was being performed. Candide found himself seated among a group of wits. This did not prevent him from weeping at various scenes that were played to perfection. One of the argumentative bores sitting near to him remarked during an interval: 'You have little cause to weep, really – the actress is atrocious; the actor playing opposite her is worse; the play is even worse than the actors; the author doesn't know a word of Arabic and yet the scene is set in Arabia.[5] What's more, he is known to reject the doctrine of innate ideas;[6] tomorrow I'll show you twenty pamphlets written against him.'[7] – 'Monsieur,' said Candide to the abbé, 'how many plays have been written in French?' – 'Five or six thousand,' came the reply. – 'That is a lot,' said Candide, 'and how many of them are any good?' – 'Fifteen or sixteen,' replied the other. – 'That is a lot,' said Martin.

Candide was rather taken with an actress who was playing Queen Elizabeth in a fairly dull tragedy[8] that sometimes gets put on. 'That actress pleases me a great deal,' he said to Martin. 'She reminds me a little of Mademoiselle Cunégonde; I would like very much to pay my respects to her.' The abbé from Périgord offered to effect an introduction. Candide, who had been brought up in Germany, inquired as to the etiquette, and asked how queens of England were treated in France.[9] 'That depends,' said the abbé. 'In the provinces you take them to a tavern. In Paris we honour them when they are beautiful, and we throw them in the public sewer when they die.' – 'Queens in the sewer!' said Candide. – 'Indeed so,' said Martin, 'the abbé is quite right. I was in Paris when Mademoiselle Monime exited, as they say, from this life to the next; she was refused what people here call "the honours of Christian burial", that is to say, the honour of rotting with all the beggars of the parish in a filthy cemetery; she was buried alone and iso-lated from the rest of her troupe at the corner of the rue de Bourgogne,[10] which would have pained her in the extreme, for she was a woman of noble mind.' – 'That was hardly a noble way for them to behave,' said Candide. – 'What do you expect?' said Martin. 'That is how these people are. Take any contradiction or inconsistency you can imagine, and you will find examples of it in the government, the courts, the churches and the theatres of this ridiculous nation.' – 'Is it true that Parisians are always laughing?' asked Candide. – 'Yes,' said the abbé, 'but with rage in their hearts; for they complain of everything amid roars of laughter; and they laugh even while doing the most abominable things.'

'So who was that fat pig,' said Candide, 'who was so critical of the play I enjoyed crying at so much, and of the actors I liked so much?' – 'He is a devil incarnate,' replied the abbé, 'someone who earns his living by vilifying every new book and play that appears; he detests anyone who succeeds, as a eunuch detests lovers: he is one of those vipers of literature who feed off dirt and venom; in short, he is a hack.' – 'And what is a hack?' said Candide. – 'A scribbler of pamphlets,' replied the abbé, 'a Fréron.'[11]

Such was Candide's conversation with Martin and the abbé from Périgord, as they stood on the staircase watching the audience file out after the play. 'Although I cannot wait to see Mademoiselle Cunégonde again,' said Candide, 'I should also like to have supper with Mademoiselle Clairon;[12] for she did seem altogether admirable.'

The abbé was not the man to effect an introduction to Mademoiselle Clairon, who moved only in superior cicles. 'She is engaged for this evening,' he said, 'but allow me the honour of taking you to the house of a lady of quality, where you will get to know Paris as well as if you had been living here for years.'

Candide, who was curious by nature, allowed himself to be taken to the lady's house, at the far end of the Faubourg Saint-Honoré;[13] there they were busy playing faro,[14] and a dozen gloomy punters were each holding a small hand of cards, the much-creased register of their misfortunes. A profound silence reigned; the punters looked pale and the banker looked uneasy, while the lady of the house, seated beside this implacable figure, kept a lynx-eyed watch on all the doubled bets and on any stakes raised by a player turning up the corners of his cards out of turn. She would make him turn them back again, severely but politely, and never lost her patience for fear of losing her clients. This lady called herself the Marquise de Parolignac.[15] Her daughter, aged fifteen, was one of the punters, and would tip the wink to her mother whenever any of these unfortunates attempted to repair the cruelties of fortune by cheating. The abbé from Périgord now entered, together with Candide and Martin; no one got up, or greeted them, or looked their way, being wholly intent on their cards. 'Her Excellency the Baroness of Thunder-ten-tronckh was more civil than this,' said Candide.

However, the abbé whispered something to the Marquise, who half rose, honouring Candide with a gracious smile and Martin with a very distant nod. She ordered a chair and a hand of cards to be dealt to Candide, who lost fifty thousand francs in two games; after which they sat down gaily to supper; everyone was surprised at how calmly Candide had taken his losses; the lackeys whispered to each other in their lackey language that this must be 'one of your English milords'.

The supper was like most suppers in Paris: silence at first, then a confused babble in which no one can make themselves heard, followed by an exchange of largely insipid witticisms, false news, pointless argument, a little politics and a quantity of slander; there was even some talk of the latest books. 'Has anyone read,' asked the abbé from Périgord, 'that gallimaufry written by Gauchat, the Doctor of Divinity?'[16] – 'Yes,' replied one of the company, 'but I couldn't finish it. We are plagued these days with the productions of impertinent scribblers, though nothing approaches the impertinence of Gauchat, Doctor of Divinity. I am so weary of this inundation of vile reading matter that I've taken refuge in gambling.' – 'And what do you think of the *Mélanges* of Archdeacon T[rublet]?'[17] asked the abbé. – 'Oh,' said Madame de Parolignac, 'such a tedious bore! How he tells you with compound interest what everyone already knows, and how he trudges through what is hardly worth skating over! How mindlessly he borrows the minds of others! How he spoils what he plunders! How he disgusts me! But he shall disgust me no more – one or two pages of our archdeacon are quite enough, thank you.'

One of the guests at table was a man of taste and learning, who confirmed what the Marquise was saying. The conversation turned to tragedies, and the Marquise asked how it was that some plays performed on stage were quite unreadable on the page. The man of taste explained very clearly how a play can be of some interest but of almost no merit. He showed in few words how it was not enough to contrive one or two of those situations that are to be found in any novel and which always captivate the audience; how one needs to be original without being far-fetched, frequently sublime but always natural; to know the human heart but also how to give it a voice; to be a poet without one's characters appearing to speak like poets; and to have perfect command of the language, using it with purity and harmony, and without ever sacrificing sense to rhyme.[18] 'Whoever fails to follow all these rules,' he added, 'may produce one or two tragedies that are applauded on the stage, but he will never be counted a good writer. There are very few good tragedies; some are merely idylls in dialogue form, however well written and well rhymed;[19] others are political tracts that send us to sleep, or pompousities that merely repel us;[20] and others still are the ravings of enthusiasts, barbarously written, with broken dialogue and lengthy apostrophes to the gods (because the author does not know how to speak to men), full of false maxims and turgid commonplaces.'[21]

Candide listened attentively to this speech, and formed a highly favourable opinion of the speaker. Since the Marquise had taken good care to place Candide at her side, he took the liberty of leaning over and asking in a whisper who this excellent talker might be. 'He is a man of learning,' said the lady, 'who does not play cards, but whom the abbé sometimes brings to my house to dine. He is a great judge of plays and books, has written a tragedy which was hissed off the stage, and a book of which only one copy has ever been seen outside the publisher's shop – the copy that he presented to me.' – 'A great man!' said Candide. 'He sounds like another Pangloss.'

So he turned to this gentleman and said: 'Sir, doubtless you are of the view that everything is for the best in the physical and moral worlds, and that nothing could be other than it is?'

– 'I, sir?' replied the man of learning. 'I believe nothing of the kind: I find everything in our world amiss; no one knows his rank or his responsibility, or what he's doing, or what he should be doing; and that, except for supper parties like this, which are gay and increase fellowship, our time here is wasted on senseless quarrels: Jansenists against Molinists, judiciary against churchmen,[22] men of letters against men of letters, courtiers against courtiers, financiers against the people, wives against husbands, relatives against relatives; it is a perpetual battlefield.'

'I have seen worse,' Candide replied. 'But a wise man, who has since had the misfortune to be hanged, taught me that there is in these things a perfect propriety; like the shadows in a beautiful painting.' – 'Your hanged man was making a mockery of us,' interjected Martin, 'and your shadows are in truth dreadful stains.'[23] – 'It is men who make these stains,' said Candide, 'and they cannot do otherwise.' – 'So it is not their fault, then,' said Martin. Most of the card players, who did not understand a word of all this, were busy drinking, while Martin disputed with the man of learning, and Candide recounted some of his adventures to the lady of the house.

After supper the Marquise took Candide to her private dressing-room and sat him down on a divan. 'Well,' she said to him, 'so are you still hopelessly in love with Mademoiselle Cunégonde of Thunder-ten-tronckh?' – 'Yes, Madame,' came the reply. The Marquise smiled tenderly and said: 'You answer like a young man from Westphalia; a Frenchman would have replied: "It is true that I was in love with Mademoiselle Cunégonde, but when I see you, Madame, I fear I can love her no longer."' – 'Alas! Madame,' said Candide, 'I shall answer as you please.' – 'Your passion for her,' continued the Marquise, 'began when you picked up her handkerchief. I want you to pick up my garter.' – 'With all my heart,' said Candide, and he picked it up. 'Now I want you to slip it back on for me,' said the lady; so Candide slipped it back on for her. 'You see,' said the lady, 'you are a visitor; sometimes I make my Parisian lovers languish for an entire fortnight, but here I am giving myself to you on the very first night, for one must do the honours of one's country to a young man from Westphalia.' The fair lady, having noticed two enormous diamonds on her young foreigner's hand, praised them so sincerely that from Candide's fingers they slipped imperceptibly to those of the Marquise.[24]

Returning home with his abbé from Périgord, Candide felt some remorse at having been unfaithful to Mademoiselle Cunégonde; the abbé commiserated with him, for he had only a small stake in the fifty thousand francs which Candide had lost at cards, or in the proceeds of the two brilliants half-given and half-extorted. His intention was to profit as fully as possible from the advantages which his acquaintance with Candide might yet procure. He asked a great deal about Cunégonde, and Candide confided that he would certainly beg that lovely creature's forgiveness for his infidelity when he saw her in Venice.

The abbé from Périgord became ever more unctuous and assiduous, and showed an affecting interest in everything that Candide said, or did, or planned to do.[25] 'And so, Monsieur, you have an assignation in Venice?' – 'Yes, Monsieur l'abbé,' said Candide. 'I must absolutely go and find Mademoiselle Cunégonde.' Then, carried away by the pleasure of talking about his beloved, he related – as he so often did – part of his adventures with that illustrious lady from Westphalia.

'I imagine,' said the abbé, 'that Mademoiselle Cunégonde has plenty of wit, and that she she must write charming letters?' – 'I have never received a letter from her,' said Candide. 'You must understand that having been kicked out of the castle on account of my for love for her, I could hardly write to her; that soon afterwards I learned that she was dead, then found her again, and then lost her; and that now I have sent a messenger to her, two thousand five hundred leagues from here, and am awaiting her reply.'

The abbé listened closely, and seemed as if lost in thought. He shortly took his leave of the two foreigners, after embracing them warmly. The next day, on waking, Candide received the following letter:

Monsieur, my dearest love, I have been lying ill in this town for the past week. I discover that you are here too. I would fly to

your arms were I able to move. I learned of your passage at
Bordeaux; I have left the faithful Cacambo and the old woman
there, and they will soon follow after. The Governor of Buenos
Aires took everything, but I still have your heart. Come to me,
your presence will restore me to life, or make me die of pleasure.

This charming letter, this unhoped-for letter, filled Candide
with an inexpressible joy, while the illness of his dear
Cunégonde overwhelmed him with grief. Torn between emotions, he takes his gold and his diamonds, and has himself and
Martin conveyed to the house where Mademoiselle Cunégonde
is staying. He enters her room, trembling with emotion, his
heart beating violently, his voice choked with sobs; he is about
to draw back the bed curtains and send for a lamp. 'You will
do no such thing,' says the maid, 'or the light will kill her,' and
she quickly closes the curtains again. 'My dearest Cunégonde,'
says Candide in tears, 'how are you feeling? If you cannot see
me, at least speak to me.' – 'She cannot speak,' says the maid.
The fair invalid now extends a plump hand from the bedclothes,
which Candide waters with his tears for a long time, and then
fills with diamonds, leaving a purse full of gold on the armchair.
    In the midst of this turmoil an officer of the watch arrives,
followed by the abbé from Périgord and a squad of men. 'So
are these the two suspicious foreigners?' he asks, and has them
arrested on the spot, ordering his flunkeys to haul them off to
prison. 'They don't treat visitors like this in Eldorado,' says
Candide. 'I am more of a Manichean than ever,' says Martin.
'But, Monsieur, where are you taking us?' says Candide. 'To
the deepest, darkest cell,' says the officer.
    Martin, having by now recovered his sang-froid, deduced that
the lady claiming to be Cunégonde was a common fraud, that
the abbé from Périgord was a fraud who had taken advantage
of Candide's innocence at the first opportunity, and that the
officer was another fraud, whom it would be easy to shake off.
    Rather than expose himself to the process of law, and enlight-
ened by Martin's advice, and impatient as ever to see the real
Cunégonde again, Candide offered the officer three little diamonds worth three thousand *pistoles* each. 'Ah, Monsieur!'

said the man with the ivory-tipped baton, 'even had you committed every imaginable crime, you are still the most honest man
alive. Three diamonds! Each worth three thousand *pistoles*! Sir,
I would lay down my life for you sooner than throw you in a
dungeon. There are orders to arrest all foreigners hereabouts,
but leave it to me. I have a brother in Dieppe, in Normandy; I
will take you there; and if you have any diamonds for him, he
will look after you as if he were looking after me.'

'And why are there orders to arrest all foreigners?' said
Candide. The abbé from Périgord now spoke up: 'It's because
an imbecile from Arras listened to some foolish talk, which was
enough to make him go and commit parricide – not like what
happened in May 1610, but like what happened in December
1594, and like several other crimes committed in other months
and other years by other wretches who have listened to similar
imbecilities.'

The officer then explained what the abbé was talking about.[26]
'Oh! What monsters!' exclaimed Candide. 'What! And are such
horrors possible, in a nation that loves dancing and singing! I
am leaving this minute! What is the quickest way out of this
country, where monkeys provoke tigers?[27] In my own country
I encountered bears; only in Eldorado have I met proper men.
For God's sake, officer, take me to Venice, where I am to wait
for Mademoiselle Cunégonde.' – 'I can only take you as far as
Lower Normandy,' said the constable. At which he ordered
Candide's leg-irons to be removed, said there had been
a mistake, sent his men away, took Candide and Martin to
Dieppe, and left them in the hands of his brother. There was a
small Dutch vessel riding at anchor. The Norman, who with the
help of three more diamonds had become the most obliging of
men, put Candide and his servants aboard the vessel, which was
about to sail for Portsmouth, England. It was not the way to
Venice, but Candide felt like a man delivered from hell, and
resolved to resume his journey to Venice at the first opportunity.

CHAPTER 23

Candide and Martin reach the shores of England – and what they see there

'Oh, Pangloss, Pangloss! Martin, Martin! Oh, my dearest Cunégonde! What sort of a world is this?' sighed Candide on board the Dutch ship. – 'A very mad and abominable one,' replied Martin. – 'You have been to England,' said Candide. 'Are they as mad there as in France?' – 'It's a different type of madness,' said Martin. 'As you know, the two countries are at war over a few acres of snow on the Canadian border, and they are spending rather more on their lovely war than the whole of Canada is worth.[1] But to say precisely if there are more people in one country who should be locked up than in another, is something beyond the limits of my feeble understanding. All I know is that by and large the people we are now going to see are disposed to be very gloomy.'

As they talked, they docked at Portsmouth; a multitude of people covered the shore, all gazing intently at a rather corpulent man who was on his knees, his eyes blindfolded, on the quarter-deck of one of the ships of the fleet; four soldiers were posted directly in front of him, each of whom now fired three bullets into his skull, as calmly as you like; after which the crowd dispersed looking extremely satisfied.[2] 'What is all this?' said Candide, 'and what devil is at work in the world?' He asked who was the fat man, who had just been so ceremoniously despatched. 'He was an admiral,' came the reply. – 'And why kill this admiral?' – 'Because,' came the reply, 'he did not get enough people killed when he had the chance: he gave battle to a French admiral, and was said not to have engaged closely enough with the enemy.' – 'In which case,' said Candide, 'surely the French admiral was just as far from the English admiral as the English admiral was from the French admiral?' – 'Unquestionably so,' came the reply, 'but in this country it is considered useful now and again to shoot an admiral, to encourage the others.'[3]

Candide was so stunned and so shocked by what he saw, and heard, that he refused even to set foot on English soil, but bargained with the Dutch captain (without caring if this one fleeced him as the other had done, in Surinam) to take him straight to Venice.

The captain was ready to leave in two days. They sailed along the coast of France, passing within sight of Lisbon, at which Candide shuddered. They entered the Straits, and the Mediterranean; finally putting in at Venice. 'Praised be God!' said Candide, embracing Martin. 'Here is where I shall see the lovely Cunégonde again. I trust Cacambo as I would myself. All is well, all goes well, all goes as well as it possibly can.'

CHAPTER 24

Concerning Paquette and Brother Girofleo

As soon as he reached Venice, he had a search made for Cacambo in all the taverns, all the coffee houses, all the brothels, but Cacambo was nowhere to be found. Each day he sent to inquire of every ship or trading vessel that came in: still no news of Cacambo. 'How do you explain this?' he said to Martin, eventually. 'I have had time to cross from Surinam to Bordeaux, travel from Bordeaux to Paris, from Paris to Dieppe, from Dieppe to Portsmouth; then to coast the length of Portugal and Spain, cross the entire Mediterranean, spend several months in Venice – and the lovely Cunégonde has still not arrived? All I have found in her place is that hussy of an imposter and an abbé from Périgord! Cunégonde is surely dead, and all that remains for me is to follow her. Alas! It would have been better to remain in the paradise of Eldorado than return to this accursed Europe. How right you are, my dear Martin! All is mere illusion and calamity.'

He fell into a black melancholy, and took no part in the fashionable operas or the other Carnival amusements; none of the Venetian ladies caused him the slightest temptation. Martin said to him: 'You are indeed a simpleton, to imagine that a half-caste valet with five or six millions in his pocket is going to comb the other side of the world for your mistress, and then bring her to you in Venice. If he finds her, he is going to keep her for himself. If he does not find her, he is going to take up with someone else: my advice to you is to forget your valet Cacambo and your mistress Cunégonde.' Martin provided little consolation. Candide's melancholy deepened, while the other continued with his relentless proofs that there is little virtue and no happiness on earth, except perhaps in Eldorado, where no one can ever go.

While debating this important question, and waiting for Cunégonde, Candide noticed a young Theatine[1] monk in Saint Mark's Square with a girl on his arm. The Theatine looked fresh, plump and vigorous; his eyes were bright, his air confident, his expression haughty, his gait proud. The girl was very pretty and was singing; she gazed lovingly at her Theatine, now and then pinching his fat cheeks. 'At least you will admit,' said Candide to Martin, 'that those two over there are happy. Until now I have encountered only unfortunate wretches, throughout the inhabited world, except in Eldorado; but as for that girl and her Theatine, I'll wager that they are happy indeed.' – 'And I'll wager the contrary,' said Martin. – 'We have only to invite them to dinner,' said Candide, 'and you will see whether I am right.'

He immediately goes up to them, presents his compliments, and invites them back to his hostelry to eat macaroni, Lombardy partridge and caviar, and to drink some Montepulciano and Lachryma Christi, not to mention wines from Cyprus and Samos. The young lady blushes; the Theatine accepts the invitation, and the girl follows, glancing at Candide with an air of surprise and confusion, her eyes filling with tears. Scarcely has she entered Candide's rooms than she says to him: 'So! Does Master Candide no longer recognize his Paquette?' On hearing these words Candide, who had not looked at her closely hitherto, having thoughts only for Cunégonde, said to her: 'My poor child! Is it you? And was it you who reduced Doctor Pangloss to that fine state in which I found him?' – 'Alas, sir,' said Paquette, 'I'm afraid so, and I see that you know the whole story. I heard afterwards about the terrible misfortunes that befell the whole household of my lady the Baroness and the lovely Mademoiselle Cunégonde. I swear to you that my own fate has been just as wretched. I was utterly innocent when you knew me. A Franciscan who was my confessor[2] had no trouble in seducing me. The consequences were terrible; I was forced to leave the castle not long after Monsieur the Baron sent you packing with great kicks to the behind. If a famous doctor had not taken pity on me, I would have surely died. Out of gratitude I was for some time the mistress of this doctor. His wife, who was jealous to the point of insanity, used to beat me every day without mercy; she was a fury. This doctor was the ugliest man alive, and I was the unhappiest of creatures, to be continually beaten on account of a man I did not love. You must know, sir, how dangerous it is for a shrewish woman to have a doctor for a husband. One day, exasperated by her behaviour, he gave her some medicine for a slight cold, of so efficacious a kind that she died two hours later in horrible convulsions. Madame's relatives brought a criminal suit against Monsieur; he fled the country, and I was thrown in prison. My innocence would not have saved me had I not been tolerably pretty. The judge released me on condition that he himself took over from the doctor. But I was soon supplanted by a rival, thrown out without a penny, and obliged to continue in this abominable profession which you men find so amusing, and which to us is nothing but an abyss of misery. I came to Venice to practise my trade. Oh, Monsieur, if you could imagine what it is like to have to caress, with the same enthusiasm, an elderly merchant, a lawyer, a monk, a gondolier and an abbé; to be exposed to every insult and affront; to be reduced often to borrowing a petticoat so as to go and have it lifted by some disgusting man or other; to be robbed by one of what you have earned with another, or have it extorted from you by officers of the law; to have nothing to look forward to but a hideous old age, the poor house and the refuse-heap;[3] then you would agree that I am one of the unhappiest creatures alive.'

Thus did Paquette open her heart to the worthy Candide as they sat in his side-room, in the presence of Martin, who remarked: 'You see, I have won half of my wager already.'

Brother Girofleo had remained in the dining-room, enjoying a glass while he waited for dinner. 'But you looked so gay, so happy, when I ran into you just now,' said Candide to Paquette; 'you were singing, you were caressing your monk so naturally and affectionately; you seemed to be as happy as you now claim to be miserable.' – 'Ah! Monsieur,' replied Paquette, 'that is another of the miseries of our profession. Yesterday I was beaten and robbed by an officer of the law; today I must seem in good humour to please a monk.'

Candide wanted to hear no more; he concluded that Martin was right. They sat down to eat with Paquette and the Theatine; the dinner was amusing enough, and by the end they were all talking quite freely. 'Father,' said Candide to the monk, 'you seem to me to enjoy a life that any of us might envy; your face glows with health, your features radiate contentment; you have a very pretty girl to amuse you, and you seem altogether happy with your monastic condition.'

'Content with it! On my faith, Monsieur,' said Brother Girofleo, 'I wish every last Theatine at the bottom of the sea. I have been tempted a hundred times to set fire to the monastery and go and turn Turk.[4] My parents forced me at the age of fifteen to wear this loathsome habit, so as to leave a larger fortune to my accursed elder brother, whom God confound! The monastery is rife with jealousies, faction and ill-feeling. It is true, I have preached a few wretched sermons which brought me a little money, half of which the prior has stolen from me: the rest I use to pay for the girls; but when I get back to the monastery in the evening I feel like dashing my brains against the dormitory walls; all my fellow friars are in the same situation.'

Martin turned to Candide with his customary coolness: 'Well?' he said, 'have I not won the whole wager?' Candide gave two thousand *piastres* to Paquette and a thousand to Brother Girofleo. 'My reply to you,' he said, 'is that they will be happy enough with this.' – 'I do not believe it,' said Martin, 'not for one moment. You may even make them unhappier still, in the end, with all your *piastres*.' – 'Be that as it may,' said

Candide. 'But one thing consoles me; I find that we often meet up with people whom we never thought to see again; it may turn out that, having run into my red sheep and then into Paquette, I may yet run into Cunégonde.' – 'I hope,' said Martin, 'that one day she may make you happy, but I doubt it very much.' – 'You are very hard,' said Candide. – 'Because I know what life is,' said Martin.

'But look at those gondoliers,' said Candide; 'do they not sing all day long?' – 'Yes, but you don't see them at home with their wives and their squalling children,' said Martin. 'The Doge⁵ has his troubles, the gondoliers have theirs. It is true that, all things considered, the lot of a gondolier is preferable to that of a Doge, but I think the difference is so slight as not to be worth arguing over.'

'I have heard talk of a certain Senator Pococuranté,'⁶ said Candide, 'who lives in that handsome palazzo on the Brenta,⁷ and who is rather welcoming to foreign visitors. They say he is a man who has never known troubles.' – 'I should like to examine so rare a specimen,' said Martin. Candide immediately sent a message to the noble Signor Pococuranté asking permission to call on him the following day.

CHAPTER 25

A visit to Signor Pococuranté, a
Venetian nobleman

Candide and Martin proceeded by gondola along the Brenta, and duly came to the palace of the noble Pococuranté. The gardens were well laid out and ornamented with fine marble statues, and the palace itself was a fine piece of architecture. The master of the house, a man of sixty, and very wealthy, received his two curious visitors correctly, but with little enthusiasm, which disconcerted Candide and suited Martin.

First, two pretty and elegantly dressed girls served hot chocolate, which they stirred into a creamy froth. Candide could not refrain from praising their beauty, their graciousness and dexterity. 'They are good creatures, it is true,' said Senator Pococuranté. 'I take them into my bed sometimes, for I am rather weary of the society ladies, with their coquetries, and their jealousies, and their quarrels, and their moods, and their spite, and their pride, and their triviality; and I'm tired of composing sonnets, or having sonnets composed, in their honour. But then, on the other hand, I also find myself getting fearfully bored of these two young girls.'

Candide, walking in a long gallery after lunch, was astonished by the beauty of the paintings. Pausing by the first two, he asked which master had painted them. 'They are by Raphael,' said the Senator. 'I bought them out of vanity, and very expensively, some years ago; I am told they are the finest in Italy, but I don't in the least care for them: the colouring is too sombre, the figures are not sufficiently rounded and lack depth, the draperies bear no resemblance to real material; in short, whatever anybody says, I do not find in them a true imitation of nature.[1] I shall only like a picture when I can believe I am looking at nature itself – and there are no such pictures. I have a great many paintings, but I no longer look at any of them.'

While they waited for dinner, Pococuranté gave orders for a *concerto*[2] to be performed. Candide thought the music delightful. 'It's a sort of noise,' said Pococuranté, 'that whiles away the odd half-hour, but if played for any longer bores everyone, though no one dares to say so. Music nowadays is merely the art of executing what is difficult to play; and in the long run what is merely difficult ceases to amuse.'

'Perhaps I might prefer opera,' he continued, 'had they not managed to turn it into a hybrid monstrosity which revolts me. Let them flock to their wretched tragedies set to music, where the story is merely the clumsy pretext for two or three ludicruous arias, designed to show off some actress's vocal chords; let them swoon with ecstasy, if they want to, at the spectacle of a castrato piping his way through the role of Caesar or Cato as he struts clumsily about the stage; for my part I have long given up on these paltry spectacles that are the glory of Italy today, and which cost its princes so much expense.'

Candide disagreed with some of this, albeit circumspectly. Martin was entirely of the Senator's opinion.[3]

They sat down to table and after an excellent dinner repaired to the library. Candide, seeing a magnificently bound copy of Homer, complimented the illustrious nobleman on his good taste. 'This book,' he said, 'was once the delight of the great Pangloss, the finest philosopher in Germany.' – 'Well, it fails to delight me,' said Pococuranté coolly. 'At one time I was deluded into believing I took pleasure in reading it; but that endless recital of battles which are all the same, those gods who are always interfering but never do anything, that Helen of his who is the cause of the war but then plays scarcely any part in the action, and that Troy which they keep besieging without ever taking – it all used to make me weep with boredom. I used to ask scholars if reading Homer bored them as much as it bored me; the honest ones admitted that the book dropped from their hands every time, but added that one had to have it in one's library, as a monument of antiquity, like those rusty coins which cannot be put into circulation.'

'Your Excellency would not say the same of Virgil, surely?' said Candide. – 'I admit,' said Pococuranté, 'that the second, fourth and sixth books of the *Aeneid* are rather fine; but as for his pious Aeneas, and his solid Cloanthus, and faithful Achates, and little Ascanius, and that imbecile King Latinus, and bourgeois Amata, and insipid Lavinia ... I cannot imagine anything more frigid and disagreeable. I prefer Tasso and those cock-and-bull tales of Ariosto.'[4]

'May I venture to ask, Monsieur,' said Candide, 'whether Horace[5] at least does not afford you real pleasure?' – 'There are one or two maxims there,' said Pococuranté, 'from which a man of the world can draw profit, and the compressed energy of the verse engraves them more easily on the memory. But I care very little for his voyage to Brindisi, or his description of a bad dinner, or his account of a vulgar squabble between – what is his name? – Pupilus, whose words he describes as "full of pus", and someone else whose words are "like vinegar". Only with extreme disgust can I bring myself to read his coarse verses against old women and witches; and I cannot see what there is to admire in his telling his friend Maecenas that if the latter will but place him among the ranks of lyric poets, his lofty forehead will strike the stars. Fools admire everything in an esteemed author. I read for myself alone; I only like what I have a use for.' Candide, who had been brought up never to judge anything for himself, was much astonished by everything he heard; Martin found Pococurante's way of thinking perfectly reasonable.

'Ah! Here is a copy of Cicero,'[6] said Candide. 'Now I cannot believe that you ever tire of reading this great man!' – 'I never read him,' replied the Venetian. 'What do I care whether he pleaded for Rabirius or for Cluentius? I have quite enough cases to judge as it is; I might have got along better with his philosophical works, but when I saw that he doubted everything I concluded that I must know as much as he, and that I needed no one's help in order to be ignorant.'

'Ah!' said Martin, 'eighty volumes of the proceedings of one of our Academies of Science; there might be something worthwhile here.' – 'There might be,' said Pococurante, 'if a single one of the perpetrators of all that rubbish had so much as invented the technique for making pins;[7] but wherever you look you find only empty systems, and not a single thing of use.' – 'What a lot of plays there are!' said Candide. 'In Italian, Spanish, French!' – 'Yes,' said the Senator, 'three thousand of them, and not three dozen decent ones. As for the collections of sermons, all of which together are not worth a page of Seneca,[8] and those fat tomes of theology likewise, you would be correct in thinking that I never open them – neither I nor anyone else.'

Martin noticed some shelves full of English books. 'I imagine,' he said, 'that a republican like yourself[9] must take pleasure in reading most of these works, written in conditions of such freedom?' – 'Yes,' replied Pococurante, 'it is a fine thing to write what one thinks; it is man's natural privilege, after all. In Italy, wherever you go, we write only what we do not think; the descendants of the Caesars and the Antonines dare not entertain an idea without the permission of a Dominican monk.[10] However, I would be happier with the freedom which inspires the English genius, except that doctrinaire passion and party spirit corrupt all that is estimable in their precious liberty.'

Candide, seeing an edition of Milton, asked him if he did not consider that author to be a great man. 'Who?' said Pococuranté, 'that barbarian who wrote an interminable commentary on the first chapter of Genesis in ten books of crabbed verse?[11] That crude imitator of the Greeks, who distorts the Creation story and, where Moses shows the Eternal Being producing the world through the Word, has the Messiah pulling a large compass out of some celestial cupboard in order to take measurements for his work? You ask me to admire the man who ruined the hell and Satan of Tasso's invention; who has Lucifer appear variously disguised as a toad or a pygmy, and has him rehash the same arguments a hundred times, and shows him quibbling over points of theology; who takes literally Ariosto's bit of comedy about the invention of firearms, and has the devils firing off cannon in heaven? Neither I nor any other Italian has ever taken pleasure in this sad extravaganza. The marriage of Sin and Death, and the adders to which Sin gives birth, must nauseate any man of remotely delicate taste, and his long description of a hospital could only interest a grave-digger.[12] This obscure, bizarre and disgusting poem was spurned at birth; I am only judging it as it was judged in its own country by its contemporaries. Anyway, I say what I think, and I care little whether others think like me.' Candide was distressed by this speech, for he admired Homer, and had some liking for Milton. 'Alas!' he said to Martin under his breath, 'I rather fear this gentleman will have nothing but contempt for our German poets.' – 'No great harm in that,' said Martin. – 'But what a superior being, this Pococuranté,' murmured Candide again, 'what a genius! There is no pleasing him.'[13]

Having thus inspected the library, they went down into the garden. Candide praised its many beauties. 'It is all in the worst possible taste,' said the owner. 'Full of trifling conceits wherever you turn. As from tomorrow I am having another one laid out on a nobler plan.'

When our two curious visitors had taken leave of His Excellency, Candide turned to Martin: 'Now then, you will agree that here is the happiest of men, for he is superior to all he possesses.' – 'Don't you see,' said Martin, 'that he is disgusted by all he possesses? Plato said long ago that the best stomachs are not those that refuse every dish.'[14] – 'But,' said Candide, 'isn't there a pleasure in being critical, in discovering faults where other men think they see excellences?' – 'Which is to say,' countered Martin, 'that there is pleasure to be had in not taking pleasure?' – 'Oh, whatever you like!' said Candide. 'In which case no one is happy but me, when I see Mademoiselle Cunégonde again.' – 'One always does well to hope,' said Martin.

Meanwhile the days, the weeks, slipped by; Cacambo did not return, and Candide was so immersed in sorrow that it did not occur to him that Paquette and Brother Girofleo had not even stopped by to thank him.

CHAPTER 26

Of a supper that Candide and Martin ate in the company of six strangers, and who they were

One evening, as Candide and Martin were about to sit down to dine with the other foreigners lodging in their hostelry, a man with a face the colour of soot came up behind him, took him by the arm and said: 'Be ready to leave with us, and do not fail.' He turned round and saw Cacambo. Only the sight of Cunégonde could have astonished and delighted him more. He was nearly mad with joy. He embraced his dear friend. 'Then Cunégonde must be here. Where is she? Take me to her, that we may both die of joy.' – 'Cunégonde is not here,' said Cacambo, 'she is in Constantinople.' – 'Constantinople! Of all places! But even were she in China, I would fly to her; let us leave now!' – 'We leave after supper,' replied Cacambo. 'I cannot say more; I am a slave, and my master is waiting for me; I must go and serve him at table: don't say a word; eat your supper and be at the ready.'

Candide, torn between joy and sorrow, delighted to see his faithful agent again, astonished to see him a slave, full of thoughts of finding his mistress, his heart in turmoil and his faculties in confusion, now sat down to eat with Martin (who observed all these goings-on impassively), and in the company of six foreigners who had come to spend Carnival in Venice.

Cacambo, who was pouring the wine for one of these strangers, inclined towards his master's ear at the end of the meal, and said to him: 'Sire, Your Majesty may depart when he pleases, the ship is waiting.' Having uttered these words, he went out. The other guests looked at each other in astonishment, without saying a word; at which point another servant came up to his master and said: 'Sire, Your Majesty's carriage is at Padua, and the boat is waiting.'[1] The master nodded, and the servant left. All the guests stared at each other again, with even greater astonishment. A third servant then came up to a third master and said: 'Believe me, Sire, Your Majesty cannot stay a moment longer; I will go and prepare everything.' At which he too disappeared.

By now, Candide and Martin were in no doubt that this was all some Carnival masquerade. A fourth servant said to a fourth master: 'Your Majesty may leave when he pleases,' and left the room like the others. The fifth servant said the same to the fifth master. But the sixth servant spoke differently to the sixth stranger, who was sitting next to Candide: 'Believe me, Sire, they won't let Your Majesty have any more credit, nor me either; if we're not careful we'll spend the night in prison, me and you; I must look out for myself, so goodbye and farewell!'

The servants having vanished, the six strangers, together with Candide and Martin, sat on in deep silence. It was broken at last by Candide. 'Gentlemen,' he said, 'this is presumably some kind of joke. How can you all be kings?[2] I can assure you that neither Martin nor I are anything of the kind.'

Cacambo's master then spoke up and said gravely in Italian: 'I am no joker, and my name is Achmed III; for several years I was Grand Sultan; I deposed my brother; my nephew deposed me; my viziers had their throats cut; I live out my days in the old seraglio; my nephew the Grand Sultan Mahmoud sometimes lets me travel for my health, and I have come to spend Carnival in Venice.'

A young man who was next to Achmed spoke next, and said: 'My name is Ivan; I was Emperor of all the Russias; I was deposed in my cradle; my father and mother were locked away; I was brought up in prison; occasionally I have permission to travel, accompanied by my guards, and I have come to spend Carnival in Venice.'

The third said: 'I am Charles Edward, King of England. My father renounced his claims to the throne in my favour; I have fought long and hard to uphold them; eight hundred of my followers had their hearts ripped out and their cheeks slapped with them; I have been put in prison; I am now on my way to Rome to visit the King my father, deposed like myself and my grandfather, and I have come to spend Carnival in Venice.'

The fourth then spoke up and said: 'I am King of Poland; the fortunes of war have deprived me of my hereditary states; my father suffered the same reverses; I entrust myself to the will of Providence, just like Sultan Achmed, Emperor Ivan and King Charles Edward, whom God preserve; and I have come to spend Carnival in Venice.'

The fifth said: 'I too am King of Poland; I have lost my kingdom twice, but Providence has given me another state, in which I have done more good than all the Sarmatian[3] kings combined have managed to do on the banks of the Vistula. I too entrust myself to Providence, and have come to spend Carnival in Venice.'

It remained for the sixth monarch to speak. 'Gentleman,' he said, 'I am not as great a ruler as any of you; but for all that I have been a king just like everyone else; I am Théodore; I was elected King of Corsica; they called me "Your Majesty", who now barely call me "Sir"; I once minted my own coin, and now do not own a farthing; I once had two secretaries of state, and now have scarcely a valet; I once sat on a throne, but then for a long time slept on straw in a London prison; I am much afraid I shall be treated in the same fashion here, although I have come like Your Majesties to spend Carnival in Venice.'

The other five kings listened to this speech with regal compassion. Each of them gave King Théodore twenty sequins[4] to buy clothes and shirts, and Candide made him a present of a diamond worth two thousand sequins. 'Who can this be?' said the five kings. 'A mere commoner who is in a position to give a hundred times as much as each of us, and who moreover gives it?'[5]

Just as they were getting up from the table, there arrived in the same hostelry four Serene Highnesses, who had likewise lost their states through the fortunes of war, and who had come to spend what remained of the Carnival in Venice. But Candide did not even notice these newcomers. All he could now think about was getting to Constantinople and finding his dear Cunégonde.

CHAPTER 27
Candide's voyage to Constantinople

The faithful Cacambo had already obtained permission, from the Turkish captain who was to escort Sultan Achmed back to Constantinople, for Candide and Martin to join them on board. They made their way to the ship, after duly prostrating themselves before His doleful Highness. On the way, Candide said to Martin: 'Six deposed kings, if you please! All of whom supped with us, and one of whom had to accept alms from me. Perhaps there are any number of other princes who are even more unfortunate. As for me, all I have lost is a hundred sheep, and here I am flying to the arms of Cunégonde. My dear Martin, once again I see that Pangloss was right: all is well.' – 'I hope so,' said Martin. – 'Nonetheless,' said Candide, 'was this not a fairly singular adventure we have just had in Venice? Who ever saw or heard of six deposed kings having supper together in a tavern.' – 'It is no more extraordinary,' said Martin, 'than most of the things that have happened to us. It is quite common for kings to be deposed, and as for the honour of dining with them, that is a mere trifle, and unworthy of our attention.'[1]

Scarcely had Candide boarded the ship than he threw his arms around the neck of his former valet, his dear friend Cacambo. 'So!' he said. 'And what is Cunégonde doing? Is she still a paragon of beauty? Does she still love me? Is she in good health? No doubt you have bought her a palace in Constantinople?'

'My dear master,' replied Cacambo, 'Cunégonde is washing dishes on the shores of the Propontide[2] for a prince who owns very few dishes – she is a slave in the household of a deposed sovereign called Ragotski,[3] to whom in his exile the Grand Sultan[4] pays an allowance of three *écus* a day; but what is far worse is that she has lost her beauty and become fearfully ugly.' – 'Oh well, beautiful or ugly,' said Candide. 'I am a man of honour, and my duty is to love her always. But how can she have been reduced to such penury, with the five or six millions that you took to her?' – 'As to that,' said Cacambo, 'did I not have to pay out two million to Señor don Fernando d'Ibaraa y Figueora y Mascarenes y Lampourdos y Souza, Governor of Buenos Aires, for permission to release Mademoiselle Cunégonde? And didn't some pirate casually relieve us of the rest of the money? And what did this pirate do but take us to Cape Matapan, and then to Milo, to Nicaria, to Samos, to Petra, to the Dardanelles, to Marmora and to Scutari?[5] Cunégonde and the old woman are now servants to the prince I mentioned, and I am a slave of the Sultan, now deposed.' – 'What a dreadful chain of calamities, each linked to the next!' said Candide. 'However, I still have a few diamonds left, after all; I will easily secure Cunégonde's release. What a shame she has become so ugly.'

Then, turning to Martin, he said: 'Well, who do you think is most to be pitied: Emperor Achmed, Emperor Ivan, King Charles Edward – or me?' – 'I have no idea,' said Martin. 'I would need to see into your hearts to know the answer to that.' – 'Ah!' said Candide, 'if Pangloss were here, he would know the answer and would tell us for certain.' – 'I am not sure what scales your Pangloss could have used to weigh the misfortunes of men and calibrate their sufferings,' said Martin. 'I can only presume that there are millions of people on this earth who are many times more to be pitied than King Charles Edward, or Emperor Ivan, or Sultan Achmed.' – 'That may well be so,' said Candide.

In a few days they reached the straits leading into the Black Sea. Candide began by ransoming Cacambo, at a very inflated price; and without delay he and his companions leapt into a galley and headed for the shores of the Propontide, to find Cunégonde, however ugly she might be.

Down in the galley were two conscripts who rowed extremely badly, and to whose naked shoulders the Levantine captain[6] periodically applied a few strokes of his lash; from natural impulse Candide looked more attentively at these two than at the other slaves, and even drew nearer to them out of pity. Something in their ravaged features reminded him vaguely of Pangloss and of that wretched Jesuit – and brother moreover of Mademoiselle Cunégonde – the Baron. The thought of which stirred and saddened him. He watched them even more closely. 'Do you know,' he said to Cacambo, 'if I had not seen Maître Pangloss hanged, and had not had the misfortune to kill the Baron, I could swear it was the two of them rowing in this galley.'

On hearing the words 'Baron' and 'Pangloss', the two galley-slaves gave a great shout, stopped rowing and let their oars drop. The Levantine captain rushed up, and his blows rained down on them with new vigour. 'Stop! Stop, good sir!' cried Candide, 'I will give you all the money you want.' – 'What! It's Candide!' said one of the convicts. – 'What! It's Candide!' said the second. – 'Is this a dream?' said Candide. 'Am I awake! Am I really on this galley? Can this be Monsieur the Baron, whom I killed? Can that be Maître Pangloss, whom I saw hanged?'

'It is we ourselves! It is we ourselves!' they repeated. – 'Oh, so is that your great philosopher?' murmured Martin. – 'Come then, sir,' said Candide to the Levantine captain, 'how much do you want for the ransom of Monsieur von Thunder-ten-tronckh, one of the first barons of the Empire, and for Monsieur Pangloss, the deepest metaphysician in all of Germany?' – 'You dog of a Christian,' replied the Levantine captain. 'Since these two Christian convict dogs are barons and metaphysicians, which must mean great honour in their country, you can pay me fifty thousand sequins for them.' – 'You shall have it, Monsieur; now take us back to Constantinople with the speed of light, and you will be paid immediately. No! In fact, take us first to Mademoiselle Cunégonde.' But on hearing Candide's offer the Levantine captain had already altered course for Constantinople, and was making his slaves row faster than a bird cleaves the air.

Candide embraced the Baron and Pangloss a hundred times. 'So how did I fail to kill you, dear Baron, after all? And you, my dear Pangloss, how can you still be alive after being hanged? And what are you both doing in a Turkish galley?' – 'Tell me, is it really true that my dear sister is here in this country?' said the Baron. – 'Yes,' said Cacambo, while Pangloss kept repeating: 'So I see my dear Candide again!' Candide introduced them to Martin and Cacambo. They all embraced; they all talked at once. The galley flew along, they were already in port. A Jew was sent for, and Candide promptly sold him a diamond worth a hundred thousand sequins for fifty thousand, while the former swore by Abraham that he could not pay a sequin more. Candide then ransomed the Baron and Pangloss. The latter threw himself at the feet of his liberator and bathed them with his tears; the other thanked him with a nod, and promised to repay the money at the first opportunity. 'But is it possible that my sister is in Turkey?' he said. – 'More than possible,' retorted Cacambo. 'She is scouring dishes in the household of a Transylvanian prince even as we speak.' Whereupon two more Jews were sent for: Candide sold more diamonds, and they all set off in another galley to the rescue of Cunégonde.

CHAPTER 28

What happened to Candide, Cunégonde, Pangloss, Martin, et cetera

'Forgive me, Reverend Father,' said Candide to the Baron, 'forgive me, once again, for running you through with my sword'. – 'Let us say no more about it,' said the Baron, 'I was a little too sharp myself, I admit. But since you want to know how I came to be rowing in a galley, I will tell you. After being cured of my wounds by the brother apothecary at the Jesuit college, I was set upon and abducted by a Spanish raiding party; I was put in prison in Buenos Aires just as my sister was leaving that city; I asked to be allowed to return to Rome, to be with the Superior General; from there I was appointed chaplain to the French Ambassador to Constantinople. Not a week after I had taken up my duties, I happened one evening to meet a young and rather good-looking icoglan.[1] It was extremely hot weather: the young man wanted to bathe; I took the opportunity to bathe as well. I was not aware that it was a capital offence for a Christian to be found stark naked with a young Muslim. A cadi[2] sentenced me to a hundred strokes on the soles of the feet, and sent me to the galleys. I don't suppose there has ever been a more flagrant miscarriage of justice. But what concerns me right now is this: why would my sister be working in the kitchens of a Transylvanian sovereign in exile in Turkey?'

'But you, my dear Pangloss,' said Candide, 'how does it come about that I see you again?' – 'It is true that you saw me hanged,' said Pangloss. 'Properly speaking I should have been burned alive, but – as you will recall – it began to pour with rain just as they were about to roast me: the downpour was so violent that they despaired of lighting the fire, and I was hanged for want of anything better; a surgeon bought my body, took it home and started dissecting me. First he made a cross-shaped incision, from the navel to the collar-bone. However, I had been poorly hanged – no one could have had a worse hanging.

The executioner charged with carrying out the orders of the Holy Inquisition was a sub-deacon who roasted people to perfection, but was not used to hanging them: the rope was wet, it would not slip through properly, and was poorly knotted. In short, I was still breathing afterwards; the surgeon's incision made me scream so loudly that he fell over backwards; and, thinking he must be dissecting the devil in person,[3] he fled in mortal panic, only to fall downstairs in his haste. At this commotion his wife came running from the next room: she saw me stretched out on the table with my cross-shaped incision, was even more terrified than her husband, took to her heels likewise and fell on top of him. When they had recovered their wits a little, I heard the surgeon's wife say to the surgeon: 'What on earth possessed you, my dear, to dissect a heretic? Don't you know that the devil takes up permanent residence in these people? I am going to fetch a priest right now, to exorcize this one.' I shuddered at these words, summoned what little strength I had left and cried out: 'Have mercy on me!' In the end this Portuguese barber[4] took his courage in both hands and sewed me up. His wife even nursed me; I was back on my feet in a fortnight. The barber found me a situation as valet to a Knight of the Order of Malta who was going to Venice; but as my new master could not afford to pay my wage, I entered the service of a Venetian merchant and followed him to Constantinople.'

'One day I took it into my head to enter a mosque; it was deserted except for an old imam and a rather pretty young devotee who was saying her paternosters; her throat was uncovered, and between her breasts she wore an attractive posy of tulips, roses, anemones, buttercups, hyacinths and primroses; she dropped the posy; I picked it up, and returned it to her with the most respectful attentions. I took so long in adjusting it that the imam flew into a rage, and, realizing I was a Christian, called out for help.[5] I was taken to the cadi, who sentenced me to a hundred strokes of the lath on the soles of my feet and sent me to the galleys. I was chained up in the very same galley and on the very same row as Monsieur the Baron. In our galley were four young men from Marseilles, five Neapolitan priests and two monks from Corfu, who told us that this sort of thing happens all the time. Monsieur the Baron kept maintaining that he had suffered a greater injustice than I; while I maintained that it was far more acceptable to replace a posy on a woman's bosom than to be found stark naked with an icoglan. We argued the whole time and were given twenty lashes a day, until the chain linking the events of this great universe led you to our galley, and you ransomed us.'

'Now tell us this, my dear Pangloss,' said Candide. 'While you were being hanged, and dissected, and beaten, and made to row in a galley, did you continue to believe that all was for the best?' – 'I hold firmly to my original views,' replied Pangloss. 'I am a philosopher after all: it would not do for me to recant, given that Leibniz is incapable of error, and that pre-established harmony[6] is moreover the finest thing in the world – not to speak of the *plenum* and the *materia subtilis*.'[7]

CHAPTER 29

How Candide was reunited with Cunégonde and the old woman

While Candide, the Baron, Pangloss, Martin and Cacambo were describing their adventures, and disputing as to whether the events in this universe are contingent or non-contingent,[1] and arguing about effects and causes, moral evil and physical evil, free will and necessity, not to mention the consolations to be found aboard a Turkish galley, they reached the shores of the Propontide, close by the house of the Prince of Transylvania. The first thing they saw was Cunégonde and the old woman, who were hanging towels out to dry on a line.

The Baron turned pale at the sight. Candide, the tender lover, on seeing his beautiful Cunégonde all weather-beaten, her eyes bloodshot, her breasts sunken, her cheeks lined, her arms red and chapped, was seized with horror; he recoiled three paces, then advanced out of sheer good manners. She embraced Candide and her brother; they embraced the old woman; Candide ransomed the pair of them.

There was a small holding in the neighborhood: the old woman suggested to Candide that he avail himself of it for the time being, until the fortunes of their whole company should improve. Cunégonde was unaware of how ugly she had become, no one having told her. She now reminded Candide of his promises, and in so peremptory a fashion that the good Candide dare not to refuse her. So he informed the Baron of his intention to marry his sister. 'Never,' said the Baron, 'will I tolerate such baseness on her part, nor such insolence on yours. Never shall I be reproached with condoning this infamous union: my sister's children would be unable to show their faces in the Chapters[2] of Germany. No, my sister shall never marry unless she marry a baron of the Empire.' Cunégonde threw herself at his feet and bathed them with her tears: he was inflexible. – 'You absolute ass,' said Candide. 'I have rescued you from the galleys; I have paid for your freedom; I have paid for your sister's freedom. She was washing dishes here; she is ugly; I have the goodness to make her my wife, and still you presume to oppose it! I would kill you all over again were I to give way to my anger!' – 'You may kill me all over again,' said the Baron, 'but you will never marry my sister while I am living.'

CHAPTER 30

Conclusion

At the bottom of his heart, Candide had no desire to marry Cunégonde; but the outrageous impertinence of the Baron determined him to go through with the ceremony, and Cunégonde was urging him on so keenly that he could not retract. He consulted with Pangloss and Martin and the faithful Cacambo. Pangloss wrote an excellent paper in which he proved that the

Baron had no authority over his sister, and that all the laws of
Empire permitted her to marry Candide with her left hand.[1]
Martin was all for throwing the Baron into the sea; Cacambo
argued that he should be returned to the Levantine captain and
put back in the galleys; after which he should be sent back to the
Superior General in Rome by the first available ship. Everyone
thought this was very sound advice. The old woman approved
it; not a word was said to the Baron's sister; the thing was
carried out with the help of a little money, and they had the
double satisfaction of duping a Jesuit and punishing the pride
of a German baron.

It would be altogether natural to suppose that Candide, after
so many disasters, would henceforth lead the most agreeable of
possible existences – married at last to his mistress, living with
the philosopher Pangloss, the philosophical Martin, the prudent
Cacambo, the old woman – having moreover brought back all
those diamonds from the land of the ancient Incas. But he had
been swindled so many times by Jews that all he had left in the
end was his little farm; his wife, growing uglier by the day, had
become shrewish and insufferable; the old woman was infirm
and even more ill-tempered than Cunégonde. Cacambo, who
worked the land and went into Constantinople to sell their
vegetables, was worn out with toil and cursed his lot. Pangloss
was in despair at not being able to shine at some German
university. As for Martin, he was firmly persuaded that people
are equally miserable wherever they are; he took things as they
came. Occasionally Candide, Martin and Pangloss discussed
metaphysics and morals. Often they saw ships through the
windows of the farmhouse, bearing effendis, pashas and
cadis[2] who were being exiled to Lemnos, or to Mitylene, or to
Erzerum. Then they would see more cadis, more pashas and
more effendis arriving to take the place of those who had been
expelled, and themselves being expelled in turn. They could see
heads neatly stuffed with straw being taken to be displayed
before the Sublime Porte.[3] Such sights gave renewed heat to
their discussions; but when they were not arguing the boredom
was so extreme that one day the old woman ventured to remark:
'I should like to know which is worse: to be raped a hundred

times by negro pirates, and have a buttock cut off, and run the gauntlet of the Bulgars, and be flogged and hanged in an *auto-da-fé*, and be dissected, and have to row in a galley – in short, to undergo all the miseries we have each of us suffered – or simply to sit here and do nothing?' – 'That is a hard question,' said Candide.

This speech gave rise to new speculations, and Martin in particular came to the conclusion that man was born to endure either the convulsions of anxiety or the lethargy of boredom. Candide did not agree with this, but he did not press the point. Pangloss conceded that he had suffered horribly, all his life, but having once maintained that everything was going splendidly he would continue to do so, while believing nothing of the kind.

Then something occurred that confirmed Martin in his detestable principles, made Candide hesitate more than ever, and further embarrassed Pangloss. This was when they saw Paquette and Brother Girofleo approaching their farm one day, in the last extremes of human misery. They had soon got through their three thousand *piastres*, left each other, been reconciled, quarrelled, been thrown in prison, escaped, and finally Brother Girofleo had turned Turk. Paquette continued to ply her trade wherever she went, but no longer earned anything by it. 'Just as I predicted,' said Martin to Candide. 'I knew that the money you gave them would soon be gone, and would only make them more wretched. As for you and Cacambo, you have squandered millions of *piastres* and are no happier than Brother Girofleo and Paquette.' – 'Aha!' said Pangloss to Paquette, 'so heaven brings you back here amongst us, my poor child! Are you aware that you cost me the end of my nose, and an eye, and an ear? And now look at the state of you, eh? What a world it is!' This new turn of events set them to philosophizing more than ever.

There lived in the neighbourhood a celebrated dervish,[4] who was said to be the greatest philosopher in Turkey; they went to consult him; Pangloss acted as spokesman, and asked him: 'Master, we have come to beg you to tell us why so curious a creature as man was ever created.'

– 'And what has it to do with you?' answered the dervish. 'Is it any business of yours?' – 'But surely, Reverend Father,' said Candide, 'there is a dreadful amount of evil in the world.' – 'And what does it matter,' said the dervish, 'if there is evil or if there is good? When His Highness the Sultan sends a ship to Egypt, does he worry whether the mice on board are comfortable or not?'[5] – 'So what must we do?' said Pangloss. – 'Keep your mouth shut,'[6] said the dervish. – 'I flattered myself,' said Pangloss, 'that you and I might have a little discussion about effects and causes, about the best of possible worlds, the origin of evil, the nature of the soul, pre-established harmony . . .' – At which the dervish slammed the door in their faces.

During this conversation news had spread that two viziers of the divan, together with the mufti,[7] had been strangled in Constantinople, and several of their allies impaled. This catastrophe caused a great stir everywhere for several hours. On their way back to their little farm, Pangloss, Candide and Martin met a worthy old man who was taking the air at his door, beneath a shady bower of orange-trees. Pangloss, who liked gossip as much as he liked argument, asked him the name of the mufti who had just been strangled. 'I have no idea,' replied the old man. 'I have never known the name of a single mufti or vizier. I know absolutely nothing of the events you describe; I assume as a matter of course that those who get involved in political affairs often come to a bad end, and that they deserve to; but I never inquire about what goes on in Constantinople; I am happy enough sending the fruits of my garden to be sold there.' Having said this, he invited the strangers into his house; his two daughters and two sons served them various home-made sorbets, some *kaimak* spiced with candied citron peel, oranges, lemons, limes, pineapples and pistachios, and some mocha coffee unadulterated by inferior blends from Batavia and the islands.[8] After this the two daughters of this good Muslim scented the beards of Candide, Pangloss and Martin.

'You must have a vast and magnificent estate,' said Candide to the Turk. – 'I have but twenty acres,' replied the Turk. 'I cultivate them with my children; our work keeps at bay the three great evils: boredom, vice, and necessity.'

Back on his little farm, Candide reflected deeply on the words of the Turk. He said to Pangloss and Martin: 'That worthy old man seems to have created for himself an existence far preferable to that of the six kings with whom we had the honour of dining.' – 'Rank and titles,' said Pangloss, 'are often dangerous, as all the philosophers agree: witness Eglon, King of the Moabites, who was assassinated by Ehud; Absalom was hanged by his hair and stabbed in the heart with three spears; King Nadab, son of Jeroboam, was killed by Baasha; King Elah by Zimri; Jehoram by Jehu; Athaliah by Jehoiada; and the Kings Jehoiakim, Jehoiachin and Zedekiah were all sold into captivity.[9] And you will recall in what manner death came for Croesus, Astyages, Darius, Dionysius of Syracuse, Pyrrhus, Perseus, Hannibal, Jugurtha, Ariovistus, Caesar, Pompey, Nero, Otho, Vitellius, Domitian,[10] Richard II of England, Edward II, Henry VI, Richard III, Mary Stuart and Charles I,[11] not to mention the three Henris of France and the Emperor Henry IV.[12] And you must also know . . .' – 'All I know,' said Candide, 'is that we must cultivate our garden.' – 'You are right,' said Pangloss, 'for when man was placed in the garden of Eden, he was put there *ut operaretur eum*,[13] so that he might work: which proves that man was not born for rest.' – 'Let us set to work and stop proving things,' said Martin, 'for that is the only way to make life bearable.'

The little society all entered into this laudable plan; each began to exercise his talents. The small farm yielded a great deal. True, Cunégonde was still very ugly, but she became an excellent pastry-chef; Paquette embroidered; the old woman took care of the laundry. Everyone made himself useful, including Brother Girofleo, who was a first-rate carpenter[14] and even became quite good company. Sometimes Pangloss would say to Candide: 'All events form a chain in this, the best of all possible worlds. After all, had you not been expelled from a beautiful castle with great kicks to the behind for the love of Mademoiselle Cunégonde, and had you not been turned over to the Inquisition, and had you not roamed America on foot, and had you not run the Baron through with a fine thrust of your sword, and had you not lost all your sheep from the good land of Eldorado, you would not be sitting here now eating candied citron and pistachios.' – 'That is well said,' replied Candide, 'but we must cultivate our garden.'[15]

Appendix 1

The Alternative Version of the Opening
of Chapter 22

*[Voltaire's manuscript contains two different versions or part-versions
of chapter 22; the cancelled version of the chapter's opening passage
follows here; it offers a rapid triptych of chronologically separate
episodes of Parisian life: the convulsionists of Saint-Médard (1728–
32), the affair of the* billets de confession *(1750), and the attempt of
Damiens to assassinate Louis XV (1757), all of which, in abridged
form, find their way into the published text.]*

Candide stopped off in Bordeaux only for as long as it took to equip
himself with a fast two-seater post-chaise, for his philosopher Martin
and himself; he was only grieved to be parting from his sheep, which
he left with the Academy of Science in Bordeaux. However, all the
travellers he met in taverns along the way told him: 'We are off to
Paris.' Such universal eagerness finally gave him a desire to see this
capital; it was not too much of a detour from the road to Venice.

He entered by the Faubourg Saint-Marceau, and it reminded him
of the meanest village in Westphalia. A moment later he passed a
cemetery; there were cries and dreadful howling, as if the dead had
been revived to play a part in this appalling sabbath. He saw little
girls, clerics, hawkers, sacristans, old women, all of them barking like
dogs, gnashing their teeth, rolling on the ground, leaping about, chanting psalms, trembling all over and frothing at the mouth, crying, 'A
miracle! A miracle!'

'Good God!' shouted Candide to Martin, 'is this what the capital
of a great kingdom is like! What a difference between this sewer and
the city of Eldorado.'

They had not walked a hundred paces when they were obstructed
by a crowd of people making even more noise than the previous mob,
gathered around a dozen coffins each covered with a black drape, and
each with a stoup for holy water at its foot. Candide and Martin

inquired as to the reason for the commotion, and an inhabitant of the neighbourhood told them, 'Messieurs, have you not heard about the tax they are now levying on corpses?' Candide swore that he knew nothing concerning the affairs of the dead or the living in this wretched city, that he was a foreigner, that he had just arrived and that all he could think of was how best to leave.

'Alas, Monsieur,' said this worthy man, 'for a few months now the dying have been presented with notes of confession, redeemable in the next world, which everyone at the point of death must sign; if they do not sign they do not get buried. Here are twelve corpses which have been refused burial. It will unleash the plague upon the city.'

The postilion who was driving our two travellers had great difficulty in getting through. When they reached the next crossroads – which stank a thousand times worse than all the assembled dead of the neighbourhood – everything was in a mad uproar. People were running this way and that without any idea where they were going. There were shouts of 'Assassin!' Everyone was running out of their houses. They were all yelling, and a thousand voices were asking Candide and Martin: 'Have you come from the court? Has he been arrested? Has he named his accomplices?' Finally, and with much difficulty, Candide and Martin learned that an outrageous attempt had been made upon the life of the King, a crime unheard of in any other nation, an assassination such as to make all men tremble and weep.

It took an entire hour before they were able to reach a half-way respectable hostelry, where they were served supper. Among their company was a little abbé from the Périgord, one of those characters who are always on the lookout for strangers passing through, to act as guides and to offer various services. This one regaled them with gossip, advised them to make a long stay, filled them in on the scandalous history of the town and ended by promising Candide that he could procure for him the first actress he set eyes on at the theatre.

Whilst appreciative of these courtesies, Candide admitted that he could not take advantage of them, since he had a rendezvous in Venice with Mademoiselle Cunégonde. The insinuating Périgordian imperceptibly drew him out on the subject of his adventures with this illustrious Westphalian beauty. 'I believe,' said the abbé . . .

Appendix 2

Voltaire's Poem on the Lisbon Disaster

[The Lisbon earthquake occured on 1 November 1755, and the Poem was written at the end of that year. Voltaire referred to it as his 'sermon' and his 'Lamentations of Jeremiah'; copies began circulating in Paris in January 1756, attributed to a certain Monsieur Liébaut, although no one was deceived as to its Voltairean provenance. It was published in March 1756.]

PREFACE

If the question of physical evil has ever deserved the attention of man, it is when those melancholy events occur which put us in mind of the feebleness of our nature – such as plagues, which have carried off a quarter of the inhabitants of the known world; or the earthquake which swallowed up four hundred thousand people in China in 1699, or those in Lima and Callao, or, most recently, those in Portugal and the kingdom of Fez. The maxim that 'whatever is, is right' can seem a little peculiar to those who have witnessed such calamities. All things are doubtless arranged and set in order by Providence, but it has long been evident that all is not ordered in such a manner as to promote our present happiness.

When the illustrious Pope published his *Essay on Man*, and expounded in immortal verses the systems of Leibniz, Lord Shaftesbury and Lord Bolingbroke, his system was attacked by a multitude of divines from every communion. These were shocked at the novelty of the proposition that 'whatever is, is right', that 'man always enjoys that measure of happiness which is suited to his constitution,' and so on. There are few writings that may not be condemned, if considered in one light, nor approved, if considered in another. It would be far more appropriate to attend to the beauties and improving parts of a work than to endeavour to put an odious construction upon the whole; but it is one of the imperfections of human nature to place a doubtful interpretation upon whatever has a doubtful sense and to run down whatever has been successful.

It was the opinion of many, therefore, that the proposition 'Whatever is, is right' was subversive of all our received ideas. 'If it be true,' they said, 'that whatever is, is right, it follows that human nature is not fallen. If the order of things requires that everything should be as it is, then human nature has not been corrupted, and consequently has no need of a Redeemer. If this world, just as it is, is the best of all possible worlds, we have no room to hope for a happier future state. If all the evils by which we are overwhelmed contribute to the general good, then all civilized nations have been misguided in endeavouring to trace out the origin of moral and physical evil. If a man devoured by wild beasts brings about the well-being of those brutes and thereby contributes to the order of the universe; if the miseries of individuals are merely the by-product of this general and necessary order, then we are nothing more than cogs which serve to keep the great machine in motion; we are no more precious in the eyes of God than the animals by which we are devoured.'

Such were the conclusions that people drew from Mr Pope's poem; and these very conclusions increased the notoriety and success of the work. But it should have been regarded from another point of view: critics might have considered the reverence for the Deity, the resignation to His supreme will, the rational morality and the spirit of toleration which breathe through this excellent poem. This is how the public have read it, and the work – translated by men equal to the task – has triumphed over criticisms, even though these turned on matters of so delicate a nature.

It is the peculiarity of violent censure to lend importance to what it attacks. A book is railed at on account of its success, a thousand errors are attributed to it, and what is the consequence? People revolt against these invectives, take for truths the very errors which these critics claim to have discovered. Censure raises phantoms on purpose to combat them, and indignant readers embrace these very phantoms.

The critics have declared that Leibniz and Pope teach fatalism; the partisans of Leibniz and Pope on the other hand maintain that, if Leibniz and Pope teach fatalism, then they must be in the right, and that invincible fatalism is what we must subscribe to.

Pope had advanced the proposition that 'Whatever is, is right' in a sense that might be freely admitted, but today his followers maintain the same proposition in a sense that deserves to be contested.

The author of the *Poem on the Lisbon Disaster* does not take issue with the illustrious Pope, whom he has always loved and admired: he agrees with him in almost every particular, but conscious of the miseries of humankind, he takes his stand against the improper uses to which that old axiom 'Whatever is, is right' may be put. He stands by that older and sadder truth, acknowledged by all men, that there is evil on earth; he maintains that the saying 'Whatever is, is right', if taken in its absolute sense and without any hopes of a happy future state, only insults us in the miseries of our present life.

When Lisbon and Meknes and Tetuan, and so many other cities, were swallowed up with so great a loss of life in the month of November 1755, had the philosophers shouted to the wretches who were escaping with their lives from the ruins: 'All this is as it should be; the heirs of those who have died will multiply their fortunes; masons will make money by rebuilding the houses; beasts will fatten themselves on the bodies buried under the ruins; this is all the necessary effect of necessary causes; your personal misfortune is as nothing, you are contributing to the general good' – such a harangue would certainly have been as cruel as the earthquake itself was fatal. And what the author of the *Poem upon the Lisbon Disaster* is saying amounts only to this.

He acknowledges, with all mankind, that there is evil as well as good to be found on this earth; he admits that no philosopher has ever explained the nature of moral and physical evil; he admits that Bayle, the greatest dialectician who has ever written, has taught us only how to doubt; and he owns that man's understanding is as weak as his existence is miserable. He gives an account of the several different systems, in as few words as possible. He says that Revelation alone can untie the great knot which philosophers have only managed to tangle further; that nothing but the hope of our continued existence in a future state can console us under present misfortunes; that the goodness of Providence is the only sanctuary in which man can take shelter during this general eclipse of his reason, and amidst the calamities to which his weak and frail nature is exposed.

P.S. Unfortunately it is as necessary as ever to warn readers to distinguish between the objections that an author proposes to his own arguments and his replies to those objections, and not to mistake what the author refutes for what he maintains.

THE LISBON EARTHQUAKE*

Or An Inquiry into the Maxim, 'Whatever Is, Is Right'

Oh wretched man, earth-fated to be cursed;
Abyss of plagues, and miseries the worst!
Horrors on horrors, griefs on griefs must show,
That man's the victim of unceasing woe,
And lamentations which inspire my strain,
Prove that philosophy is false and vain.
Approach in crowds, and meditate awhile
Yon shattered walls, and view each ruined pile,
Women and children heaped up mountain high,
Limbs crushed which under ponderous marble lie;
Wretches unnumbered in the pangs of death,
Who mangled, torn, and panting for their breath,
Buried beneath their sinking roofs expire,
And end their wretched lives in torments dire.
Say, when you hear their piteous, half-formed cries,
Or from their ashes see the smoke arise,
Say, will you then eternal laws maintain,
Which God to cruelties like these constrain?
Whilst you these facts replete with horror view,
Will you maintain death to their crimes was due?
And can you then impute a sinful deed
To babes who on their mothers' bosoms bleed?
Was then more vice in fallen Lisbon found,
Than Paris, where voluptuous joys abound?
Was less debauchery to London known,
Where opulence luxurious holds her throne?
Earth Lisbon swallows; the light sons of France
Protract the feast, or lead the sprightly dance.
Spectators who undaunted courage show,
While you behold your dying brethren's woe;
With stoical tranquillity of mind
You seek the causes of these ills to find;
But when like us Fate's rigors you have felt,
Become humane, like us you'll learn to melt.
When the earth gapes my body to entomb,
I justly may complain of such a doom.

* Translated by Tobias Smollett and others; all footnotes are Voltaire's.

Hemmed round on every side by cruel fate,
The snares of death, the wicked's furious hate,
Preyed on by pain and by corroding grief
Suffer me from complaint to find relief.
'Tis pride, you cry, seditious pride that still
Asserts mankind should be exempt from ill.
The awful truth on Tagus' banks explore,
Rummage the ruins on that bloody shore,
Wretches interred alive in direful grave
Ask if pride cries, 'Good Heaven, thy creatures save.'
If 'tis presumption that makes mortals cry,
'Heav'n, on our sufferings cast a pitying eye.'
All's right, you answer, the eternal cause
Rules not by partial, but by general laws.
Say what advantage can result to all,
From wretched Lisbon's lamentable fall?
Are you then sure, the power which could create
The universe and fix the laws of fate,
Could not have found for man a proper place,
But earthquakes must destroy the human race?
Will you thus limit the eternal mind?
Should not our God to mercy be inclined?
Cannot then God direct all nature's course?
Can power almighty be without resource?
Humbly the great Creator I entreat,
This gulf with sulphur and with fire replete,
Might on the deserts spend its raging flame,
God my respect, my love weak mortals claim;
When man groans under such a load of woe,
He is not proud, he only feels the blow.
Would words like these to peace of mind restore
The natives sad of that disastrous shore?
Grieve not, that others' bliss may overflow,
Your sumptuous palaces are laid thus low;
Your toppled towers shall other hands rebuild;
With multitudes your walls one day be filled;
Your ruin on the North shall wealth bestow,
For general good from partial ills must flow;
You seem as abject to the sovereign power,
As worms which shall your carcasses devour.
No comfort could such shocking words impart,
But deeper wound the sad, afflicted heart.

When I lament my present wretched state,
Allege not the unchanging laws of fate;
Urge not the links of the eternal chain,
'Tis false philosophy and wisdom vain.
The God who holds the chain can't be enchained;[1]
By His blest will are all events ordained:

[1] The universal chain is not, as some have thought, a regular gradation which connects all beings. There is, in all probability, an immense distance between man and beast, as well as between man and substances of a superior nature; there is likewise an infinity between God and all created beings whatever. There are none of these insensible gradations in the globes which move round our sun in their several periods, whether we consider their mass, their distances, or their satellites.

If we may believe Pope, man is not capable of discovering the reason why the satellites of Jove are less than Jove himself; he is herein mistaken; such an error as this may well be overlooked in so fine a genius. Every smatterer in mathematics could have told Lord Bolingbroke and Mr Pope, that if the satellites of Jove had equalled him in magnitude, they could not have moved round him; but no mathematician is able to discover the regular gradation in the bodies of the solar system.

It is not true, that the world could not exist if a single atom was taken from it: This was justly observed by Mr Crousaz, a learned geometrician, in a tract which he wrote against Pope. He seems to have been right in this point, though he was fully refuted by Mr Warburton and Mr Silhouette.

The concatenation of events was admitted and defended with the utmost ingenuity by the celebrated philosopher Leibniz; it is worth explaining. All bodies and all events depend upon other bodies and other events. That cannot be denied; but all bodies are not essential to the support of the universe, and the preservation of its order; neither are all events necessary in the general series of events. A drop of water, a grain of sand more or less, can cause no revolution in the general system. Nature is not confined to any determinate quantity, or any determinate form. No planet moves in a curve completely regular; there is nothing in Nature of a figure exactly mathematical; no fixed quantity is required for any operation: Nature is never very strict or rigid in her method of proceeding. It is, therefore, absurd to advance, that the removal of an atom from the earth might be the cause of its destruction.

This holds, in like manner, with regard to events. The cause of every event is contained in some precedent event; this no philosopher has ever called in question. If Caesar's mother had never gone through the Caesarian operation, Caesar had never subverted the commonwealth; he could never have adopted Octavius, and Octavius could never have chosen Tiberius for his successor in the empire. The marriage of Maximilian with the heiress of Burgundy and the Low Countries gave rise to a war which lasted two hundred years. But Caesar's spitting on the right or left side, or the Duchess of Burgundy's dressing her head in this manner or in that, could have altered nothing in the general plan of Providence.

He's just, nor easily to wrath gives way,
Why suffer we beneath so mild a sway:[2]
This is the fatal knot you should untie,
Our evils do you cure when you deny?
Men ever strove into the source to pry,
Of evil, whose existence you deny.
If he whose hand the elements can wield,
To the winds' force makes rocky mountains yield;
If thunder lays oaks level with the plain,
From the bolts' strokes they never suffer pain.
But I can feel, my heart oppressed demands
Aid of that God who formed me with His hands.
Sons of the God supreme to suffer all
Fated alike; we on our Father call.
No vessel of the potter asks, we know,
Why it was made so brittle, vile, and low?
Vessels of speech as well as thought are void;
The urn this moment formed and that destroyed,

It follows, therefore, that there are some events which have consequences and others which have none. Their chain resembles a genealogical tree, some branches of which disappear at the first generation, whilst the race is continued by others. There are many events which pass away without ever generating others. Thus in every machine there are some effects indispensably necessary toward producing motion, and others which are productive of nothing at all. The wheels of a coach make it go; but whether they raise more or less dust, the journey is finished alike. Such is the general order of the world, that the links of the chain would not be in the least discomposed by a small increase or diminution of the quantity of matter, or by an inconsiderable deviation from regularity.

The chain is not in an absolute *plenum*; it has been demonstrated that the celestial bodies perform their revolutions in an unresisting medium. Every space is not filled. It follows then, that there is not a progression of bodies from an atom to the most remote fixed star. There may of consequence be immense intervals between beings imbued with sensation, as well as between those that are not. We cannot then be certain, that man must be placed in one of these links joined to another by an uninterrupted connection. That all things are linked together means only that all things are regularly disposed of in their proper order. God is the cause and the regulator of that order. Homer's Jupiter was the slave of destiny; but, according to more rational philosophy, God is the master of destiny. (See Clarke's Treatise 'Upon the Existence of God'.)

[2] *Sub Deo justo nemo miser nisi mereatur* – St Augustine. The meaning of this *ipse dixit* of the Saint is, no one is miserable under the government of a just God, without deserving to be so.

The potter never could with sense inspire,
Devoid of thought it nothing can desire.
The moralist still obstinate replies,
Others' enjoyments from your woes arise,
To numerous insects shall my corpse give birth,
When once it mixes with its mother earth:
Small comfort 'tis that when Death's ruthless power
Closes my life, worms shall my flesh devour.
Remembrances of misery refrain
From consolation, you increase my pain:
Complaint, I see, you have with care repressed,
And proudly hid your sorrows in your breast.
But a small part I no importance claim
In this vast universe, this general frame;
All other beings in this world below
Condemned like me to lead a life of woe,
Subject to laws as rigorous as I,
Like me in anguish live and like me die.
The vulture urged by an insatiate maw,
Its trembling prey tears with relentless claw:
This it finds right, endowed with greater powers
The bird of Jove the vulture's self devours.
Man lifts his tube, he aims the fatal ball
And makes to earth the towering eagle fall;
Man in the field with wounds all covered o'er,
Midst heaps of dead lies weltering in his gore,
While birds of prey the mangled limbs devour,
Of Nature's Lord who boasts his mighty power
Thus the world's members equal ills sustain,
And perish by each other born to pain:
Yet in this direful chaos you'd compose
A general bliss from individuals' woes?
Oh worthless bliss! in injured reason's sight,
With faltering voice you cry, 'What is, is right'?
The universe confutes your boasting vain,
Your heart retracts the error you maintain.
Men, beasts, and elements know no repose
From dire contention; earth's the seat of woes:
We strive in vain its secret source to find.
Is ill the gift of our Creator kind?
Do then fell Typhon's cursed laws ordain
Our ill, or Arimanius doom to pain?

Shocked at such dire chimeras, I reject
Monsters which fear could into gods erect.
But how conceive a God, the source of love,
Who on man lavished blessings from above,
Then would the race with various plagues confound
Can mortals penetrate His views profound?
Ill could not from a perfect being spring,
Nor from another, since God's sovereign king;
And yet, sad truth! in this our world 'tis found,
What contradictions here my soul confound!
A God once dwelt on earth amongst mankind,
Yet vices still lay waste the human mind;
He could not do it, this proud sophist cries,
He could, but he declined it, that replies;
He surely will, ere these disputes have end,
Lisbon's foundations hidden thunders rend,
And thirty cities' shattered remnants fly,
With ruin and combustion through the sky,
From dismal Tagus' ensanguined shore,
To where of Cadiz' sea the billows roar.
Or man's a sinful creature from his birth,
And God to woe condemns the sons of earth;
Or else the God who being rules and space,
Untouched with pity for the human race,
Indifferent, both from love and anger free,
Still acts consistent to His first decree:
Or matter has defects which still oppose
God's will, and thence all human evil flows;
Or else this transient world by mortals trod,
Is but a passage that conducts to God.
Our transient sufferings here shall soon be o'er,
And death will land us on a happier shore.
But when we rise from this accursed abyss,
Who by his merit can lay claim to bliss?
Dangers and difficulties man surround,
Doubts and perplexities his mind confound.
To nature we apply for truth in vain,
God should His will to human kind explain.
He only can illume the human soul,
Instruct the wise man, and the weak console.
Without Him man of error still the sport,
Thinks from each broken reed to find support.

Leibniz can't tell me from what secret cause
In a world governed by the wisest laws,
Lasting disorders, woes that never end
With our vain pleasures real sufferings blend;
Why ill the virtuous with the vicious shares?
Why neither good nor bad misfortunes spares?
I can't conceive that 'what is, ought to be',
In this each doctor knows as much as me.
We're told by Plato, that man, in times of yore,
Wings gorgeous to his glorious body wore,
That all attacks he could unhurt sustain,
By death ne'er conquered, ne'er approached by pain.
Alas, how changed from such a brilliant state!
He crawls 'twixt heaven and earth, then yields to fate.
Look round this sublunary world, you'll find
That nature to destruction is consigned.
Our system weak which nerves and bone compose,
Cannot the shock of elements oppose;
This mass of fluids mixed with tempered clay,
To dissolution quickly must give way.
Their quick sensations can't unhurt sustain
The attacks of death and of tormenting pain,
This is the nature of the human frame,
Plato and Epicurus I disclaim.
Nature was more to Bayle than either known:
What do I learn from Bayle, to doubt alone?
Bayle, great and wise, all systems overthrows,
Then his own tenets labours to oppose.
Like the blind slave to Delilah's commands,
Crushed by the pile demolished by his hands.
Mysteries like these can no man penetrate,
Hid from his view remains the book of fate.
Man his own nature never yet could sound,
He knows not whence he is, nor whither bound.[3]

---

[3] It is self-evident that man cannot acquire this knowledge without assistance. The human mind derives all its knowledge from experience; no experience can give us an insight into what preceded our existence, into what is to follow it, nor into what supports it at present. In what manner have we received life? What is the spring upon which it depends? How is our brain capable of ideas and memory? In what manner do our limbs obey every motion of the will? Of all this we are entirely ignorant. Is our globe the only one that is inhabited? Was it created after other globes, or at the same instant? Does every particular

Atoms tormented on this earthly ball,
The sport of fate, by death soon swallowed all,
But thinking atoms, who with piercing eyes
Have measured the whole circuit of the skies;
We rise in thought up to the heavenly throne,
But our own nature still remains unknown.
This world which error and o'erweening pride,
Rulers accursed between them still divide,
Where wretches overwhelmed with lasting woe,
Talk of a happiness they never know,
Is with complaining filled, all are forlorn
In seeking bliss; none would again be born.
If in a life midst sorrows past and fears,
With pleasure's hand we wipe away our tears,
Pleasure his light wings spreads, and quickly flies,
Losses on losses, griefs on griefs arise.
The mind from sad remembrance of the past,
Is with black melancholy overcast;
Sad is the present if no future state,
No blissful retribution mortals wait,
If fate's decrees the thinking being doom
To lose existence in the silent tomb.
All may be well; that hope can man sustain,
All now is well; 'tis an illusion vain.
The sages held me forth delusive light,
Divine instructions only can be right.
Humbly I sigh, submissive suffer pain,
Nor more the ways of Providence arraign.
In youthful prime I sung in strains more gay,
Soft pleasure's laws which lead mankind astray,
But times change manners; taught by age and care
Whilst I mistaken mortals' weakness share,
The light of truth I seek in this dark state,
And without murmuring submit to fate.

---

species of plants proceed from a first plant? Is every species of animals produced by two first animals? The most profound philosophers are no more able to solve these questions than the most ignorant of men. All these questions may be reduced to the vulgar proverb: Was the hen before the egg, or the egg before the hen? The proverb is rather low, but it confounds the utmost penetration of human wisdom, which is utterly at a loss with regard to the first principles of things without supernatural assistance.

A caliph once when his last hour drew nigh,
Prayed in such terms as these to the most high:
'Being supreme, whose greatness knows no bound,
I bring thee all that can't in Thee be found;
Defects and sorrows, ignorance and woe.'
Hope he omitted, man's sole bliss below.

Appendix 3

Entries from Voltaire's Philosophical Dictionary*
(Dictionnaire philosophique portatif)

[First published in 1764, this volume of articles was begun as early as 1752, and was to be steadily enlarged over the next decade, finding its completion as Questions sur l'encyclopédie *(Encyclopaedic Questions, 1770), and comprising several hundred articles. One of Voltaire's objections to the great multi-volume* Encyclopédie, *to which he had contributed several articles, was its scale. As he wrote in a letter (5 April 1762): 'Twenty folio volumes will never achieve a revolution. It is the little portable volumes of thirty sous that are to be feared. If the Gospel had cost twelve hundred sesterces the Christian religion would never have been established.' Secondly, the* Encyclopédie *had itself been suppressed in 1759; Voltaire's 'one-man Encyclopedia' would take up the slack, and present Enlightenment ideas in portable form to a wider public.*

The Philosophical Dictionary *is also in effect a companion volume to* Candide, *and the following articles offer Voltairean contexts for some of the concerns debated in the 'conte philosophique'.]*

Bien (Tout Est): All Is Good

There was a fine row in the schools, and even among people who think, when Leibniz, paraphrasing Plato, built his edifice of the best of possible worlds, and imagined that all was for the best. He affirmed in the north of Germany that god could make only a single world. Plato had at least left him free to make five, because there are only five regular solids: the tetrahedron or three-faced pyramid with uniform base, the cube, the hexahedron, the dodecahedron, the icosahedron. But our world is not shaped like any of Plato's five bodies, he had allowed god a sixth manner.

* These extracts are taken from Voltaire's *Philosophical Dictionary*, translated by Theodore Besterman (London, 1972). All footnotes are by Besterman.

That will do for Plato. Leibniz, who was certainly a better geometer than he, and a more profound metaphysician, did mankind the service of explaining that we ought to be entirely satisfied, and that god could do no more for us, that he had necessarily chosen, among all the possibilities, what was undeniably the best one.

'What will become of original sin?' they shouted at him. 'It will become what it can,' said Leibniz and his friends; but in public he wrote that original sin was necessarily part of the best of worlds.

What! to be chased from a place of delights, where we would have lived for ever if an apple had not been eaten! What! produce in wretchedness wretched children who will suffer everything, who will make others suffer everything! What! to undergo every illness, feel every sorrow, die in pain, and for refreshment be burned in the eternity of centuries! Is this really the best lot that was available? This is not too *good* for us; and how can it be good for god?

Leibniz realized that these questions were unanswerable: so he wrote thick books in which he did not agree with himself.

A Lucullus in good health, dining well with his friends and his mistress in the house of Apollo, can say laughingly that there is no devil; but let him put his head out of the window and he will see unhappy people; let him suffer a fever and he will be unhappy himself.

I do not like to quote; it is usually a ticklish job: what precedes and follows the passage quoted is passed over, and one exposes oneself to a thousand quarrels. Still, I must quote Lactantius, church father, who, in his chapter XIII, of his *On the Wrath of God*[1] puts these words into the mouth of Epicurus:

Either god wants to remove the evil from this world, and cannot, or he can, and does not want to; or he neither wants to nor can; or he wants to and can. If he neither wants to nor can, this is impotence, which is contrary to the nature of god; if he can but does not want to, this is wickedness, which is no less contrary to his nature; if he neither can nor wants to this is at once wickedness and impotence; if he wants to and can (which is the only one of these possibilities fitting for god) whence then comes the evil which is on earth?

The argument is powerful; so that Lactantius answers it very badly, saying that god wants evil but that he has given us the wisdom with

[1] The exact date of *De ira dei* is not known; Lactantius Firmianus flourished c.300.

which one acquires the good. It must be admitted that this answer is quite weak in comparison with the objection, for it assumes that god could create wisdom only by producing evil; besides our wisdom is pretty ridiculous!

The origin of evil has always been an abyss whose bottom nobody has been able to see. This is what reduced so many ancient philosophers and legislators to have recourse to two principles, one good, the other bad. Typhon was the bad principle of the Egyptians, Ahriman of the Persians. It is well known that the Manicheans adopted this theology; but as these people had never spoken to the good nor the bad principle, we should not take their word for it.

Among the absurdities with which this world overflows and which can be counted among our evils, it is not a trivial one to have imagined two all-powerful beings fighting each other to see which of them would put more of himself into this world, and entering into a treaty like the two doctors in Molière: Pass me the emetic, and I'll pass you the lancet.

Basilides[2] alleged as early as the first century of the church, following the Platonists, that god had entrusted the creation of the world to his lowest angels, and that these, not being skilful, arranged matters as we see them. This theological fable crumbles into dust before the terrible objection that it is not in the nature of an all-powerful and all-wise God to entrust the building of the world to incompetent architects.

Simon,[3] who appreciated the objection, met it by saying that the angel who directed the workshop was damned for having done his work so badly; but the burning of this angel does not remedy our ills.

Among the Greeks the adventure of Pandora does not meet the objection any better. The box in which all ills reside, and at the bottom of which hope remains, is certainly a charming allegory; but this Pandora was created by Vulcan only to avenge himself against Prometheus, who had made a man out of mud.

The Indians have no better solution: having created man god gave him a drug that ensured his permanent health; man loaded his donkey with the drug, the donkey was thirsty, the serpent told him about a fountain; and while the donkey drank the serpent took the drug for himself.

[2] Basilides was a second-century gnostic, one of the most important links between Persian dualism and Manicheism.
[3] Probably Simon of Gitta as reported in the *Clementine homilies*.

The Syrians imagined that man and woman, having been created in the fourth heaven, took it into their heads to eat a pancake instead of the ambrosia which was their natural food. The ambrosia was exhaled through the pores, but after having eaten pancakes they had to go to stool. The man and woman begged an angel to tell them where the closet was. 'Well,' replied the angel, 'you see that little planet, though it is so small, which is about 60 million leagues from here; it is the universe's privy; hurry there.' They went there, they were left there, and since then our world has been what it is.

We must still ask the Syrians why god allowed man to eat the pancake, and so appalling a host of ills to descend on us in consequence.

I move quickly, before I get bored, from this fourth heaven to milord Bolingbroke. This man, who was undoubtedly a great genius, gave the celebrated Pope his notion of the *All is good*. It was in effect found later word for word in the posthumous works of lord Bolingbroke, and had previously been set out by lord Shaftesbury in his *Characteristics*. Read Shaftesbury's chapter on moralists; you will find these words in it:

> Much is alleged in answer to show why nature errs, and how she came thus impotent and erring from an unerring hand. But I deny she errs ...'Tis ... from this order of inferior and superior things that we admire the world's beauty, founded thus on contrarieties: whilst from such various and disagreeing principles, a universal concord is established ... The vegetables by their death sustain the animals: and animal bodies dissolved, enrich the earth, and raise again the vegetable world ... The central powers, which hold the lasting orbs in their just poise and movement, must not be controlled to save a fleeting form, and rescue from the precipice a puny animal, whose brittle frame, however protected, must of itself so soon dissolve.[4]

Bolingbroke, Shaftesbury and Pope, who embodied their ideas, do not resolve the question any better than the others: their *All is good* means nothing more than that all is controlled by immutable laws. Who does not know that? You tell us nothing new when you observe,

[4] *Characteristics: the Moralists* I. iii. (I have modernized the original text.) The intellectual descent from Shaftesbury to Pope through Boling-broke has been much debated, but what Voltaire says here is still basically sound.

as all little children have done, that flies are born to be eaten by spiders, spiders by swallows, swallows by shrikes, shrikes by eagles, eagles to be killed by men, men to kill one another, and to be eaten by worms, and then, all but one in a thousand, by devils.

Here we have a clear and fixed order among every kind of animal. There is order everywhere. When a stone is formed in my bladder it is by means of admirable mechanics: calculous juices pass little by little into my blood, they filter into the kidneys, pass through the ureters, deposit themselves in my bladder, and assemble there by an excellent Newtonian attraction; the stone is formed, gets bigger, I suffer pains a thousand times worse than death, by the most elegant arrangement in the world. A surgeon, having perfected the art invented by Tubalcain,[5] comes to thrust a sharp and cutting iron into the perineum, and takes hold of my stone with his pincers. It breaks under his efforts by a necessary mechanism; and by the same mechanism I die in frightful torments. *All this is good*, all this is the evident consequence of inalterable physical principles. I agree with them, and I knew it as well as you did.

If we were without feeling there would be no reason to object to this cause and effect. But that is not the point. We are inquiring whether there are any perceptible evils, and whence they come. 'There are no evils,' says Pope in his fourth essay on the *All is good*; 'or if there are particular evils, they form the common good.'[6]

A strange general good! composed of the stone, the gout, all crimes, all suffering, death and damnation.

The fall of man is the plaster we stick on all these particular diseases of the body and the soul, which are called 'general health'. But Shaftesbury and Bolingbroke derided original sin; Pope does not refer to it; it is obvious that their system undermines the Christian religion at its foundations, and explains nothing at all.

Nevertheless this system has recently been approved by several theologians who readily accept contradictions. Capital! we must not begrudge anybody the consolation of reasoning as best he can about the deluge of evils by which we are inundated. It is right to allow the incurable to eat what they like. It has even been claimed that this system is consoling. 'God', says Pope, 'sees perish with equal eye the

[5] Tubalcain, the descendant of Cain, was 'the forger of every cutting instrument of brass and iron' (*Genesis* iv. 22).
[6] Pope's most lapidary rendering of this view is 'All partial Evil universal Good' (*Essay on Man*, i, 292).

hero and the sparrow, an atom or a thousand planets precipitated into ruin, the formation of a soap-bubble or a world.'[7]

Here, I must admit, we have a pleasant consolation. Do you not find a great palliative in the prescription of lord Shaftesbury, who says that god is not going to upset his eternal laws for so puny an animal as man? It must at least be admitted that this puny animal has the right to cry out humbly, and to seek to understand, in crying, why these eternal laws are not made for the well-being of every individual.

This system of *All is good* represents the author of nature only as a powerful and maleficent king, who does not care, so long as he carries out his plan, that it costs four or five hundred thousand men their lives, and that the others drag out their days in want and in tears.

So far from the notion of the best of possible worlds being consoling, it drives to despair the philosophers who embrace it. The problem of good and evil remains an inexplicable chaos for those who seek in good faith. It is an intellectual exercise for those who argue: they are convicts who play with their chains. As for the unthinking mass, it rather resembles fish who have been moved from a river to a reservoir. They do not suspect that they are there to be eaten in lent: nor do we know anything by our own resources about the causes of our destiny.

Let us put at the end of nearly all chapters on metaphysics the two letters used by Roman judges when they could not understand a lawsuit: *N. L., non liquet*, this is not clear.

Chaîne des Evénements: Chain of Events

It is said that the present gives birth to the future. Events are linked to each other by an invisible fate: destiny, which in Homer is superior to Jupiter himself. This master of gods and men declared plainly that he could not prevent his son Sarpedon from dying at the appointed time. Sarpedon was born at the moment at which he had to be born, and could not have been born at any other. He could not die anywhere

[7] *Essay on Man*, i. 87–90, reads:

> 'Who sees with equal eye, as God of all,
> A hero perish, or a sparrow fall,
> Atoms or systems into ruin hurled,
> And now a bubble burst, and now a world.'

The difference is not trivial, for Voltaire, unlike Pope, has included creation in god's indifference.

but before Troy. He could not be buried elsewhere than in Lycia. At the appointed time his body had to produce vegetables which had to be changed into the substance of some Lycians. His heirs had to establish a new order in his states. This new order had to influence neighbouring kingdoms. From this resulted a new disposition of war and peace with the neighbours of the neighbours of Lycia. Thus by degrees the destiny of the whole world depended on the death of Sarpedon, which depended on another event, which was bound up with others back to the origin of all things.

If a single one of these facts had been arranged differently a different universe would have resulted; it was not possible for the actual universe to exist and not to exist; therefore it was not possible for Jupiter to save his son's life, for all he was Jupiter.

This system of necessity and fatality was invented in our times by Leibniz, so he claims, under the name of *sufficient reason*. It is nevertheless very old: it is hardly a discovery that there is no effect without a cause, and that the smallest cause often produces the greatest effects.

Lord Bolingbroke admitted that the petty quarrels of the duchess of Marlborough and lady Masham gave him the opportunity to make the special treaty between queen Anne and Louis XIV. This treaty led to the peace of Utrecht. This peace of Utrecht confirmed Philip V on the throne of Spain. Philip V took Naples and Sicily from the house of Austria. The Spanish prince who is today king of Naples clearly owes his kingdom to lady Masham; and he would not have had it, he would perhaps not even have been born, if the duchess of Marlborough had been more indulgent towards the queen of England. His existence in Naples depended on one foolishness more or less at the court of London. Examine the situations of all the peoples of the universe. They are established in the same way on a succession of facts which appear to be connected with nothing, but which are connected with everything. All is wheels, pulleys, ropes, springs in this immense machine.

So it is in the physical order. A wind that blows from deepest Africa and the southern seas brings part of the African atmosphere, which falls as rain in the valleys of the Alps. These rains fertilize our land. Our north wind in its turn sends our vapours to the blacks. We benefit Guinea, and Guinea benefits us in its turn. The chain extends from one end of the universe to the other.

But it seems to me that the truth of this principle is sadly misused. People conclude from it that there is no atom so small that its movement has not influenced the present arrangement of the entire world;

that there is no phenomenon too small, whether among men or among animals, to be an essential link in the great chain of destiny.

Let us be clear about this. Every effect obviously has its cause, which can be retraced from cause to cause into the abyss of eternity; but every cause does not have its effect to the end of time. I admit that all events are produced by one another. If the past gives birth to the present, the present gives birth to the future. All things have fathers, but not all things have children. This is exactly like a genealogical tree: we know that every house goes back to Adam, but plenty of people in the family died without posterity.

There is a genealogical tree of this world's events. It is unquestionable that the inhabitants of Gaul and of Spain are descended from Gomer, and the Russians from Magog, his younger brother: this genealogy is found in so many heavy books.[8] It is undeniable that the grand Turk, who is also descended from Magog, owes it to him that he was thoroughly defeated in 1769 by the empress of Russia, Catherine II. This adventure is clearly connected with other great adventures. But whether Magog spat to the right or to the left near mount Caucasus, whether he made two rings in a well or three, whether he slept on his left side or his right, I do not see that this has much influenced our present affairs.

We must reflect that nature is not a plenum, and that all movement is not communicated from one thing to another until it has gone round the world. Throw a body of similar density into water, and you can easily calculate that at the end of a certain time the movement of this body and that which it communicated to the water will have disappeared. Movement is lost and restored. Therefore the movement Magog may have produced when he spat into a well cannot have had any influence on what is happening today in Moldavia and Wallachia. Therefore the events of the present are not the children of all past events. They have their direct lines of descent, but a thousand little collateral lines are of no use to them. Once again, every being has its father, but not every being has children.

Destin: Fate

Of all the western books that have come down to us Homer is the oldest. It is there that we find the customs of profane antiquity, gross heroes, gross gods made in the image of man. But it is also there that we find the seeds of philosophy, and above all the notion of fate,

[8] All deriving ultimately from the table of nations in *Genesis* x.

which is the master of the gods, as the gods are the masters of the world.

When the magnanimous Hector absolutely insisted on fighting the magnanimous Achilles, and for that purpose fled with all his strength and went three times round the town before fighting in order to increase his vigour; when Homer compares to a sleeping man the light-footed Achilles who pursues him (mme Dacier goes into ecstasies of admiration for the art and deep meaning of this passage); then Jupiter in vain tries to save Hector; he consults the fates; he weighs in the balance the fates of Hector and Achilles, he finds that the Trojan absolutely must be killed by the Greek; he cannot resist; and from that moment Apollo, Hector's guardian genius, is obliged to abandon him. It is true that Homer is often prodigal in his poem with quite contrary ideas, as was permitted in antiquity; but still he is the first in whom the notion of fate is found. It must therefore have been quite current in his time.

The Pharisees, among the little Jewish people, did not adopt fate until several centuries later; for these Pharisees, who were the first literate Jews, were themselves quite new. In Alexandria they mixed part of the dogmas of the Stoics with the ancient Jewish ideas. Saint Jerome even alleges that their sect is not much older than our common era.

Philosophers never needed either Homer or the Pharisees to convince themselves that all events are governed by immutable laws, that all is arranged, that all is a necessary effect.

Either the world subsists by its own nature, by its physical laws, or a supreme being formed it in accordance with his supreme laws. In either case these laws are immutable. In either case all is necessary. Heavy bodies tend towards the centre of the earth, incapable of tending to rest in the air. Pear trees can never bear pineapples. The instinct of a spaniel cannot be the instinct of an ostrich. All is arranged, geared and limited.

Man can have only a certain quantity of teeth, hair and ideas. A time comes when he necessarily loses his teeth, his hair and his ideas.

It is a contradiction to say that what was yesterday was not, that what is today is not. It is also a contradiction to say that what must be does not have to be.

If you could alter the fate of a fly there would be nothing to prevent you from creating the fate of all the other flies, all the other animals, all men, all nature. When all is said and done, you would find yourself more powerful than god.

Idiots say: 'My doctor saved my aunt from a fatal illness, he made

her live ten years longer than she should have lived.' Other idiots, who
affect to know better, say: The prudent man makes his own fate.

> *Nullum numen abest, si sit prudentia, sed nos*
> *Te facimus, fortuna, deam, coeloque locamus.*
> *La fortune n'est rien; c'est en vain qu'on l'adore.*
> *La prudence est le dieu qu'on doit seul implorer.*[9]

But the prudent man, far from making his own fate, often succumbs
to it. Prudent men are made by fate.

Profound statesmen assert that if Cromwell, Ludlow, Ireton and a
dozen other parliamentarians had been assassinated a week before
Charles I's head was cut off, this king could have gone on living and
died in his bed. They are right. They can also claim that if the whole
of England had been engulfed in the sea, this monarch would not have
died on a scaffold in Whitehall (which in English means a white room).
But things were arranged in such way that Charles had to have his
neck cut.

Cardinal d'Ossat was no doubt more prudent than a madman in
the Petites-maisons; but is it not obvious that the organs of the wise
Ossat were not made in the same way as those of the lunatic, just as
the fox's organs are different from those of a crane and a lark?

Your doctor saved your aunt; but he certainly did not gainsay the
order of nature to do so: he obeyed it. It is obvious that your aunt
could not prevent herself from being born in a given town, that she
could not prevent herself from having a certain illness at a given time,
that the doctor could not be elsewhere than in the town in which he
was; that your aunt had to send for him; that he had to prescribe the
drugs that cured her.

A peasant thinks that hail fell by chance on his field; but the philosopher knows that there is no chance, and that the world being
constituted as it is, it was impossible for the hail not to fall that day
on that spot.

There are people who, afraid of this truth, grant half of it, like
debtors who offer half to their creditors, and ask to be let off the rest.
There are, they say, necessary events, and others that are not necessary.
It would be laughable for one part of this world to be arranged, and

[9] Juvenal, *Satires* x. 365–6: 'Fate would have no divinity if we were wise: it is
we who make her a goddess and place her in heaven.' Voltaire's French version
is so free that it must also be translated: 'Fortune is nothing; it is adored in
vain. Prudence is the only god to whom we should pray.'

not the other, if one part of what happens had to happen, and another part of what happens did not have to happen. When one examines this closely it is seen that the doctrine opposed to fate is absurd. But there are many people fated to reason badly, others not to reason at all, others to persecute those who reason.

There are people who tell you: 'Don't believe in fatalism; for, every-thing then appearing to be inevitable, you won't work at anything, you'll wallow in indifference, you'll love neither wealth, nor honours, nor praise; you won't want to acquire anything; you'll believe yourself to be equally without value and power. No talent will be cultivated; everything will perish in apathy.'

Fear not, gentlemen, we shall always have passions and prejudices, since it is our fate to be subject to prejudices and to passions. We would be well aware that it no more depends on us to have much merits and great talents than to have a good growth of hair and a beautiful hand. We would be convinced that vanity is not to be drawn from anything, and yet we shall always be vain.

I have *from necessity* the passion to write this; and you, you have the passion to contradict me: we are both equally foolish, equally the playthings of fate. Your nature is to do evil, mine is to love the truth and to publish it in spite of you.

The owl, who feeds on mice in his shanty, said to the nightingale: 'Stop singing in your shady trees, come into my hole for me to devour you'; and the nightingale replied: 'I was born to sing here and to laugh at you.'

You ask me what will become of freewill. I don't understand you. I do not know what this freewill is that you speak of. You have been arguing for so long about its nature that you assuredly do not know it. If you want peacefully to examine with me what it is, or rather if you can, turn to the letter L.[10]

[10] The French word for freewill is *liberté*.

Notes

Title-page

1. *Optimism*: A recent and specialized term in French (only one recorded use, 1737, prior to *Candide*), it appears only twice in the text (see Introduction), in a passage that is a late addition. The word is not used by Voltaire in its modern sense of a psychological attitude, but denotes a philosophical position, expounded notably by Gottfried Wilhelm Leibniz (1646–1715): that this world is the best possible world, because God, being all-wise, must know all possible worlds, being all-powerful, must be able to create whatever he chooses, and being all-good, must choose the best. Optimism tries to reconcile goodness and the perfection of God with the existence of evil. In maintaining the necessity of things being as they are, however, the word is suggestive of fatalism. Voltaire wrote to Elie Bertrand in February 1756: 'We need a God who talks to the human species. Optimism is a counsel of despair, a cruel philosophy with a consoling name.'
2. *Ralph*: The subtitle was added in the 1761 edition (hereafter 1761); Monsieur le Docteur Ralph is a fictitious German academic (rather than medical doctor) with a mystificatory Anglo-Saxon name, possibly inspired by a character in Samuel Butler's (1612–80) satirical poem *Hudibras* (1663), or by James Ralph, a minor poet lampooned by Alexander Pope (1688–1744) in *The Dunciad* (1728).
3. *additions*: These refer particularly to the long passage added to chapter 22 in 1761.
4. *Minden*: The battle of Minden, fought in the German province of Westphalia in August 1759, resulted in a heavy defeat for the French army ('a flourishing army led to butchery' was Voltaire's comment at the time). Actual historical events succeeding the first publication of *Candide* gave added satirical impetus to Voltaire's

choice of this impoverished rustic province as the setting for his earthly paradise. In a letter to his niece, Mme Denis, in 1750, he had already pondered the 'vast, sad, sterile, detestable countryside of Westphalia' through which he was then travelling.

CHAPTER I
How Candide was brought up in a beautiful castle, and how he was driven from the same

1. *seventy-one quarterings*: Divisions in heraldry, indicated on a coat of arms: a noble has as many quarterings as he has maternal and paternal ancestors among the nobility. Admission to knighthood was granted on the basis of sixteen quarterings. To possess seventy-one is to possess an absurd impossibility; Cunégonde possesses seventy-two – such is the intransigent pride of the German petty princes.

2. *Pangloss*: See A Note on Names. In composing the character of Pangloss, Voltaire may have been thinking of Leibniz's disciple Christian Wolff (1679–1754), and perhaps also of the French philosopher and writer Jean-Jacques Rousseau (1712–78). In 1756 Voltaire had written an attack on Rousseau entitled *Lettre au docteur Jean-Jacques Pansophe* (*Letter to Doctor Jean-Jacques Pansophe* – 'pansophe' means 'all-knowing').

3. *metaphysico-theologico-cosmo-nigology*: Voltaire's assault on cosmic optimism is a compound-caricature of Leibniz, Pope and Wolff, the latter a rigidly systematic thinker who introduced the word 'cosmology' to a wider world; 'nigology' comes from *nigaud* ('booby').

4. *no effect without cause*: Leibniz: 'Nothing ever happens without a cause or at least a sufficient [determining] reason' (*Théodicée* (1710), I, 44; translated as *Essays in Theodicy on the Goodness of God, the Liberty of Man, and the Origin of Evil*), which Voltaire here reduces to tautology. Voltaire's comedy habitually separates cause and effect.

5. *all is for the best*: The passage is a burlesque *reductio* of the principle of final causes, or the argument from design. Voltaire accepted a moderate form of the principle, but attacked extreme materialist versions of it. Cf. his article on 'Final Causes' in the *Philosophical Dictionary* (transl. Theodore Besterman, London, 1972, pp. 205–7). Philosophically, 'all is for the best' means that each thing is justified by its purpose in the plan of Creation, but common parlance turns the expression into abject enthusiasm for the world as it is.

6.   *sufficient reason*: A Leibnizian term (referring to that quality, in
     each thing, which explains and justifies its existence), satirically
     redirected here from metaphysical to physical concerns. The vol-
     itions of God are 'sufficient reasons' determined by our percep-
     tion of the good. Leibniz intended his principle as a criterion of
     truth in the sphere of the contingent, that is, of experience. It
     suggests a rationally constructed universe and so is connected
     with his Optimism. Voltaire judged the principle to be a case of
     obfuscation, and reduces it to the simple notion of cause and
     effect.

CHAPTER 2
What became of Candide among the Bulgars

1.   *Valdberghoff-trarbk-dikdorff*: A composite name which mocks
     the German language and its compounds: *vald* (*Wald*) – 'wood';
     berg (*Berg*) – 'mountain'; *hoff* (*Hof*) – 'court'; *dorff* (*Dorf*) –
     'village'. The title-page of *Candide* describes it as a work 'trans-
     lated from the German'.
2.   *Two men dressed in blue*: The uniform of Frederick the Great's
     feared recruiting officers.
3.   *écus*: Old form of French currency.
4.   *King of the Bulgars*: The Abars and the Bulgars, whom Voltaire
     had encountered while researching his *Essai sur l'histoire génér-
     ale et sur les mœurs et l'esprit de nations* (*Essay on General
     History and on the Manners and Spirit of the Nations*, 1756),
     were two barbarian nations who laid waste the Byzantine empire
     in the eighth and ninth centuries. In the contemporary setting of
     the Seven Years' War (1756–63), the references to recruiting
     officers and to the tallness of recruits suggest that the Bulgars
     represent the Prussians and the Abars the French. Etymologically,
     'Bulgars' also imputes homosexuality to Frederick and his tall
     troops ('bulgar' – *bougre*, 'bugger').
5.   *your glory is assured*: By accepting the King's money and toasting
     the King's health, Candide has unwittingly signed up for military
     service.
6.   *ramrod*: Used for pressing the charge down the muzzle of the
     gun. The manoeuvres described by Voltaire were newly essen-
     tial to success on the field of battle in the eighteenth century;
     by increasing their speed and synchronization, the Prussians
     increased their mobility as a fighting force and reduced their
     losses. Voltaire had witnessed the militarization of the Prussian
     army in Potsdam during his stay with Frederick (1750–53), and

he closely followed developments in military tactics, as evidenced in the opening of the next chapter.

7. *freedom of the will*: Under Frederick's influence Voltaire had abandoned the doctrine of freedom of the will, which he had formerly defended (in his *Eléments de la philosophie de Newton* (*Elements of the Philosophy of Newton*), 1740) and would subsequently mock.

8. *thirty-six times*: In his *Mémoires pour servir à la vie de M. de Voltaire* (*Memoirs Relating to the Life of M. Voltaire*, written 1759–60), Voltaire describes this punishment being meted out to deserters from the Prussian army, while Frederick watched from his windows. There is also a reminiscence here of a French nobleman press-ganged by Prussian officers, who deserted, was recaptured and bastinadoed 'thirty-six' times. Voltaire interceded on his behalf.

9. *sung in all the newspapers for all the ages*: A satire on Frederick's gift for propaganda; the phrase 'in all the newspapers' was an addition, not present in the manuscript.

10. *Dioscorides*: A first-century AD Greek doctor, satirically cited by François de Rabelais (*c.* 1493–1553) in *Gargantua* (1534), and hardly an up-to-date medical authority (though still cited in the eighteenth century).

CHAPTER 3
*How Candide ran away from the Bulgars, and
what became of him*

1. *a harmony such as was never heard in hell*: An ironic reference to Leibniz's theory of pre-established harmony. The Seven Years' War was being waged during the composition and publication of *Candide*. According to the 1761 title-page, Doctor Ralph, purported author of *Candide*, perished in this same war in 1759. Voltaire wrote to an English correspondent, George Keith, on 4 October 1759: 'The present war is the most hellish that ever was fought. Your Lordship saw formerly one battle a year at most; but nowadays the earth is covered with blood and mangled carcasses almost every month. Let the contented lunatics who say that "All that Is, Is Well" be confounded! 'Tis not so, indeed, with twenty provinces exhausted and three hundred thousand men murdered. I wish your Lordship the peace of mind necessary in this lasting hurricane of horror.'

2. *scoundrels who were infesting its surface*: Soldiers were commonly seen as recruited from the dregs of the population.

3. *First the cannon . . . a few thousand more*: Voltaire's description
    follows the usual sequence of eighteenth-century battles: artillery
    exchanges followed by infantry, followed by hand-to-hand fight-
    ing with bayonets. He omits the cavalry charge.

4. *Te Deums*: Hymns of thanksgiving in the Catholic liturgy, tra-
    ditionally sung after victories: 'a ceremony established to encour-
    age the people, whom it is essential always to deceive' (Voltaire,
    Le Siècle de Louis XIV (*The Age of Louis XIV*), 1751). That the
    Te Deum was often sung simultaneously in both camps, for
    propaganda purposes, had already been criticized as ludicrous
    by the philosopher Pierre Bayle (1647–1706) in his *Diction-
    naire historique et critique* (*Historical and Critical Dictionary*,
    1695–7), and is one of the commonplaces of Voltaire's anti-
    religious polemic.

5. *international law*: Theorists of international law, such as Hugo
    Grotius (1583–1645), had tried to legalize what they could not
    proscribe: hence the theoretical justification of pillage or slavery,
    for example, which outraged Voltaire.

6. *Here old men . . . arms and legs*: The description in this passage
    is faithful to contemporary accounts of the realities of war: a
    synthesis rather than an exaggeration. 'None of the atrocities
    in *Candide* is invented' (Jean Starobinski, 'Voltaire's Double-
    Barrelled Musket', in *Blessings in Disguise* (California, 1993),
    p. 85).

7. *dealt with it accordingly*: In his manuscript Voltaire originally
    added the sentence: 'Virtually the entire province had been
    destroyed.'

8. *He begged alms . . . how to earn his living*: Begging was pro-
    hibited in Holland, and Voltaire was a supporter of such
    measures.

9. *This orator*: A Protestant pastor; after the Revocation of the
    Edict of Nantes (1685), Holland became one of the centres of
    asylum for free-thinkers, Protestants and proselytizers against
    Rome.

10. *a chain of necessity*: The Leibnizian principle that all phenomena
    are of necessity linked to one another, though the satire here is
    anti-determinist rather than specifically anti-Leibnizian.

11. *Anti-Christ*: A view maintained by orthodox Calvinists.

12. *Anabaptist*: A member of a sixteenth-century Protestant sect,
    widespread in Holland and Westphalia. Anabaptists rejected
    infant baptism, maintaining that only adults could choose Chris-
    tianity. Having originally been unpopular for their sanguinary

and radical views on property and religious discipline, they had settled down in the eighteenth century, becoming peaceful burghers – industrious, altruistic, tolerant of other sects – and as such had earned Voltaire's approval.

13.   *two legs, no feathers and a soul*: The Anabaptist adds a soul to this famously minimal definition of man, coined – according to Aristotle – by one of the philosophers of the Academy (whereupon Antisthenes, the Cynic, presented him with a chicken).

CHAPTER 4
How Candide encountered his old philosophy tutor, Doctor Pangloss, and what came of it

1.   *brought him to his senses . . . in the stable*: The manuscript reads: 'brought him to his senses by giving him a beaker of cow's urine' – more likely to be found in a stable than 'vinegar'.

2.   *not one stone remains standing on another*: Cf. Mark 13:2: 'There shall not be left one stone upon another.'

3.   *a very learned Franciscan*: The epithet is in jest: the mendicant orders were widely regarded as ignorant and morally lax, corrupted by their comings and goings in society.

4.   *Jesuit*: There was a routine jest that Jesuits were homosexual, on account of their passion for pedagogy. Voltaire elsewhere criticized their 'pride' and 'thirst for power', but he also praised their 'austerity' and 'virtue'.

5.   *genealogy*: A parody of biblical genealogies; the venereal theme was a favourite of Voltaire, partly because of its force as a proof against Optimism (a benevolent God would hardly meddle with the machinery of procreation). He had read widely on the subject, and in this passage he follows the physician Jean Astruc's (1684–1766) *Treatise on Venereal Illnesses* (1734), which located the origins of syphilis in the Caribbean. It was generally believed that syphilis was introduced into Europe by followers of Columbus returning from the Americas. 'The venom which poisons the source of life originated in the Caribbean; each climate on this unhappy globe has its poison, where nature has blended a little good with a lot of evil' (*Essay on the Manners and Spirit of the Nations*).

6.   *necessary ingredient*: A parody of the Optimist doctrine that evil is necessary to the 'universal harmony'.

7.   *cochineal*: An insect imported from Mexico, from which a scarlet dye was produced.

8.   *peculiar to the inhabitants of our continent*: The manuscript
      reads: 'peculiar to Christians'.

9.   *men are not born wolves, yet they have become wolves*: An
      allusion to the Latin motto of Thomas Hobbes's (1588–1619)
      philosophy: *homo homini lupus* ('man is a wolf to man'). Voltaire
      may be alluding satirically to Rousseau and the primitivist view
      that man had degenerated from his original state of natural
      goodness. The notion that man had corrupted nature was univer-
      sal in the eighteenth century, if variously nuanced. Voltaire did
      not consider the primitive state to be superior to civilized society
      – his target is the doctrine of original sin, with its suggestion that
      individuals are born evil.

10.   *neither twenty-four-pounders nor bayonets*: Twenty-four-
      pounders were the largest cannon deployed by the French, whose
      cannon-balls weighing twenty-four pounds caused heavy losses
      to the enemy; bayonets were invented in 1670 and became wide-
      spread in infantry regiments during the eighteenth century,
      making hand-to-hand fighting a great deal more murderous.

11.   *the courts which seize . . . creditors*: In 1754 Voltaire lost 8,000
      livres of income from the bankruptcy of the son of the famous
      banker Samuel Bernard, in whose hands he had placed part of
      his fortune. In 1758 he tried to recover some of these losses. A
      bankrupt's creditors could normally hope to be compensated by
      division of the bankrupt's estate, but the law delayed the process
      by seizing all of the estate in the first instance, from which it
      would then deduct costs.

12.   *private ills make up the general good*: A philosophical view which
      rested on a Newtonian vision of the world, and which became a
      cliché of Leibnizian 'Optimism'. Voltaire was an adherent of this
      view, but turned against it prior to *Candide* (cf. *Zadig, Memnon,
      Poem on the Lisbon Disaster*). In Panglossian caricature, all evils
      are part of the general good: the more evil, so to speak, the better.

CHAPTER 5
Storm, shipwreck, earthquake, and what became of
Dr Pangloss, Candide and Jacques the Anabaptist

1.   *Lisbon harbour was built expressly . . . should one day drown in
      it*: A satire on providentialism: the wicked survive. But there is a
      further jest: 'only death by involuntary and permanent immersion
      will do for a man who believes in the necessity of adult immer-
      sion' (Roger Pearson, *The Fables of Reason: A Study of Voltaire's
      'Contes Philosophiques'* (Oxford, 1993)).

2. *a priori proofs*: Arguments from logic rather than from experience are ironized as endemic to Leibnizian philosophy.

3. *feel the earth tremble beneath them*: The earthquake that shook Lisbon at 9.40 a.m. on 1 November 1755 killed between 15,000 and 60,000 people (contemporaries estimated that 30,000 people died), setting off a tsunami that reached England by 2 p.m. and the West Indies by 6 p.m. Most of the city was destroyed, and the subsequent conflagration was spread by cooking fires, alight for mealtime. The catastrophe convulsed European belief systems. Voltaire consulted various published and eyewitness accounts for his description in *Candide*. In a letter dated 24 November, he wrote: 'This is indeed a cruel piece of natural philosophy! We shall find it difficult to explain how the laws of motion can produce such fearful disasters *in the best of all possible worlds* – when a hundred thousand ants, our neighbours, are crushed to death in seconds in one of our ant-heaps, half of them undoubtedly dying in inexpressible agonies, beneath debris from which it was impossible to extricate them; families all over Europe reduced to beggary, and the fortunes of a hundred merchants – Swiss, like yourself – swallowed up in the ruins of Lisbon. What a game of chance is human life! What will the preachers say now – especially if the Palace of the Inquisition is left standing! I flatter myself that those reverend fathers, the Inquisitors, have been crushed just like everyone else; which ought to teach men not to persecute men: for, while a few sanctimonious hypocrites are burning a few fanatics, the earth opens up and swallows them all.' In a later letter dated 16 December, Voltaire wrote; 'Like you, I pity the Portuguese; but men make even more evil for themselves on their little molehill than nature makes for them. More men have their throats cut in wars than are swallowed up in earthquakes. If there were nothing more to fear in this world than the Lisbon earthquake, we should all be a lot better off.' Cf. Voltaire's *Poem on the Lisbon Disaster* (see Appendix 2).

4. *Batavia*: The capital of Java, a Dutch colony; now called Jakarta, it is the capital of modern Indonesia.

5. *four times I've trampled on the cross*: Originally receptive to Europeans, Japan began to suspect the Christian missions of being the advance guard of imperialism, and in 1638 closed its ports to foreigners. Only the Dutch were permitted to continue trading; Voltaire's claim that they had to repudiate their religion symbolically by trampling on a crucifix is incorrect, although the

Japanese working for the Dutch in Batavia were required to do so.

6. *some oil and wine*: These were used to wash wounds.

7. *a seam of sulphur running underground from Lima to Lisbon*: This was one of the theories current at the time to explain the origin of earthquakes, adopted by the naturalist Georges-Louis Leclerc, comte de Buffon (1707–88), and popularized by the Swiss pastor Elie Bertrand (*Mémoire sur les tremblements de terre* (*Dissertation on Earthquakes*), 1756), with whom Voltaire corresponded on this subject. Lima, in Peru, had been destroyed by an earthquake in 1746.

8. *things could not be otherwise*: The manuscript, together with one of the 1759 editions, offers a different ending to this paragraph: '"For," he said, "it is necessary, if a universe is to exist, that it be the best of universes. And, in the best of universes, all is good, all is well, all is for the best. Console yourselves, rejoice and let us drink."'

9. *it cannot be anywhere else*: Conversely, if the world were made for man by a benevolent God, volcanoes would only occur in uninhabited regions.

10. *neither Fall nor punishment*: Voltaire slyly insists on the difficulty of reconciling the providentialism of Leibnizian Optimism with Christianity proper and the orthodox dogma of original sin. Optimism is heretical in so far as it sidesteps the Fall: if all is well, 'it follows that human nature is not fallen. If the order of things requires that everything should be as it is, then human nature has not been corrupted, and consequently has no need of a Redeemer' (Preface to the *Poem on the Lisbon Disaster*, see Appendix 2). The man in black's argument is that Optimism removes all grounds for belief in supernatural punishment or reward, and by making God directly responsible for the misery of the world, destroys the possibility of human freedom.

11. *predetermined*: Pangloss's Leibnizian argument here is determinist, but also recognizably scholastic in attempting vainly to reconcile providence with free will. Orthodox Catholics were required to believe in the doctrine of free will.

12. *Porto, or rather Oporto*: They are one and the same Portuguese city – a moment of pedantry (and a late addition, not present in the manuscript) which reminds us that this is a tale being told by the obscure German with the English name, Doctor Ralph.

CHAPTER 6
How they had a magnificent auto-da-fé *to prevent earthquakes, and how Candide was flogged*

1. *a fine auto-da-fé*: During this ceremony the charges of heresy brought by the Inquisition were read out to the accused and the crowd, and the accused were invited to make an 'act of faith' (*auto-da-fé*); executions were carried out by the secular authority. Voltaire relied for his details upon the *Relation de l'Inquisition de Goa* (*Account of the Inquisition of Goa*, 1688) by C. Dellon. In reality, no *auto-da-fé* took place in response to the Lisbon disaster. Three *autos-da-fé* were held in Lisbon – on 8 October 1756, 28 September 1757, 27 August 1758 – but these were unconnected with the earthquake, and there were no executions.

2. *Coïmbra*: The seat of the university of Lisbon, which is by implication in thrall to the Inquisition, rather as in Voltaire's eyes the university of the Sorbonne was in the pay of religion.

3. *Biscayan*: A Spanish Basque – another foreigner, like Candide and Pangloss.

4. *marrying his fellow godparent . . . eating a chicken*: The relation between godmother and godfather was regarded as a spiritual kinship, and an ecclesiastical interdiction forbade them from marrying each other – an empty superstition, as far as Voltaire was concerned (and satirized in his later tale *L'Ingénu* (*The Ingenu*)). The two Portuguese converts are secretly Jews, *marranos*, who betray their allegiances by removing the rashers of bacon, as food proscribed by Mosaic dietary law; the Inquisition was on the lookout for cases of false conversion. Voltaire's sympathy for Jewish victims of the Inquisition was unaffected by his congenital anti-Semitism.

5. *san-benito*: A short smock or sackcloth over-garment painted with flames, figures of devils, the victim's own portrait, etc., and worn by the condemned as they were led to the stake at an *auto-da-fé*. The *san-benito* came to symbolize the abominations of organized religious intolerance.

6. *his flames were upright*: The crime of Pangloss, who has spoken heresy, is greater than that of Candide, who has merely listened; hence the flames painted on the former's *san-benito* point upwards, while those on the latter's point downwards. Generally, the penitent wore inverted flames, while those deemed to be impenitent wore upright flames.

7. *plainchant monotony*: 'Faux-bourdon', a fourteenth-century version of polyphony (i.e. music in more than one part), consisting of an improvised part above or below a plainchant original – for voices rather than instruments. It was long extinct by the eighteenth century; what is intended here is therefore uncertain, other than – to Voltaire's ears – sinister and tedious music ironically characterized as 'delightful'. It is the *Miserere* that is being sung in this fashion (cf. chapter 8).

8. *hanging was not the custom at an auto-da-fé*: Those condemned by the Inquisition were invariably burned to death; Pangloss is hanged (so that he can come back to life again when required to do so).

9. *That same day the earth quaked once more with a terrifying din*: This second, minor, shock in fact took place two months after the earthquake, on 21 December 1755, as Voltaire noted in his correspondence.

CHAPTER 7
How an old woman took care of Candide, and how he was reunited with his beloved

1. *may Our Lady of Atocha . . . watch over you*: A statue in Madrid, the site of a cult of the pregnant Virgin: 'This Lady is made of wood; every year she weeps on her feast-day, and the people weep too. Once on this occasion the preacher, seeing a carpenter with dry eyes, asked him how it was that he did not dissolve in tears when the Holy Virgin wept. "Ah, reverend Father," he replied, "it was I who refastened her in her niche yesterday; I drove three great nails into her behind: it is then she would have wept had she been able" ' (Voltaire, annotation to the *Journal* of the Marquis de Dangeau, 1769). Saint Anthony is the patron saint of Portugal (notwithstanding the reference here to Padua in Italy), and was the saint to invoke when looking for things lost – in this case Cunégonde; Saint James is the patron saint of Spain.

CHAPTER 8
Cunégonde's story

1. *to the old law or to the new*: The Old Law is the law of Moses, the New Law is the law of Christ; the uncertainty is as to whether the night in question belongs to Saturday (Jewish) or to Sunday (Christian).

2. *miserere*: Psalm 50, one of the penitential psalms.

CHAPTER 9
What became of Cunégonde, Candide, the Grand Inquisitor and a Jew

1. *the Babylonian Captivity*: Jerusalem was captured in 596 BC by Nebuchadnezzar, King of Babylon; the Jewish king together with his court were taken in captivity to Babylon.

2. *moidores*: Old Portuguese gold currency; *moidores* are replaced by *pistoles* (a French term for the Spanish *escudo*) in chapters 10 and 22.

3. *the Holy Hermandad*: The Holy Brotherhood of the Inquisition, a semi-religious order with police powers, active in eighteenth-century Spain.

4. *Avacena*: An invented name.

CHAPTER 10
In what distress Candide, Cunégonde and the old woman arrive in Cadiz, and of their embarkation

1. *everyone has an equal right to them*: Here and elsewhere (chapters 15 and 16) Pangloss's utopian socialism parrots the arguments of Rousseau's *Discours sur l'origine de l'inégalité* (*Discourse on the Origins of Inequality*, 1755), whose proposal that all men are equal in a state of nature, and that social inequalities are artificial, had been ironized by Voltaire: 'I have received, Monsieur, your new work against the human species . . . Never has so much wit been expended in an effort to make brutes of us all. Reading your book makes one feel like crawling on all fours' (letter to Rousseau, 30 August 1755).

2. *maravedi*: A Spanish copper coin of little value.

3. *Benedictine prior*: The Benedictines were thought to be very wealthy.

4. *Lucena . . . Chillas . . . Lebrija . . . Cadiz*: The names are real, but the itinerary is fantastical. Cadiz was the centre of trade with Spanish America. Voltaire invested heavily in this trade. In 1756 he had invested part of his capital in the fitting-out of a ship to transport Spanish troops from Cadiz, to quell a Paraguayan Indian uprising, supposedly backed by the Jesuits (the ship was named the *Pascal*, after their Jansenist enemy). Candide, Cunégonde and the old woman embark on a ship effectively owned by Voltaire.

5. *San Sacramento*: Eighteenth-century Paraguay covered a far greater area than today, much of it controlled by Jesuit missions.

In 1750 the Spanish government ceded the town of San Sacramento – situated inside the mission settlements – to Portugal; the Indians rebelled against the prospect of passing under Portuguese rule, and the Jesuits were held responsible (in Voltaire's manuscript, 'who were accused of having incited' reads: 'who had incited'). In 1755 Spain and Portugal sent an expedition to repress the uprising, and guerilla activity continued for several years; Candide becomes – briefly – a commanding officer on such an expedition.

6. *another world*: 'If all is well, how can the followers of Leibniz concede that one world could be better than another? This idea of a better world, is it not proof in itself that all is not well?' (Voltaire, letter to Elie Bertrand, 18 February 1756).

7. *seventy-two quarterings*: Voltaire had at first written 'seventy-one', but this number of heraldic quarterings on a coat of arms was considered insufficient in Westphalia (chapter 1, note 1).

CHAPTER II
The old woman's story

1. *the daughter of Pope Urban X and the Princess of Palestrina*: A non-existent Pope. Voltaire had originally written 'Clement XII', an actual and recent Pope. According to his secretary Wagnière, he intended to add the following footnote, which appeared only in posthumous editions of *Candide*: 'Note the extreme discretion of our author at this point! Until now there has never been a Pope Urban X. He is afraid to attribute a bastard daughter to an existent Pope. What circumspection! What delicacy of conscience!' Palestrina was an Italian principality, near Rome, which produced a Pope named . . . Urban VIII.

2. *Massa-Carrara*: A small Italian duchy, in Tuscany.

3. *Gaeta*: An Italian port, north of Naples.

4. *Salé*: A Moroccan port, near Rabat, and in the eighteenth century a notorious centre of piracy targeted at Christian vessels. It is likewise a corsair from Salé that swoops in Daniel Defoe's (1660–1731) *Robinson Crusoe* (1719).

5. *in articulo mortis*: 'At the point of death'. Only priests are authorized to give absolution, but in their despair the soldiers have lost all sense of the proprieties and are demanding Christian absolutions of a Muslim pirate.

6. *Knights of Malta*: An order of soldier-monks based in Malta, whose mission was to defend Christian pilgrims against the infidel.

7. *Muley Ismaël*: Emperor of Morocco, who reigned ruthlessly for

over fifty years, and whose sons (two, not fifty) engaged in a protracted struggle for power after his death in 1727.

8. *without anyone omitting ... as required by Mahomet*: Voltaire, like Bayle before him, denies any connection between religious protocol and ethical conduct.

9. *O che sciagura d'essere senza coglioni*: 'Oh, what a misfortune to be without balls!'

CHAPTER 12
The misfortunes of the old woman, continued

1. *some are sent off to govern provinces*: An allusion to the Neapolitan castrato Farinelli (1705–82), celebrated for his voice and subsequently for his role as advisor to the Spanish kings Philip V and Ferdinand VI. Paul Valéry (1871–1945) remarked on the frequency with which Jesuits and eunuchs appear in eighteenth-century satire – Jesuits as a punishment for having educated most of the writers concerned, but why so many eunuchs? 'I wonder is there a secret and profound reason for the almost obligatory presence of these figures, so cruelly separated from so many things, and in some sense cut off from themselves?' (Preface to the Baron de Montesquieu's (1689–1755) *Lettres persanes* (*Persian Letters*, Paris, 1926)).

2. *to conclude a treaty ... Christian powers*: This refers to the negotiations by certain enemies of France, such as Portugal, to ally themselves with Muley Ismaël at the outset of the War of Spanish Succession (1701–13). Voltaire's target is Christians arming Moors against other Christians, and more generally, the economic basis of modern warfare. Cf. *The Age of Louis XIV*, chapter 18.

3. *Ceuta*: An African port opposite Gibraltar.

4. *the Dey of that province*: Algeria was a dependency of the Sultan of Constantinople, whose representative was the Dey, or governor.

5. *It is very common in Africa*: Epidemics of the 'Black Death' (bubonic plague) continued to ravage the Mediterranean during the eighteenth century, notably in Marseilles in 1720, and Messina in 1743.

6. *janissaries*: Slaves, prisoners, or captured Christians who serve as mercenary infantrymen under the command of the aga.

7. *the Russians who were besieging it*: Peter the Great had captured the port of Azov from the Turks after a protracted siege (1695–7), which gave Russia an outlet on the Black Sea.

8.   *Maeotian Marshes*: The Roman name for the sea of Azov, a
     swampy lake outside the city.
9.   *imam*: A Muslim cleric.
10. *Cut off one buttock . . . you will be rescued*: Voltaire came across
     references to buttock-eating in a history of the Celtic peoples
     published in 1741, which in turn cites St Jerome, according
     to whom the Scots would feast on the buttocks of young boys,
     and the breasts of young girls, when they had no game to eat.
     (Cf. the entry 'Anthropophages', *Philosophical Dictionary*,
     pp. 38–40).
11. *boyar*: Russian minor nobility, repressed and abolished by Peter
     the Great, in 1698, after a conspiracy was discovered ('the petty
     intrigue at Court' mentioned below). The leaders were tortured
     by being broken on the wheel. (Cf. Voltaire's *Histoire de la
     Russie sous Pierre le Grand* (*History of the Russian Empire*,
     1759), chapters 8 and 10).
12. *carrying a fardel*: The old woman appears to be recalling Hamlet's
     soliloquy on suicide ('Who would these fardels bear?' III, i, 75).
13. *three negroes, four Englishmen, four Genevans and a German
     professor named Robeck*: Negroes: an allusion to the high suicide
     rate among negro slaves. Englishmen: the English were thought
     in the eighteenth century to be especially prone to melancholy
     and suicide. Genevans: added to the list in 1761, probably as a
     jibe at Rousseau, whose *La Nouvelle Héloise* (*The New Eloise*,
     1761, with its two letters on suicide, nos. 21–2) Voltaire had
     read in the interim. Robeck: Johann Robeck, a Swede, wrote a
     treatise advocating suicide in 1736, before following his own
     example and drowning himself in the river Weser at Bremen
     in 1739. The debate about suicide had an important place in
     eighteenth-century philosophy and letters, because it acutely
     focused issues of Christian morality and human contradiction;
     Voltaire had no doctrinal objections to suicide and he debated
     the question on several occasions.

CHAPTER 13
How Candide was obliged to part from the lovely
Cunégonde and from the old woman

1.   *and although this white lie . . . the Moderns*: A biblical allusion
     inserted in 1761: Abraham and Isaac, being less scrupulous than
     Candide, mendaciously passed their wives off as sisters (Genesis
     12:11–20, 26); this was a favourite example in the Voltairean
     and deist polemic against the morality of the Bible; it was the

subject of a celebrated article in Bayle's *Dictionary* ('Sara'), and is discussed in Voltaire's *Philosophical Dictionary* (p. 18).

2.   *You have been raped . . . enjoyed your favours*: The old woman speaks more candidly of Cunégonde's ordeals than Cunégonde herself, in the version of her story offered to Candide in chapter 8.

3.   *an alcalde and some alguazils*: A magistrate and accompanying policemen.

CHAPTER 14
How Candide and Cacambo were received by the Jesuits of Paraguay

1.   *a quarter Spanish*: i.e. a quadroon: his father is a half-caste, his mother an Indian.

2.   *the Tucuman*: In the eighteenth century a province; today an Argentinian city, at the foot of the Andes.

3.   *their kingdom*: A deliberately incorrect usage, suggestive of the autocracy of the Jesuits; it was rumoured in 1755–6 that the Indians had crowned a Jesuit as their king. 'With regard to the supposed kingdom of the Jesuits in Paraguay, I tell you, with all of Europe as my witness, that nothing is more certain . . . I know very well, gentlemen, that they do not have the title of king, and therefore you may say it is a wretched fable to talk of the kingdom of Paraguay. But even though the Dey of Algiers is not a king, he is nonetheless master of that country' (pseudonymous letter from Voltaire to the *Journal encyclopédique*, 15 July 1762, in response to a review of *Candide* that had appeared on 15 March 1759).

4.   *Asunción*: The capital of the Jesuit-administered territory in Paraguay. The college, or Colegio de la Asunción, was the centre of Jesuit administration in South America.

5.   *Los Padres*: A less than affectionate Spanish term for the Jesuit fathers, by whom Voltaire had himself been educated.

6.   *leagues*: One league equals three miles.

7.   *justice and reason*: In this chapter Voltaire is openly sceptical of the supposed communalism introduced by the Jesuits in Paraguay, who had organized their Indian parishes into autonomous villages. But he preferred the conduct of the Jesuit missions to the 'horrors' which had accompanied the conquests of Mexico and Peru. (Cf. *Essay on the Manners and Spirit of the Nations*, chapter 154.)

8.   *spontoon*: A short pike; a weapon carried by infantry officers and used for signalling orders to the regiment. (It was in fact

contrary to Canon law for a priest to carry weapons or engage in war.)

9. *three hours*: The text reads 'three hours', but 'hours' is either an exaggeration or a corruption of 'days': according to Voltaire's letter to the *Journal encyclopédique* of 15 July 1762, 'They do not permit any Spaniard to remain for more than three days in their territories.' The Jesuits are also accused in this letter (and cf. the *Essay on the Manners and Spirit of the Nations*, chapter 154) of not allowing Spanish visitors to speak to the natives, for fear of their influencing the indigenous population adversely.

10. *kissing his spurs*: A parodic variation on a custom ridiculed elsewhere by Voltaire, according to which it was a sign of respect towards the Pope to kiss his mule.

11. *arbour*: Not a rustic hut, but a lavishly appointed residence. The jest notwithstanding, the austerity of the lives led by Jesuits was universally acknowledged, not least by Voltaire.

12. *gold vessels*: In the communal system introduced by the Jesuits, gold was banished as a currency and therefore lost its customary value; in the tendentious universe of the tale, it is transformed into a material reserved for the exclusive use of Jesuits.

13. *negro slaves*: The Jesuits were authorized to have negro slaves, along with everyone else.

CHAPTER 15
How Candide killed the brother of his dear Cunégonde

1. *my sister raped*: The Baron omits to mention what Pangloss has already told us: that he received 'exactly the same treatment' as his sister.

2. *Father Croust*: Rector of the Jesuit college in Colmar, and an enemy of the *philosophes* (i.e. the group of free-thinkers – writers, scientists and philosophers – associated with the *Encyclopédie* (1751–72), the great collective French Enlightenment project of a multi-volume illustrated encyclopedia which summarized the current state of human knowledge across the arts and sciences), Croust treated Voltaire with hostility when the latter tried to settle at Colmar in 1754, after his return from Prussia. Croust is here homosexualized, and referred to elsewhere by Voltaire as 'the most brutalized member of the Society'.

3. *colonel and priest*: An invidious conjunction, for Voltaire; the Jesuit order was founded on principles of military discipline, with military titles.

4.   *that all men are equal*: Another reference to Pangloss's Rous-
      seauist socialism.

CHAPTER 16
What became of our two travellers when they encountered two girls, two apes and the savages named the Oreillons

1.   *Journal de Trévoux*: A critical but scrupulously informative peri-
      odical published by the Jesuits at Trévoux under the title
      Mémoires pour servir à l'Histoire des Sciences et des Beaux-Arts
      (*Memoranda Relating to the History of the Sciences and the
      Arts*). It ran from 1701 to 1767, and carried out a sustained
      offensive against the *philosophes* and the *Encyclopédie*. Voltaire
      counter-attacked from 1759 onwards (cf. 'An Account of the
      Illness of the Jesuit Berthier', in *Micromégas and Other Short
      Fictions*, edited by Haydn Mason (London, 2002)).

2.   *they are one-quarter human . . . one-quarter Spanish*: Rousseau's
      Discourse on the Origins of Inequality, with its emphasis on the
      proximity of the higher apes to man, may have been a satirical
      starting point for this chapter, though the idea that apes were
      close to humans – or were perhaps human – was a commonplace.

3.   *aigypans*: A form of Pan, with the feet of a buck and a hirsute body.

4.   *fables*: A widely known work entitled *La Mythologie et les fables*
      (*Mythology and Fables*, 1740), by the Abbé Antoine Banier, had
      argued that mythological beings such as satyrs and fauns were
      in reality large monkeys, refracted through the imaginations of
      the ancients. Voltaire's view – advanced by several eighteenth-
      century naturalists and philosophers – was that such creatures
      were hybrids produced by the coupling of humans with other
      species, a notion which called into question the radical metaphys-
      ical distinction between man (beneficiary of salvation) and the
      rest of creation.

5.   *the Oreillon tribe*: Or Orejones; according to Garcilaso de la
      Vega's *Historia General del Perú* (*History of the Incas of Peru*,
      1704), this was the name of an Indian tribe of the upper Amazon,
      with large ears (*oreilles*) on account of the heavy pendants that
      they wore.

6.   *ropes made of bark*: Doubtless inspired by familiarity with Lilli-
      putian tactics – Voltaire had read Jonathan Swift's (1667–1745)
      Gulliver's Travels (1726) with great gusto while he was living in
      England in the 1720s.

7.   *'Let's eat Jesuit!'*: Within weeks of the publication of *Candide*,

the expression 'Mangeons du Jésuite!' had acquired proverbial status with a public increasingly hostile to the order, which was to be expelled from France in 1764.

8. *state of nature*: The Rousseauist doctrine that men in a natural state are free of evil is under attack throughout *Candide*. Voltaire was unpersuaded of the supposed advantages of primitive life over civil society: 'Good houses, good clothing, a good standard of living, with good laws and freedom are better than want, anarchy and slavery. Those who are unhappy with London just have to go off to the Orkneys; there they will live as everyone used to in London in Caesar's time; they'll eat oat bread, and cut each others' throats for sun-dried fish and a straw hut. Those who recommend it should set the example' ('The ABC: Seventh Conversation: That modern Europe is better than Ancient Europe', in *Voltaire's Political Writings*, edited by David Williams (Cambridge, 1994), p. 131).

9. *If we Europeans ... ravens and crows*: The defence of primitive by comparison with 'civilized' customs goes back to Michel de Montaigne's (1533–92) essay 'Des Cannibales' ('Of Cannibals') in *Essais* (*Essays*, 1580–88), Book 1, essay 31. Cacambo's eloquence here draws on Voltaire's article 'Anthropophages' in the *Philosophical Dictionary*, to the effect that eating your enemy is not as bad as killing him in the first place. (Cf. also the discussion of cannibalism in the *Essay on the Manners and Spirit of the Nations*, chapter 146).

10. *the enemy of your enemies*: A piece of sophistry on Cacambo's part; nothing so far suggests that the Oreillons are inimical to the Jesuits (who in Paraguay claimed to defend the indigenous peoples against the ravages of colonialism) – they are merely out to avenge Candide's murder of the two apes.

CHAPTER 17
Arrival of Candide and his manservant in the land of Eldorado, and what they saw there

1. *Eldorado*: From the fifteenth century onwards, Spanish conquistadors had speculated about a region abounding in gold and precious stones, to which the last Incas were thought to have retreated. Numerous attempts were made to discover this fabled but literal land lying between the Orinoco and the Amazon. By the eighteenth century it had largely become another name for Utopia. Voltaire's main source for the local colour of the Eldorado episode was Garcilaso de la Vega's *History of the Incas*.

Voltaire frequently mocked the obstinacy with which Spanish travellers sought out this imaginary land; he summarizes accounts of Eldorado in the *Essay on the Manners and Spirit of the Nations*, chapter 151.

2. *Cayenne*: The capital of French Guiana, and a considerable distance from Paraguay.

3. *the useful was joined to the agreeable*: Horace (65–8 BC): 'omne tulit punctum qui miscuit utile dulci' ('he who has joined the useful to the agreeable has won every vote'), *Ars Poetica* (*The Art of Poetry*), ll. 343–4. Cf. also Julie's garden in Rousseau's *Nouvelle Héloïse*, Book 4, letter 11.

4. *large red sheep*: Llamas: a South American ruminant related to the camel; they were sometimes described by travellers as of a reddish colour, were used as pack-animals, and were notable for their speed.

5. *to despise gold and gems*: Contempt for gold was part of the regime in Sir Thomas More's (1478–1535) *Utopia* (1517).

6. *they were speaking Peruvian ... where nothing else is spoken*: There is no Peruvian language as such; either the joke is on Cacambo as self-appointed linguist, or Voltaire is thinking of the lost language of the Incas.

7. *All the inns ... are paid for by the government*: Prior to the Spanish conquest, according to Garcilaso, free hostelries 'well stocked with provisions', were maintained by the Inca government for the benefit of travellers.

CHAPTER 18
What they saw in the land of Eldorado

1. *wiped out by the Spaniards*: 'It is said that the family of Incas retreated to this vast country whose limits extend to Peru, where the majority of Peruvians escaped the avarice and cruelty of the Christians from the Old World, that they lived nearby a lake whose sands were made of gold, and that there was a city whose roofs were covered in gold; the Spaniards called this city El Dorado' (*Essay on the Manners and Spirit of the Nations*, chapter 151, composed at the same time as *Candide*).

2. *the consent of the people*: This detail has been taken to suggest that, unlike most utopias, Eldorado is governed by a constitutional monarchy (cf. J. H. Brumfitt, *Candide* (London, 1968), p. 178); elsewhere in the chapter it is also clear that Eldorado is a utopia replete with servants.

3. *Raleigh*: An allusion to the exploration of Guiana by Sir Walter

Raleigh (1554–1618), who was sent there by Queen Elizabeth. Voltaire was familiar with the account of Eldorado, which Ralegh located near Guiana, in his *The Discovery of Guiana* (1591).

4. *from night till morning*: The deism which characterizes Eldoradean beliefs, in addition to being Voltaire's own conviction, is based on accounts in Garcilaso and the utopian novels inspired by his writings. The curious expression 'from night till morning', however, suggests some recondite irony.

5. *two Gods, or three, or four*: A statement of Voltaire's rational aversion to the Christian doctrine of the Trinity. By contrast, Deist confidence in a providential design suffuses the whole passage: there is a single all-powerful and all-virtuous God, creator of the universe, who rules by unchangeable universal laws; who neither punishes nor rewards, but gives man the reason by which to apprehend the moral law. This chapter also draws on Voltaire's admiration for Quaker customs in Pennsylvania (cf. *Lettres anglaises ou philosophiques* (*Philosophical Letters*, 1734), chapters 1 and 4). As a Deist, Voltaire believed that the existence of a supreme being can be inferred by natural reason from the evidences of design in the world.

6. *lick the dust off the parquet*: Gulliver, before being admitted to an audience at the court of Luggnag, must first 'sweep the floor with his tongue'.

7. *large squares*: The Incas were famed for their engineering feats and lavish public works.

8. *the law courts and the court of appeal*: In Voltaire's time France had a dozen *parlements*, the main one being in Paris. In addition to combining the functions of high court and court of appeal, the *parlements* claimed the right to participate in legislation by registering royal edicts and remonstrating against those of which they disapproved. Voltaire found these claims invalid in law and reactionary in politics, and he supported the royalist party throughout his career; his version of Eldorado thus has an enlightened constitutional monarch whose powers have not been eroded by the judiciary.

9. *that species of tyranny ... our customs or our laws*: An allusion to the 'tyranny' of Frederick II, who in 1753 had tried farcically to prevent Voltaire from leaving Prussia.

10. *twenty million pounds ... the currency of that country*: The currency of Eldorado is English sterling, or less improbably a currency whose measure – like the English pound – is pure silver rather than (valueless) gold.

CHAPTER 19

*What happened to them in Surinam, and how
Candide made the acquaintance of Martin*

1. *Surinam*: Candide and Cacambo were heading for Cayenne, capital of French Guiana, but they end up in Surinam, a neighbouring Dutch colony.

2. *in Dutch*: As is essential for a picaresque hero, Candide is polyglot. His mother tongue is German; he may have learned his Dutch in the house of the Anabaptist; he converses freely with the old woman (in Portuguese, or perhaps Italian), with the Governor of Buenos Aires (in Spanish), with the Parisians, with the English, with the Venetians – and he even understands the Levantine captain and the Turkish dervish. He only baulks at the native languages of the Oreillons and the Eldoradeans: but Cacambo is there to help him out. (Cf. *Candide*, edited by René Pomeau (Oxford, 1980), p. 195).

3. *It is the price we pay for the sugar you eat in Europe*: The inhumane treatment of slaves traded from European colonies to the Americas (in numbers exceeding 100,000 per year in the mid-eighteenth century) was condemned by Montesquieu in *De l'Esprit des lois* (*Spirit of the Laws*, 1748, Book 15, chapter 5), and likewise by Claude Adrien Helvétius (1715–71). Voltaire, a great consumer of sugar, was especially struck by a footnote in the latter's *De l'Esprit* (*Essays on the Mind*, 1758), which he read on its publication in autumn 1758, denouncing the connection between slavery and sugar: 'It is well known that not a barrel of sugar arrives in Europe but is stained with human blood'. Voltaire seems to have interpolated the episode of the Surinam slave (the second and third paragraphs of this chapter) at a late stage, after reading Helvétius, for it does not appear in the manuscript. The details regarding cloth shirts and amputations are adapted from the *code noir* for slaves, an edict of Louis XIV (summarized in the *Encyclopédie* article on 'Slavery').

4. *Patagonian écus*: Spanish and Flemish silver coinage.

5. *Dutch fetishes*: The word 'fetish' is of Portuguese origin, designating a sacred object worshipped by primitive peoples; used here to refer to the Dutch Protestant pastors, considered as sorcerers or witch doctors.

6. *giving up on your Optimism ... What is Optimism*: These are the only appearances of the word in the text of *Candide*.

7. *a free state*: Candide is thinking of Venice's reputation for

pleasure. Until Napoleon's campaign against Austria in 1797, Venice was a free and independent republic, but its aristocratic government was not noted for tolerating either political liberty or freedom of thought.

8. *Monsieur Vanderdendur ... presented himself*: The following passage alludes to Voltaire's personal disputes with the Dutch publisher Van Duren, who kept increasing the amount agreed for the printing of Frederick II's treatise *Anti-Machiavel*, the publication of which Voltaire had supervised.

9. *piastres*: Spanish silver coinage.

10. *publishing houses of Amsterdam ... could more disgust a man*: Amsterdam was a major European centre for the book trade. Authors flocked there from all points of the compass, often refugees or fugitives, and wrote to order for – in their view – exploitative publishers (also known as 'booksellers' or 'printers'), an opinion shared by Voltaire, who had perennial trouble with publishers, since piracy flourished in an age of censorship, and copyright law had yet to be established.

11. *preachers ... had decided he was a Socinian*: Like tradesmen and booksellers, preachers (i.e. Protestant pastors) were fixtures of Dutch society, enjoying official status and considerable influence. Socinians were a sect who proposed a form of 'rational' Christianity, exalting individual conscience and minimizing or denying such mysteries as the divinity of Christ, the Trinity, original sin, the person of the devil and the eternity of hell. They were regarded as outright heretics in many European countries during the eighteenth century, even by those Protestants most closely allied to the *philosophes*. Voltaire attacked their ingrained optimism but approved their rationality; his impoverished scholar is reminiscent of Pierre Bayle, eking out his exile in Rotterdam, drudging for publishers and under suspicion for his religious beliefs.

CHAPTER 20
What happened to Candide and Martin at sea

1. *physical evil and moral evil*: Philosophical questions much in debate in the aftermath of the Lisbon earthquake, not least by Rousseau, who discusses the origins of evil in his *Lettre sur la providence* (*Letter on Providence*, 1756), which proffered a modified version of Christian providentialism in response to Voltaire's poem on the disaster.

2. *Manichean*: Bayle's sympathetic article on 'Manicheans' in his

Dictionary had revived interest in this third-century heresy, according to which the created world is the work of two equally powerful deities or principles, both of which must be propitiated: God rules only half the universe, and is incapable of controlling the operations of the devil, who rules the other half. The Manicheans disposed of the problem of the origin of evil by saying that it had no origin as such, but was present in the very constitution of the universe. Thus God is absolved from responsibility, but at the cost of reducing his omnipotence. Voltaire's fascination with Manichean dualism was tempered by his belief that an eternal struggle between good and evil could only have produced chaos, rather than the self-evident Newtonian harmony which we see around us (*Philosophical Dictionary*, article 'Bien (Tout Est): All Is Good', see Appendix 3).

3. *globule*: The term had been used by the philosopher and physicist Blaise Pascal (1623–62) to refer to a 'particle of matter', but Voltaire was the first to employ it as a not very affectionate diminutive for the terrestrial globe.

4. *assassins in regimental formation*: Mercenaries were in the pay of all European armies in the eighteenth century, and are a salient feature of Voltaire's critique of war as organized murder; and the figure of 'a million' would be reasonably close to the total strength of the European armies mobilized in the Seven Years' War by 1758.

CHAPTER 21
Candide and Martin approach the coast of France philosophizing all the way

1. *talking nonsense*: The flightiness of the French character was proverbial in the eighteenth century.

2. *But have you been to Paris, Monsieur Martin?*: 'Voltaire was a Parisian at heart, and the great drama of his life was to have been obliged, from the 1750s onwards, to live away from the capital. Hence the rancour expressed in these pages: Candide will only find happiness in a marginal life, a life at the *periphery*' (Frédérick Deloffre and Jacques van den Heuvel (eds.), *Voltaire romans et contes*, (Paris, 1979), p. 875). The Parisian chapter is the longest in *Candide*, and the most densely worked and reworked (see Appendix 1).

3. *the Saint-Germain fair*: The most famous Parisian fair, held annually between February and April, and frequented by many foreign visitors.

4. *religious convulsions*: Martin, on his visit to Paris, had seen only a range of questionable human types; the doors of good society are not open to him. As usual, Voltaire has his sights on journalists, men of letters, sectarians, Jansenists. The latter are caricatured by recalling an episode (1729–32) in which Jansenist zealots fell into 'convulsions' or miraculous trances before the Paris tomb of one of their deacons, in the cemetery of Saint-Médard. So great were the crowds, and so violent the enthusiasm, that in 1732 the authorities closed the cemetery. Voltaire was profoundly affected by this spectacle, and it remained one of his salient examples of religious fanaticism. The 'convulsionist rabble' appears onstage in the manuscript version of the opening of chapter 22 (see Appendix 1), but are banished to the wings in subsequent versions of the chapter.

5. *that fat volume belonging to the captain*: Possibly the Bible; more likely to be a recent history of polar navigation, *Histoire des navigations* (*History of Navigation*, 1756) by Charles de Brosses (1709–77), which followed the naturalist Buffon in explaining the presence of marine fossils on mountain tops as evidence of an aboriginal flood. Voltaire tirelessly mocked this theory of origins, which bore so uncomfortable a resemblance to the biblical story of a Flood.

6. *why do you expect men to have changed theirs?*: Voltaire attacks the primitivist idea (whether the Christian doctrine of the Fall, or the classical conception of a Golden Age) that man was formerly good and, corrupted by freedom, has since degenerated into the evil state in which he now appears to exist. Voltaire always insisted that the essential character of human beings has persisted unchanged, whatever their histories or cultures.

CHAPTER 22
What happened to Candide and Martin in France

1. *A plus B minus C divided by Z*: Voltaire's target is the Academies which had sprung up in the French provinces, with their enthusiasm for sterile debate (he had in fact been an associate member of the Academy of Bordeaux since 1746). The 'scholar from the North' is probably the philosopher and mathematician Pierre-Louis Moreau de Maupertuis (1698–1759), director of the Academy of Berlin, whose *Essai de Cosmologie* (*Essay on Cosmology*, 1756) had claimed to represent the laws of creation by a mathematical formula, and whom Voltaire accused of trying to prove the existence of God by algebra.

2. *Faubourg Saint-Marceau*: During the eighteenth century this was the main southern approach to Paris, an impoverished district 'whose disgusting rusticity offends the eye', as Voltaire remarks elsewhere. Rousseau described in similar terms his first visit to Paris via this Faubourg (*Confessions*, 1782, Book 1, chapter 159).

3. *a note of confession*: This refers to the notorious *billets de confession*, introduced in 1750, according to which the dying were required to present proof of confession, signed by a priest who had formally accepted the 1713 papal bull *Unigenitus* (condemning Jansenism as a heresy). Those without a *billet* could not receive absolution, or be admitted to the last sacraments, or be buried in consecrated ground – all of which Voltaire found abhorrent: 'I will neither return to Berlin to endure the cruel caprices of a King, nor to Paris to expose myself to its *billets de confession*' (letter to the Duchess of Saxe-Gotha, 25 March 1755).

4. *a little abbé from Périgord*: An *abbé* was a young man of good breeding who, without being a clergyman, wore a clerical habit in return for a modicum of theological study, in the hope of acquiring an education and a benefice; the Périgord gentry in particular were mocked for their social ambition and impecuniousness.

5. *the scene is set in Arabia*: The play alluded to – and snubbed – is Voltaire's own tragedy, *L'Orphelin de la Chine (The Orphan from China*, 1755).

6. *innate ideas*: In the manuscript, this reference to the Cartesian doctrine of innate ideas was preceded by the sentence: 'He is someone who esteems Locke.' Voltaire, the author of the play under question, did indeed esteem John Locke (1632–1704), who held that ideas are produced by sense-experiences rather than existing prior to all sense-experience (cf. Voltaire's *Philosophical Letters*, chapter 13).

7. *twenty pamphlets written against him*: Here begins the long passage interpolated by Voltaire in 1761. See Note on the Text.

8. *a fairly dull tragedy*: Le Comte d'Essex (1678), by Thomas Corneille (1625–1709).

9. *how queens of England were treated in France*: Candide's whole-hearted view of the stage leads him to confuse stage queens with historical queens.

10. *at the corner of the rue de Bourgogne*: Adrienne Lecouvreur (1692–1730), a famous actress and close friend of Voltaire, died

suddenly in 1730 and was buried by stealth at night in unconsecrated ground, having been refused Christian burial. Actors were automatically excommunicate in France, and were denied last rites unless they had previously repented. Voltaire campaigned at length against this rule, and when the polemic over the excommunication of actors was renewed in 1760, he interpolated this passage into the Parisian chapter.

11. *a Fréron*: Elie-Catherine Fréron (1718–76) was a celebrated journalist, a tenacious and gifted opponent of the *philosophes*, a personal enemy of Voltaire and an indefatigable critic of the latter's tragedies. He had reviewed *Candide* for the *Année littéraire* on its anonymous first appearance, in 1759, dismissing the possibility that it could have been written by Voltaire.

12. *Mademoiselle Clairon*: An actress who had recently played with great success in Voltaire's tragedy *Tancrède* (1760). She appears in *Candide* only from 1761 onwards.

13. *Faubourg Saint-Honoré*: A wealthy district of the city.

14. *faro*: A game resembling baccarat, with players competing against the bank. Voltaire did not play cards, but in the mid-1740s he had often accompanied his mistress, Mme du Châtelet, to aristocratic gambling places.

15. *Marquise de Parolignac*: In the game of faro, a *paroli* is the term for a raised stake; the termination *-gnac* indicates a Périgord origin (like Balzac's Rastignac); the hostess would seem to be a compatriot as well as an accomplice of the little abbé.

16. *Gauchat, the Doctor of Divinity*: The abbé Gauchat had participated in the campaigns against the *philosophes*, denounced Helvétius as an 'impious beast' and repeatedly 'refuted' Voltaire in the course of his *Lettres critiques, ou Réfutation d'écrits modernes contre la religion (A Refutation of Modern Works Written against Religion)* in twelve volumes, 1753–63.

17. *Archdeacon T[rublet]*: Archdeacon Trublet (1677–1770) was another enemy of the *philosophes*; and had in addition accused Voltaire's epic poem *La Henriade (The Henriad*, 1728) of being boring.

18. *sacrificing sense to rhyme*: The paragraph as a whole is a defence of Voltaire's ideas on theatre, in response to criticisms of *Tancrède*.

19. *however well written and well rhymed*: Such as those of Jean Racine (1639–99).

20. *pomposities that merely repel us*: Such as those of Pierre Corneille (1606–84).

21. *false maxims and turgid commonplaces*: Such as those of Prosper Jolyot, Sieur de Crébillon (1674–1762).

22. *Jansenists against Molinists, judiciary against churchmen*: The Jansenists were a party of strict religious reform, who believed in predestination and moral austerity. The Molinists were Jesuits, so named after Luis Molina, a sixteenth-century Jesuit whose views on freedom of the will had been adopted by the order. The controversy referred to here, between Jesuits and Jansenists, concerned the relative importance accorded to free will in the scheme of human salvation. Jansenism was in direct, bitter conflict with the more relaxed theology of the Jesuits, and was always in a minority. By turns accommodated and persecuted, Jansenism was finally condemned by the papal bull *Unigenitus*, though it continued to maintain its hold thereafter. The *parlements*, or judiciary, comprised of the anti-papal minor aristocracy, were Jansenist in outlook and took sides in religious controversy throughout the century, often against the Church and in favour of weakening the ties between French Catholicism and Rome.

23. *your shadows are in truth dreadful stains*: In his *Essays in Theodicy*, Leibniz justified the existence of 'apparent defects' in the fabric of this world, on the grounds that these 'stains' enhance the beauty of the whole and procure a greater good.

24. *After supper ... those of the Marquise*: The episode of Candide's visit to the Marquise de Parolignac, added in *1761*, is a parodic version of Saint-Prieux's visit to the brothel in Rousseau's *Nouvelle Héloïse*.

25. *or planned to do*: The passage which Voltaire interpolated in *1761* ends here. Pre-*1761*, the transition was effected as follows. After the speech by the 'argumentative bore' (above, p. 61), ending 'tomorrow I'll show you twenty pamphlets written against him', the text continues:

> 'Sir,' said the abbé, 'do you see that young creature over there with the beguiling look and the delicate figure? She would only cost you ten thousand francs a month, and for fifty thousand écus of diamonds you could ...' – '... I could spare her only a day or two,' replied Candide, 'because I have a pressing appointment in Venice.' The next night after supper the sly Périgordian became ever more unctuous and assiduous ...

26. *what the abbé was talking about*: The abbé is talking in a guarded way about regicides. Robert François Damiens (born in Arras,

1715–57), attempted to stab Louis XV to death in the courtyard
of Versailles in January 1757; François Ravaillac assassinated
Henri IV in May 1610, after an earlier attempt on his life had
been made in December 1594. Voltaire emphasizes the element
of religious fanaticism common to all three attacks, and in the
case of Henri IV the conviction that it was right to kill a king
who had been excommunicated by the Pope.

27. *monkeys provoke tigers*: The 'monkeys' are priests who incite
assassins like Damiens and Ravaillac.

CHAPTER 23
*Candide and Martin reach the shores of England –
and what they see there*

1. *the two countries . . . than the whole of Canada is worth*: The
colonial struggle in North America was at its height during the Seven Years' War. The conflict concerned an ill-defined
frontier region between the French and British colonies, but
which controlled access to Canada (and which was to be secured
for England in 1763); Voltaire is concerned more with what he
sees as the prodigal waste of a long-drawn-out war over 'a few
acres of snow' than with the consequences, which cost France
her American provinces. Voltaire's much-quoted 'few acres of
snow' were in fact a vast and fertile region; he shared the general
indifference towards colonies characteristic of France in the eighteenth century.

2. *a multitude of people . . . the crowd dispersed looking extremely
satisfied*: Admiral John Byng commanded the British naval forces
when they were defeated by the French off the coast of Minorca
in 1756. He was court-martialled for insufficiently engaging with
the enemy, and on 14 March 1757 was executed by firing squad
on his own quarter-deck, in Portsmouth harbour, to satisfy public
opinion and City traders. Voltaire had met Byng during his residence in England, was incensed by this injustice and tried to
intercede on his behalf.

3. *to encourage the others*: 'Pour encourager les autres', the second
most famous and most quoted phrase from *Candide*, which has
taken on a life of its own.

CHAPTER 24
Concerning Paquette and Brother Giroflée

1. *Theatine*: A regular order founded in 1524, dedicated to
reforming standards of ecclesiastical behaviour, Brother Giroflée

notwithstanding. Unfortunately for their reputation in *Candide*, one of their members was an enemy of Voltaire.

2. *A Franciscan who was my confessor*: Presumably the same syphilitic Franciscan already encountered in chapter 4. 'Confessor' implies that the religion practised in the castle of Thunderten-tronckh would seem to be Catholicism (and the 'billets de confession' episode in chapter 22 makes sense only if Candide is understood to be a Catholic).

3. *refuse-heap*: Where the remains of prostitutes and actresses were thrown, rather than buried in consecrated ground.

4. *turn Turk*: i.e. convert to Islam.

5. *Doge*: The constitutional head of the Venetian state.

6. *Senator Pococurante*: The Venetian Senate was all-powerful, and was recruited from a handful of aristocratic families. 'Pococuranté' means 'one who cares for little' (cf. A Note on Names). Voltaire acknowledged, in a letter to his friend Thieriot in 1759, that he had something in common with this figure: the same age, wealthy, independent, with luxurious tastes and a tendency to judge writers and artists with maximum severity.

7. *Brenta*: The river which runs from Padua into the Venetian lagoon.

CHAPTER 25
A visit to Signor Pocuranté, a Venetian nobleman

1. *a true imitation of nature*: The aesthetic judgements on painting, music and literature dispensed by Pococuranté in this chapter are for the most part versions of Voltaire's own opinions, filtered through the exaggerated sensibility of a disillusioned Venetian aristocrat.

2. *a concerto*: Possibly a composition for soloist and orchestra (the 'concerto' was evolving into its modern meaning at this time); more likely an instrumental ensemble for a group of players.

3. *perhaps I should like ... the Senator's opinion*: The passage alludes to an eighteenth-century musical controversy between two schools of music, broadly French and the Italian: the former as exploring complex harmonies and polyphony (exemplified by Jean Philippe Rameau, 1683–1764), the latter as favouring melodic line and the refinements of *bel canto*. Pococuranté seems to reject both, the former for its academicism, the latter for its addiction to virtuosity and unnatural or 'hybrid' combinations of recitative and aria.

4. *Tasso ... Ariosto*: Ludovico Ariosto (1474–1533) and Torquato

Tasso (1544–95), two Italian epic poets who were widely read in France during the eighteenth century; Voltaire preferred Ariosto to Homer; the judgements of Pococuranté on Homer, Virgil, Tasso and Ariosto are reproduced almost verbatim from Voltaire's *Essai sur la poésie épique* (*Essay on Epic Poetry*, 1733).

5. *Horace*: The passage below alludes to various poems by Horace (*Satires* I.5, I.7 and II.8 (the character is named Rupilius, not 'Pupilus'); *Epodes* V, VIII, XII; *Odes* I.1), who was widely admired throughout Europe in the eighteenth century.

6. *Cicero*: Cicero (146–43 BC) was in fact Voltaire's favourite classical author; he wrote a play about him, quoted him incessantly, and called his *De Divinatione* (*On Divination*) and *De Officiis* (*On Duties*) the best books of antiquity.

7. *technique for making pins*: Possibly the least ironic statement in the chapter: metallurgy was undergoing a rapid evolution during this period, and Voltaire greatly admired practical inventions.

8. *Seneca*: (4? BC–AD 65), Roman stoic philosopher, dramatist and statesman. It was an Enlightenment commonplace to compare Christianity unfavourably with stoicism.

9. *a republican like yourself*: Venice was a republic, but with an effective system of censorship; whereas for Voltaire the English enjoyed a freedom of thought and expression almost unique in Europe. 'Pascal is only amusing at the expense of the Jesuits; Swift entertains and educates us at the expense of the human race! How I love the English boldness! How I love people who say what they think! People who only half think are only half alive' (Letters D5704 – *Correspondence*, ed. Theodore Besterman, Paris, 1977–90).

10. *a Dominican monk*: The Dominicans played a leading role in the Inquisition.

11. *that barbarian ... crabbed verse*: The reference is to John Milton's (1608–74) *Paradise Lost*, first published in ten books in 1667 (thereafter in twelve books), towards which Voltaire was consistently severe, and towards which Pococuranté is severe to the point of caricature.

12. *and his long description of a hospital could only interest a gravedigger*: An interpolation added in 1761.

13. *Candide was distressed by this speech ... There is no pleasing him*: An interpolation appearing in certain editions of 1759, and in all editions of 1761.

14. *Plato said ... not those that refuse every dish*: A résumé of Plato's *Republic*, 475 BC.

CHAPTER 26
Of a supper that Candide and Martin ate in the company of six strangers, and who they were

1. *the boat is waiting*: Travel between Venice and Padua was by water.

2. *How can you all be kings?*: The six deposed rulers are, respectively: Achmed III, who ruled Turkey from 1703 to 1730, and was deposed by a revolt; Ivan IV of Russia (1740–64), who was deposed while still an infant by Peter the Great's daughter Elizabeth, spent the rest of his days in prison and was later strangled on the orders of Catherine the Great (several years after the composition of *Candide*); Charles Edward, the Young Pretender (1720–88), grandson of the deposed Stuart king, James II; Augustus III, King of Poland and Elector of Saxony (1696–1763), who lost Saxony in 1756 to Frederick II; Stanislaus I (1677–1766), King of Poland from 1704 to 1709, whose daughter married Louis XV in 1726 (on the death of Augustus II in 1733 he briefly regained the throne, but lost it to Augustus III the following year; he was granted the Duchy of Lorraine and was host to Voltaire at his court in Lunéville on several occasions, the last being when Mme du Châtelet (Voltaire's companion and former mistress) died there in 1749); Théodore, Baron von Heuhoff (1670–1756), an adventurer who helped the Corsicans in their revolt against their Genoese masters, and was proclaimed King of Corsica on several occasions; he was subsequently imprisoned as a debtor in England, where he died. It is worth noting that, although it is impossible for these six kings to have met together, five of them might have been able to do so without any anachronism.

3. *Sarmatian*: Properly speaking, an inhabitant of ancient Sarmatia, a region north of the Black Sea; but the word was often used, as here, to designate Poland and its inhabitants.

4. *sequins*: Venetian gold coinage.

5. *and who moreover gives it*: According to Wagnière, Voltaire intended to add the following sentences: 'Are you a king too, Monsieur?' – 'No, and I have no desire to be one.' Cf. Henry James: 'Ever since the *table d'hôte* scene in *Candide*, Venice has been the refuge of monarchs in want of thrones – she wouldn't know herself without her *rois en exil* [kings in exile]' ('The Grand Canal', in *Italian Hours*, (London, 1909)). The wealthy Voltaire – also a mere 'commoner' – was at the time extending financial

credit to three rulers: the duc de Wurtenberg, the Elector Palatine and the duc de Saxe-Gotha.

CHAPTER 27
Candide's voyage to Constantinople

1. *unworthy of our attention*: According to Wagnière, Voltaire had intended to add the following sentence: 'What does it matter with whom one sups, as long as one sups well?' to sharpen the satire on royalty.
2. *Propontide*: The Sea of Marmora.
3. *a deposed sovereign called Ragotski*: Rácózy (1676–1735), Prince of Transylvania; supported by Louis XIV and by the Turks, he mounted a Hungarian uprising against Emperor Joseph II; the uprising was quelled and he took refuge on the Sea of Marmora, near Constantinople.
4. *Grand Sultan*: The Ottoman emperor.
5. *to Cape Matapan, and then . . . to Scutari*: An Eastern Mediterranean itinerary; Marmora is the name of the principal island in the Sea of Marmora, between the Dardanelles and the Bosphorus. Scutari is a suburb of Istanbul on the shores of the Bosphorus.
6. *Levantine captain*: Commander of the 'levantis' (galley soldiers); also: native of the countries of the Levant (*levant* – 'rising'), i.e. the Eastern Mediterranean.

CHAPTER 28
What happened to Candide, Cunégonde, Pangloss, Martin, et cetera

1. *icoglan*: A young boy raised in the Sultan's seraglio with a view to fulfilling high functions in the Turkish state.
2. *cadi*: A Muslim judge.
3. *must be dissecting the devil in person*: The superstitious barber imagines that the shape of the cross has roused the devils in possession of the body of this heretic.
4. *Portuguese barber*: Traditionally, barbers also practised surgery. In the early eighteenth century French surgeons finally freed themselves from their humiliating association with the Barbers' Guild.
5. *One day I took it into my head . . . called out for help*: The scene is a compound fabrication: Christians were not allowed inside mosques; Islamic law moreover forbade the simultaneous presence of men and women in a mosque (or any form of *décolletage*).

6.   *pre-established harmony*: The most generally known aspect of
     Leibniz's philosophy: the monads of which the Leibnizian uni-
     verse is composed are spiritual entities; they cannot 'observe' the
     world – are 'windowless' – but they 'reflect' it, by virtue of a
     correspondence which God has established between them, hence
     'pre-established' harmony; Leibniz's theory is here evoked
     explicitly, for the first time in the *conte*, as the philosophy of
     Optimism.

7.   *the plenum and the materia subtilis*: Two characteristic elements
     of Cartesian metaphysics: the universe as a system of vortices
     consisting of ethereal fluid (*materia subtilis*), which support and
     transport all matter inside a *plenum* – a cosmos 'full' of matter,
     with no empty spaces, since Leibniz denied the possibility of a
     vacuum. Both concepts are required for the operations of opti-
     mistic determinism, and are refuted by Newton (and mocked by
     Voltaire) in favour of a lucid void ordered by the operations of
     gravitational law.

CHAPTER 29
How Candide was reunited with Cunégonde and the old woman

1.   *contingent or non-contingent*: A traditional distinction in logic,
     whereby events are either contingent (may happen) or non-
     contingent (must happen).

2.   *Chapters*: Assemblies of military and religious dignitaries and
     orders of nobility.

CHAPTER 30
Conclusion

1.   *with her left hand*: i.e. conclude a morganatic marriage, whereby
     a prince could marry beneath him without bestowing his goods
     or title upon his partner or offspring.

2.   *effendis, pashas and cadis*: Turkish dignitaries, governors and
     judges.

3.   *Sublime Porte*: The gate of the Sultan's palace.

4.   *dervish*: Member of a religious brotherhood; Voltaire elsewhere
     compares dervishes to mendicant friars.

5.   *whether the mice on board are comfortable or not*: Voltaire had
     employed the same image in his correspondence: 'With regard to
     events in the north of Germany, I think we are no better informed
     than the mice as to the intentions of those who steer the ship'
     (9 November 1757).

6. *Keep your mouth shut*: In the manuscript, the dervish's advice begins: 'Cultivate your land, drink, eat, sleep and [keep your mouth shut].'

7. *two viziers of the divan, together with the mufti*: Two ministers (viziers) of the Turkish council of state (the divan), as well as the principle religious dignitary of Constantinople (the mufti).

8. *Batavia and the islands*: Indonesia and the East Indies.

9. *witness Eglon ... sold into captivity*: Examples from the Old Testament.

10. *Croesus ... Domitian*: Examples from the history of Greece and Rome.

11. *Richard II ... Charles I*: Examples from English history: Edward II (1284–1327; King 1307–27) was deposed from the throne and murdered in captivity; Henry VI (1421–71; King 1422–61, 1470–71) was dethroned by his rival Edward IV and died, probably murdered, in captivity; Richard III (1452–85; King 1483–5) was killed at the battle of Bosworth Field; Mary Stuart, known as Mary Queen of Scots (1542–87), was executed on the orders of Elizabeth I; Charles I (1600–1649; King 1625–49) was deposed by the Parliamentary forces led by Oliver Cromwell and was later executed.

12. *The three Henris of France and the Emperor Henri IV*: 'The three Henris' were Kings of France: Henri II (1519–59; King 1547–59) was killed in a tournament; Henri III (1551–89; King 1574–89) and Henri IV (1553–1610; King 1589–1610) were assassinated. Henri IV (1050–1106), Holy Roman Emperor (1056–1106), died in exile.

13. *ut operaretur eum*: Genesis 2:15 (in the Latin Vulgate translation): 'And the Lord took the man, and put him into the garden of Eden, *to dress it and to keep it*.'

14. *carpenter*: In the manuscript Voltaire had initially described Girofleo as a first-rate 'tapestry-maker' (*tapissier*).

15. *we must cultivate our garden*: 'Garden': plot of land. Gustave Flaubert commented on the conclusion: 'The end of *Candide* is for me incontrovertible proof of genius of the first order; the stamp of the master is in that laconic conclusion, as stupid as life itself.'

PENGUIN CLASSICS

DEERBROOK
HARRIET MARTINEAU

'If you do a thing which a village public does not approve, there will be offence in whatever else you say and do, for some time after'

When the Ibbotson sisters, Hester and Margaret, arrive at the village of Deerbrook to stay with their cousin Mr Grey and his wife, speculation is rife that one of them might marry the village apothecary, Edward Hope. Although he is immediately attracted to Margaret, Edward is persuaded to wed the beautiful Hester, and becomes trapped in an unhappy marriage. But his troubles are compounded when he becomes the victim of a malicious village gossip, whose rumours threaten his entire career. A powerful exploration of the nature of ignorance and prejudice, *Deerbrook* proved an inspiration for both Charlotte Brontë and Elizabeth Gaskell. It may be regarded as one of the first Victorian novels of English domestic life.

New to Penguin Classics, this edition of *Deerbrook* contains the full text of the original three-volume novel. Valerie Sanders's introduction outlines the novel's themes and considers its unique position in nineteenth-century women's literature. This volume also contains a chronology, further reading and detailed notes.

Edited with an introduction and notes by Valerie Sanders

Penguin Classics

CRANFORD
ELIZABETH GASKELL

'It is very pleasant dining with a bachelor ... I only hope it is not improper; so many pleasant things are!'

A portrait of the residents of an English country town in the mid-nineteenth century, *Cranford* relates the adventures of Miss Matty and Miss Deborah, two middle-aged spinster sisters striving to live with dignity in reduced circumstances. Through a series of vignettes, Elizabeth Gaskell portrays a community governed by old-fashioned habits and dominated by friendships between women. Her wry account of rural life is undercut, however, by tragedy in its depiction of such troubling events as Matty's bankruptcy, the violent death of Captain Brown and the unwitting cruelty of Peter Jenkyns. Written with acute observation, *Cranford* is by turns affectionate, moving and darkly satirical.

In her introduction, Patricia Ingham discusses *Cranford* in relation to Gaskell's own past and as a work of irony in the manner of Jane Austen. She also considers the implications of the novel as to class and empire. This edition also includes further reading, notes and an appendix on the significance of 'Fashion at Cranford'.

Edited with an introduction and notes by Patricia Ingham

PENGUIN CLASSICS

THE HISTORY OF TOM JONES
HENRY FIELDING

'He was indeed a thoughtless, giddy youth, with little sobriety in his manners, and less in his countenance'

A foundling of mysterious parentage brought up by Mr Allworthy on his country estate, Tom Jones is deeply in love with the seemingly unattainable Sophia Western, the beautiful daughter of the neighbouring squire – though he sometimes succumbs to the charms of the local girls. But when his amorous escapades earn the disapproval of his benefactor, Tom is banished to make his own fortune. Sophia, meanwhile, is determined to avoid an arranged marriage to Allworthy's scheming nephew and escapes from her rambunctious father to follow Tom to London. A vivid Hogarthian panorama of eighteenth-century life, spiced with danger and intrigue, bawdy exuberance and good-natured authorial interjections, *Tom Jones* (1749) is one of the greatest and most ambitious comic novels in English literature.

In his introduction to this new Penguin Classics edition, Thomas Keymer discusses narrative techniques and themes, the context of eighteenth-century fiction and satire, and the historical and political background of the Jacobite Rebellion. This volume also includes a chronology, further reading, notes, a glossary and an appendix on Fielding's revisions.

Edited by Thomas Keymer and Alice Wakely

With an introduction by Thomas Keymer

PENGUIN CLASSICS

CHEKHOV: A LIFE IN LETTERS
ANTON CHEKHOV

'Medicine is my lawful wedded wife, and literature my mistress. When I've had enough of one, I can go and spend the night with the other'

From his teenage years in provincial Russia to his premature death in 1904, Anton Chekhov wrote thousands of letters to a wide range of correspondents. This fascinating new selection tells Chekhov's story as a man and a writer through affectionate bulletins to his family, insightful discussions of literature with publishers and theatre directors, and tender love letters to his actress wife. Vividly evoking landscapes, people and his daily life, the letters offer revealing glimpses into Chekhov's preoccupations – the onset of tuberculosis, his dual careers as doctor and writer, and his ambivalence about his growing reputation as Russia's foremost playwright and author. This volume takes us inside the mind of one of the world's great writers, and the character that emerges from these pages is resilient, generous, charming and life enhancing.

This is the first uncensored edition of the letters in any language, including previously unpublished material from the Russian archives, and the translation conveys the humour and warmth of Chekhov's prose.

Translated by Rosamund Bartlett and Anthony Phillips

With an introduction and notes by Rosamund Bartlett

PENGUIN CLASSICS

THÉRÈSE RAQUIN
EMILE ZOLA

'It was like a lightning flash of passion, swift, blinding, across a leaden sky'

In a dingy apartment on the Passage du Pont Neuf in Paris, Thérèse Raquin is trapped in a loveless marriage to her sickly cousin Camille. The numbing tedium of her life is suddenly shattered when she embarks on a turbulent affair with her husband's earthy friend Laurent, but their animal passion for each other soon compels the lovers to commit a crime that will haunt them forever. *Thérèse Raquin* caused a scandal when it appeared in 1867 and brought its twenty-seven-year-old author a notoriety that followed him throughout his life. Zola's novel is not only an uninhibited portrayal of adultery, madness and ghostly revenge, but is also a devastating exploration of the darkest aspects of human existence.

Robin Buss's new translation superbly conveys Zola's fearlessly honest and matter of fact style. In his introduction, he discusses Zola's life and literary career, and the influence of art, literature and science on his writing. This edition also includes the preface to the second edition of 1868, a chronology, further reading and notes.

Translated with an introduction and notes by Robin Buss

PENGUIN CLASSICS

THREE TALES
GUSTAVE FLAUBERT

'When she went to church, she would sit gazing at the picture of the Holy Spirit and it struck her that it looked rather like her parrot'

First published in 1877, the *Three Tales*, dominated by questions of doubt, love, loneliness and religious experience, form Flaubert's final great work. 'A Simple Heart' relates the story of Félicité – an uneducated serving-woman who retains her Catholic faith despite a life of desolation and loss. 'The Legend of Saint Julian Hospitator', inspired by a stained-glass window in Rouen cathedral, describes the fate of Julian, a sadistic hunter destined to murder his own parents. The blend of faith and cruelty that dominates this story may also be found in 'Herodias' – a reworking of the tale of Salome and John the Baptist. Rich with a combination of desire, sorrow and faith, these three diverse works are a triumphant conclusion to Flaubert's creative life.

Roger Whitehouse's vibrant new translation captures the exquisite style of the original prose. Geoffrey Wall's introduction considers the inspiration for the tales in the context of Flaubert's life and other work. This edition includes a further reading list and detailed notes.

Translated by Roger Whitehouse

Edited with an introduction by Geoffrey Wall

PENGUIN CLASSICS

THE SHOOTING PARTY
ANTON CHEKHOV

'Why did I marry him? Where were my eyes? Where were my brains?'

The Shooting Party, Chekhov's only full-length novel, centres on Olga, the pretty young daughter of a drunken forester on a country estate, and her fateful relationships with the men in her life. Adored by Urbenin, the estate manager, whom she marries to escape the poverty of her home, she is also desired by the dissolute Count Karneyev and by Zinovyev, a magistrate, who knows the secret misery of her marriage. And when an attempt is made on Olga's life in the woods, it seems impossible to discover the perpetrator in an impenetrable web of deceit, lust, loathing and double-dealing. One of Chekhov's earliest experiments in fiction, *The Shooting Party* combines the classic elements of a gripping mystery with a story of corruption, concealed love and fatal jealousy.

Ronald Wilks's new translation of this work is the first in thirty years. It brilliantly captures the immediacy of the dialogue that Chekhov was later to develop into his great dramas. This edition also includes suggestions for further reading and explanatory notes.

Translated and edited by Ronald Wilks

PENGUIN CLASSICS

DEAD SOULS   NIKOLAI GOGOL

'It's not a question of the living. I've nothing to do with them. I'm asking for the dead'

Chichikov, a mysterious stranger, arrives in the provincial town of 'N', visiting a succession of landowners and making each a strange offer. He proposes to buy the names of dead serfs still registered on the census, saving their owners from paying tax on them, and to use these 'souls' as collateral to re-invent himself as a gentleman. In this ebullient masterpiece, Gogol created a grotesque gallery of human types, from the bear-like Sobakevich to the insubstantial fool Manilov, and, above all, the devilish conman Chichikov. *Dead Souls*, Russia's first major novel, is one of the most unusual works of nineteenth-century fiction and a devastating satire on social hypocrisy.

David Magarshack's introduction discusses Gogol's plan for a novel in three parts, tracing Chichikov's progress from sin to redemption, and tells how Gogol destroyed part of the manuscript in the grip of madness. The surviving sections, volume one and a fragment of volume two, are translated here.

'Gogol was a strange creature, but then genius is always strange'
Vladimir Nabokov

Translated with an introduction by David Magarshack

PENGUIN CLASSICS

A HERO OF OUR TIME   MIKHAIL LERMONTOV

'I'm still in love with her ... I'd give my life for her. But she bores me'

Proud, wilful and intensely charismatic, Pechorin is bored by the stifling world that envelops him. With a predatory energy for any activity that will relieve his ennui, he embarks on a series of adventures – encountering smugglers, brigands, soldiers, lovers and rivals – and leaves a trail of broken hearts behind him. With its cynical, immoral hero, Lermontov's novel outraged many critics when it was published in 1840. Yet it was also a literary landmark: an acutely observed psychological novel, narrated from a number of different perspectives, through which the true and complex nature of Pechorin slowly emerges.

Paul Foote's fine translation is accompanied by an introduction discussing the figure of Pechorin within the literary tradition of 'superfluous men' and the novel's influence on Tolstoy, Dostoyevsky and Chekhov. The edition also includes a chronology, explanatory notes and a historical note on the Caucasus.

'Vigorous and audacious ... it retains its power as a psychological study'
Julian Barnes

Translated with an introduction by Paul Foote

THE STORY OF PENGUIN CLASSICS

Before 1946 ...'Classics' are mainly the domain of academics and students, without readable editions for everyone else. This all changes when a little-known classicist, E. V. Rieu, presents Penguin founder Allen Lane with the translation of Homer's *Odyssey* that he has been working on and reading to his wife Nelly in his spare time.

1946 *The Odyssey* becomes the first Penguin Classic published, and promptly sells three million copies. Suddenly, classic books are no longer for the privileged few.

1950s Rieu, now series editor, turns to professional writers for the best modern, readable translations, including Dorothy L. Sayers's *Inferno* and Robert Graves's *The Twelve Caesars*, which revives the salacious original.

1960s The Classics are given the distinctive black jackets that have remained a constant throughout the series's various looks. Rieu retires in 1964, hailing the Penguin Classics list as 'the greatest educative force of the 20th century'.

1970s A new generation of translators arrives to swell the Penguin Classics ranks, and the list grows to encompass more philosophy, religion, science, history and politics.

1980s The Penguin American Library joins the Classics stable, with titles such as *The Last of the Mohicans* safeguarded. Penguin Classics now offers the most comprehensive library of world literature available.

1990s The launch of Penguin Audiobooks brings the classics to a listening audience for the first time, and in 1999 the launch of the Penguin Classics website takes them online to a larger global readership than ever before.

The 21st Century Penguin Classics are rejacketed for the first time in nearly twenty years. This world famous series now consists of more than 1300 titles, making the widest range of the best books ever written available to millions – and constantly redefining the meaning of what makes a 'classic'.

The Odyssey continues ...

The best books ever written

PENGUIN CLASSICS

SINCE 1946

Find out more at www.penguinclassics.com